NATHALIE SARRAUTE

MARTEREAU

A NOVEL

TRANSLATION BY
MARIA JOLAS

DALKEY ARCHIVE PRESS

Originally published in French under the same title by Éditions Gallimard, 1953
Originally published in English by George Braziller, Inc., 1959

Library of Congress Cataloging-in-Publication Data available
ISBN: 1-56478-348-0

Partially funded by a grant from the Illinois Arts Council, a state agency.

Dalkey Archive Press books are published by the Center for Book Culture,
a nonprofit organization, located at Milner Library, Illinois State University.

www.centerforbookculture.org

Printed on permanent/durable acid-free paper and bound in the United States of America

MARTEREAU

Nothing about me that might put her on her guard or in any way arouse her mistrust. Not a sign, not the slightest tremor on my part when she quivers imperceptibly and says ironically, putting "important people" and "big shots" between quotes: We were obliged to entertain a lot of "important people." We were entertained by a lot of "big shots." I adhere strictly to the rules of the game. I remain in the desired position. I look at her without flinching even at those moments when we feel a bit abashed and flustered, when we shift our gaze in spite of ourselves, so people won't notice that we've seen; even at such moments, I look straight at her with an innocent, approving expression.

And so with me she can enjoy herself to the full. They can all enjoy themselves to the full with me. Never do I put up the slightest resistance. It is doubtless precisely this strange passivity, this sort of docility which I have never succeeded in explaining very well to myself, that excites them and makes them secrete irresistibly, when they come into contact with me, a substance like that which certain animals eject in order to blind their prey . . . "A lot of 'important people,' 'big shots.' So-and-so . . . do you know him? But you've surely heard of him. I dined with him the other evening . . . he told me . . ."

It's amusing to see the look they have at the very beginning, when they don't yet know what to expect, their look of prudent apprehension. How they examine you cautiously from every side, how they sniff. My extreme self-effacement must occasionally, at first, arouse their mistrust. Then they begin to gather courage, still somewhat apprehensive, not entirely sure of themselves. I never know whether it's something in them that makes them uncomfortable or whether it is I who cause them to feel ashamed of themselves, without intending to, and despite all my efforts, but it seems to me as though they too would like to look somewhere else while they are telling it to me in as negligent, natural a manner as possible: "It was X who told me that. You don't know him. He's a good friend of ours, he's absolutely charming. Recently he has aged a good deal. His wife's death was hard on him, but you know he's still brilliant in his good moments, and so simple . . ." Nor have I yet succeeded in explaining to myself the painful, slightly nauseating pleasure that I experience when I feel them little by little gaining in courage, trying to jostle me with little knocks, watching me amusedly out of the corner of their eyes, while I force myself to stand decently on my two feet and answer in a tone consisting of as exact doses as I can mix of detachment and admiration . . . "No, I don't know him. But I can imagine . . . in fact, I have heard people say that he was quite delightful . . ." Yes, with me they're sure to win.

With her, once she's over that hardly perceptible discomfiture, the sort of embarrassed start she gives to begin with, even with me, then she can frolic about freely . . . "Big shots . . . All sorts of important people . . . My husband's position . . . You didn't know your uncle then. We didn't live like hermits the way we do now. We went out almost every evening, we entertained a great deal . . ." In the same way that the well-trained male dancer in a ballet, at a certain note, leaps aside and takes up his position at the desired distance while the star ballerina advances towards mid-stage, it seems to me that I change places right away, ever so slightly. I step a little to one side and stand motionless, leaning forward a bit; she blushes, or rather flushes, hardly, she doesn't cough, but almost does, she must be holding it in: "I had succeeded in gathering a few friends about me . . . Le Brix, you know, the painter . . ." I nod, earnestness itself . . . "we were very intimate at that time; his reputation was limited to a small group. He has rather forgotten it, but I did a lot to launch him then . . . Ducret . . ." she is wriggling gently . . . "you know, the well-known collector, I had invited them to dinner, I had almost forced Ducret to buy one of his pictures. Now when we happen to meet, he reminds me of that, and we laugh over it: do you remember how I had to be coaxed to buy that Le Brix? The fact is, I must tell you . . ." it seems to me that she is trembling very slightly, excited by her own boldness . . . "the fact is, I must tell you . . . at that time, in a certain set . . . the way some people say: in a certain 'élite' " . . . she lowers her eyes, then looks up again right away, courageously: "my opinion was of some importance. People used to say about me—I was told this—you know that apparently feather-brained little woman . . ." she fairly coos, dragging one syllable after the other . . . fea-ther-brained . . . "well, that little woman with her air of not lifting a finger, is all-powerful just now. That made your uncle very proud. He was never very much interested in all that kind of thing . . . always absorbed in his business, but in reality he was very proud of me . . ." It wouldn't need much to set her to twisting about with that simpering, falsely innocent manner that certain precocious little girls assume when they want to play the baby . . . "For him, wherever we went, I was always the best-looking . . ." she gives a roguish glance in my direction and leans towards my ear: "And just between ourselves, to tell you the truth, I don't believe he's ever got over it . . . I often tell him that he's an old silly-billy . . . He used to say that I was his mascot . . . I had to be the smartest of all . . . Sometimes I used to kick over the traces and tell him: you know I'm fed up with acting as your sandwich-man. But I adored to dress well . . . Paquin . . . Patou . . . Poiret . . . Ah! you should have known Poiret . . . What a delightful man! He used to say that I had missed my vocation, that I could have made a fortune. It was true that sometimes I used to amuse myself by making clothes out of nothing at all. He would stare at me with his big eyes—because he took in everything at one glance! nothing escaped him—and say: But where in the devil did she unearth that? I remember one dress . . ." she puckers her eye-lids, pouting amorously: "Oh! it was nothing at all, a simple linen smock with purple and green stripes. But he was crazy about it! I told him—and you know it was true—why . . . I cut it out of an old curtain . . . That delighted him." Now she feels confident, entirely at her ease; she lays her hand on my arm: "But you know, in spite of all that, I didn't like Paris much. No, I went there principally in the Spring . . . Is there anything more beautiful than Paris in the Spring with all the horse-chestnuts in bloom? And then, I wanted to see the collections and take in all the exhibits. But in winter, oh, in winter I preferred the Riviera. Or else, traveling around . . . ah, traveling . . . my husband traveled a lot on business at that time. He would telegraph me to meet him in Constantinople, or in Rome, or in Cairo . . . I used to take along two or three dresses, I knew he would drag me to a lot of parties. But on the way back, I always asked for what I called 'my little bonus' . . . We would stop off in Naples or else leave the Orient-Express in Venice. He balked a bit. He used to say: 'My dear child, you make me do some reckless things.' Naturally, for him, for a man as busy as he was, every day lost counted. But I insisted. Ah! Italy . . . Venice . . . for me, that was like Paradise . . . We used to stay at the Danieli . . . In Venice you have to stay at the Danieli. What a view you have from those windows . . . San Georgio . . . The lagoon . . ."

She can rest assured, it's been there inside me, all ready, all prepared for a long time. A few carelessly sketched lines, a few rapid, roughly drawn hatchings and the picture appears by itself the way it does in one of those children's albums in which it suffices to cover a white page with pencil scribblings to make a drawing appear . . . Venice . . . The Grand Canal . . . The old palaces all lighted up . . . pink lanterns swinging from the silver-trimmed prows of gondolas . . . men in dress-clothes, women in evening-gowns, leaning on balconies enjoying the fresh air . . . behind them, high ceilings, gold panel-ing, glass chandeliers, tall carved cabinets, silver chests, paintings, Oriental carpets, the pink marble terrace on which Aretinus once rested his arms, from which Tintoretto had once leaned . . . and against this background, like Carpaccio's princesses, she herself, the far-away princess, the lady with the unicorn, the little fairy . . . her "artfully gloved hand" brushes the gondolier's outstretched arm, she jumps lightly on to the steps, advances with her tripping gait, mysterious, exotic, detached, "frail among enormous bows of ribbon," towards the lounge all shimmering with light, "an ape in a brocade vest," "a little scarlet nigger-boy" follow, precede her, the old *concierge* rises to greet her as she passes, the elevator-boy tips his cap, she is a vase of great price, a Tanagra statuette, a bit of delicate porcelain to which each one in passing gives a touch of chisel or brush, in order to perfect its exquisite form, she receives from each one, she feels it, as she passes in front of him, returning his greeting, a sense of joyous freedom, of liberty, meetness and litheness, an air of delicate graciousness—dreamy, melancholy, somewhat distant; she is gliding along in a mellow, velvety, perfumed universe, with well-oiled wheels and muffled sounds, like the silky click of the elevator door which the boy discreetly holds open for her, like the warm purring of the blue-tinged water in the alabaster tub . . . The chamber-maid catches her veil-draped hat on the wing when she tosses it towards her with a weary gesture. She is lost in thought as she draws her long gloves from her "slender broad-ringed fingers," Lady Hamilton, the Belle Ferronière, Camille . . .

But something is happening. Something is changing. She puckers her lids and stares nostalgically at some distant point, she sighs . . . "Ah, yes, those were happy days . . . I was young then . . . We had good times . . ." But I feel that her heart isn't in it any more. She is thinking of something else. Mechanically, she repeats: "Ah, yes, those were happy days. Yes, I used to love all that . . ." She seems to have arrested her momentum, to be slowing down, imperceptibly . . . "Yes . . . All that was very fine . . . But you know . . ." she is looking at me earnestly: it seems to me that she is pulling herself together, then she takes her decision: "Well, one fine day, I realized that that was not everything, that life wasn't just that. And then, I didn't hesitate one second . . ." her gesture makes me think of that skillful movement of the hips and shoulders thanks to which well-trained skiers are able to perform their slaloms . . . she turns . . . she swings round . . . "not one second, you understand, to leave all that behind" . . . She has felt something, that is certain, she is on her guard . . . she is watching me . . . she hasn't stopped spying on me from below while she appeared to be babbling along so innocently, preening herself casually, while I thought I was so safe, locked in, guarded on every side—but no matter what precautions you take, or what efforts you make, you can never succeed in deceiving them—she has noticed all at once, she has seen something, a vibration, hardly a breath, a movement in the fold of my lips, a waver of my glance, she has understood: it is not what is called for, there has been a misdeal, she has made a mistake, as when she reaches into her closet and instead of a "small dinner" dress, takes down an evening gown, it is not suitable at all. She had been letting herself go heedlessly, she hadn't thought about it again, and suddenly it came back to her: what she knew, what she had discovered about me, amassed, collected little by little, or else what she realized all at once in a flash of clairvoyance, thanks to one of those illuminations, one of those sudden divinations, such as do occur: sometimes practically nothing, an intonation, a word spoken by chance suffices for them, or even less than that, signs visible to them alone inform them; something I had let drop without thinking, something undefinable in my walk or in the cut of my clothes, perhaps one day when she had seen me strolling along the quays, or in the street, believing myself far from them, rid of them for an instant, letting myself go, carefree, relaxed (how uncomfortable I feel, when she says to me with that little pointed laugh of hers: "hm, hm, you know I saw you, I was in the bus"); or else that time when I saw her trotting busily along on the opposite sidewalk, ferreting about, staring with the eyes of a watch-dog at the things in the shop-windows, when she could have seen me, she too,—nothing escapes her, she sees everything—when she may have caught something on my face while I was seated on a café terrace, lolling in the sunshine; or again—this is what frightens me most—some-one deposited that in her, slipped it to her insidiously (a mere word, or a smile when I was mentioned) and every-thing that was floating about in her, in suspense, had crystal-lized around that—I can't tell, nor she either probably, but in any case, she has felt, of this I am certain, that it is preferable to treat me to something else: be that as it may, it takes more than that to upset her, she has more than one string to her bow, her repertoire is an extensive one . . . "Yes, I waked up one fine morning—it's when we wake up in the morning that we see those things clearly—I sat up in bed and I said to myself: 'My poor girl, what are you doing here, anyway? What on earth are you doing with your life? A bird in a golden cage, that's what they've made of you. An object of luxury.' You understand, all that was

very fine, devouring entire libraries, bringing people together, or helping others get started, but I knew I was
worth more than that, I wanted to do something on my
own, to work, to live my own life, as people said. So then
—you know I've always been a bit of a madcap—one fine
day, I just cleared out bag and baggage, of course that's a
manner of speaking, it boiled down to very little, I only
wanted to take what I absolutely needed, and I didn't take
a single piece of jewelry: just the jewelry I had as a girl
and what my mother left, that was all, and a little cameo
your uncle gave me, that I was very fond of . . . and so I
left. People couldn't get over it. My father was furious.
But my husband was a good sport. He is always very nice
when it's a question of something important. Sometimes I
tell him: 'It's too bad that important things don't happen
more often, because then, you behave perfectly.' He came
to see me. At first he was unable to take me seriously, then
later, when he had taken it in, he did all he could to get
me back; he was ready to promise everything . . . He offered me money to found an art review, to open a picture
gallery, or a publishing house, or a dress-making establish-
ment . . . anything I wanted . . . but at that time I wouldn't
give in. You understand, it seemed to me that I had been
living in a sort of lethargy. I felt all of a sudden, that I had
not yet really lived, I wanted to throw myself headlong into
life, I wanted to struggle, to really suffer . . ." she hesitated
a moment . . . "to fall in love . . . I was a child when I
married. That's the trouble with marrying girls off so
young. Imagine: I was only seventeen! I was flattered that

such a fine man, respected by everybody—my father thought very highly of him—, that such an educated, intelligent man should be interested in a chit of a girl like me. My parents were so happy when he asked for my hand . . . They were already old, and they had begun to wonder what would become of me without them . . . As for me, I didn't worry. I was very proud, from one day to the next I felt that I had become someone very important. You don't know what that feeling means to a young girl . . . Your uncle was on his knees to me, naturally, and did everything I asked him to do . . . It was like a wonderful dream . . . And then one day I waked up . . ." I acquiesce understandingly, I am moved in spite of everything, vaguely flattered too, one always is a bit in such cases: they know that and they play a sure game . . . small change that they distribute generously to the Chinese pedicure squatting at their feet, to their hairdresser, or to their masseur; well aware of the value of the gracious gift they are bestowing; remaining themselves untouched, distant, ice-cold, Madame Récamier smiling at the little chimney-sweep, great ladies opening their heart generously to some bewildered *petit-bourgeois*—whom they consider so "nice," so "likeable," who really deserves to be encouraged—with an air of sincerity, exquisite modesty, perfect simplicity, complete equality "which, you may say what you want, they alone have" the one they have thus favored will say later to his admiring, moved friends, "really, they are the only ones who have retained the secret of such grace and simplicity." He accepts, he collects—delighted, like myself vaguely embarrassed, somewhat surprised, but flattered, even at times with a sort of infatuated, intimate little smile —he is determined to preserve reverently these relics which they do him the honor ("he's so different from the others, isn't he, so comprehending, so quick") to entrust into his hands. But sometimes the slightest thing, a little too great an effort to abolish the distance between them, or to efface in him a last remaining trace of timidity, of humility, an awkward stiffness that makes them ill at ease, in which they fear to detect somewhat hostile mental reservations, a certain resistance . . . perhaps they go a little too fast, a little too far, and suddenly, at the very heart of that exquisite intimacy, nascent friendship and unhoped for rapprochement, something rises up in him, a chill little breath, a doubt to which he hardly dares give expression—how is it possible to believe them to be so cynical, so hypocritically cold, so exaggeratedly convinced of the hierarchies—something rises up to which he will never give entire freedom of the city, or only much later, one of those semi-hatreds of the most dangerous kind, one of those unacknowledged, larval resentments that are almost impossible to appease.

But between her and me, it is not that. Not that at all, of course. Something in me had just stirred, an echo, a reflection, less than a reminiscence, a vague recollection of something that I had perhaps myself not experienced, but had seen, had read somewhere, caught a glimpse of, brushed against, got a whiff of, I'm not too sure where or when. It was rather, while she was speaking, like the furthermost point of a distant land, a promontory that had appeared to me thanks to a brief clearing, I just saw it for an instant, then it grew dim and disappeared.

No, between her and me, it is not that. Or so little. She can't have towards me such a feeling of condescension. She doesn't seek to gratify me, or hardly. Her chief aim—because there are always several, we'd be surprised, if we consented to look a little more closely, to see how they throng, much more numerous than we could ever imagine, about what are apparently the most insignificant words— her aim, conscious or not, must be elsewhere . . . "Yes, one fine day I waked up . . . Oh! I can assure you that it wasn't as easy as it sounds. I went through some hard times. The friends I lived with were as poor as I was then; we struggled hard for a living. We lived in a studio in the Rue de la Grande Chaumière, that was a change for me after having had every comfort: we froze in winter and in summer it was like a furnace. But how we worked! And the fun . . . It was marvelous! What a life . . . I took up painting . . . that had always been my dream . . . I had always wanted to paint ever since I was so high . . . My friends gave me great encouragement . . . Ah! if you could see the spirit of those people, what pluck, what marvelous faith in their own genius! When we had worked till we dropped in our tracks, then we went out . . . Montparnasse was in full swing . . . We used to meet at the Dôme, or the Jockey, or the Rotonde . . . I felt I was in the very heart of things . . ." In the heart of the world. On top of it. On the highest peaks where the spirit breathes. On warm spring evenings, or on hot summer nights, they leave their work-tables or

13

their studios and scatter abroad the surplus strength that has gathered in them, the result of difficult research, of the bitterest, most exquisite effort. They stride lithely along in their loose-flowing garments, their pockets stuffed with books and papers; their throats unconfined in open collars or turtle-neck sweaters, hair blowing, casual, extravagant, freed of all restraints, all conventions, of all sordid cares, sanctified by the single purpose they are bent on pursuing, by their noble obsession, overcoming all obstacles . . . jungle conquerors . . . their ferocious eyes, pitiless, piercing, tender, profound, scan the terraces in search of friends, of the elect . . . an entire life of abnegation, and the most arduous work would not permit just anyone to sit down beside them—one must possess a heaven-sent grace, a gift, —while they dream away, solitary, impenetrable, inaccessible, revolving under their vast foreheads magnificent projects, strange, new thoughts . . .

No matter how hard I become, how much I lie to myself, or smile at the childish picture that her rough pencil strokes have evoked, this time, I am obliged to recognize that she has aimed straight: like the astronomer who, from his calculations alone, succeeded in discovering the existence and situation of invisible planets, the bits of information she has obtained about me without my knowledge (I see clearly now what they are and am suffused with rage and shame) have allowed her to play a sure game. It's there inside me, she knows it—no effort on my part would succeed this time in deceiving her—there it is: mixed with admiration—an exquisite amalgam—in an infinitesimal dose, however, but they don't need more, an infinitesimal dose suffices for them: a mere dash of slightly shame-faced nostalgia, of secret envy. At present, whether I do or don't flinch, whether my glance wavers, or my voice falters, or not, is of little importance. She catches, she foresees all the movements, all the attempts to curl up in a ball, on the part of the frightened little animal that hides as best it can deep down in its hole. The game becomes serious, more exciting: "Yes indeed . . . And you know I earned my living. I had begun to make African style jewelry, pendants and necklaces . . . African Art was all the rage at the time . . . At first I had difficulty, then gradually I received a lot of orders. Almost too many. Sometimes I would sit up all night . . . because during the day I painted . . . But what a joy it was when I received my first cash! Money earned by me, 'by the sweat of my brow,' you can imagine! Now I didn't need to ask anything from anybody . . . I was independent . . ." The little animal she had never stopped teasing, which she had finally succeeded in smoking out, crawls shamefacedly from out of its hole . . . What a treat to watch it reeling and blinking at the light, to see at last in broad daylight its look of cunning, contemptuous, humiliated rage, and its desire, curbed by fear, to bite.

No, there is no way of defending oneself against them, no way of resisting them—they are too over-powering. There would of course be one way for me, a heroic, desperate way, the one used by people who know that they have nothing more to lose. That would be, to let myself go completely, to give up everything, release all my brakes, and shout at them that I am no fool, either, that I see through their cowardly little game . . . cowardly and cruel . . . I don't earn my living, I don't, and I feel uncomfortable about it, which they well know . . . incapable of getting rid of them, or of escaping . . . caught in their toils, cornered, ill, and they take advantage of that fact . . . I'm ill, I'd shout that at her, I can't live in an unheated studio and you know that perfectly well, I can't sit up all night. . . . That's why I'm stagnating here, listening to your stupid twaddle, taking part in your dubious amusements, people amuse themselves as best they can, don't they? You know where my weak spot is and you hit me there, in order to humiliate and annihilate me—you always do it—that picks you up for a while, gives you confidence, excites you . . .

But I shall never dare. Nobody ever dares to do such a thing. They know that, and can therefore rest easy. They don't run the slightest risk. If ever some madman, in a moment of fury, should dare, out of a blue sky, to indulge in such an indecent outburst as that, we know very well what would happen to him. He would see them suddenly leave, withdraw, as they know how to do, far away, at immense distances, setting between them and him all their sad amazement, their incomprehension, their innocence, their unawareness; he would be alone, abandoned by everybody, in a desert, with no other partner, no other adversary, than himself; scratching, biting, embracing nobody but himself, turning in circles round himself, a stupid dog that bites its own tail, a ludicrous dervish.

I must confess that it took me a long time to understand more or less what it was all about. At first, when I was a child, it seemed to me that it came from the things that surrounded me, from the dreary and even slightly sinister setting: it emanated from the walls, from the mutilated sycamores, from the sidewalks, from the overly gleaming lawns, from the falsely brisk music of the merry-go-round behind the hedge, from the icy clink of the rings . . . something stealthily hostile, an obscure threat. And then I realized that things had nothing to do with it, or very little, that they were at best accomplices, vague allies, faithful servants who take on the style of their masters. Things could very easily have assumed a familiar, kindly aspect, they had all that was needed for that, or in any case, a perfectly neutral, unobtrusive, harmless one, if it hadn't been for the others, the people. Everything came from them: a smile, a glance, a word dropped in passing by them and it sprang up suddenly from just anywhere, from the most insignificant of objects—a stealthy onslaught, a threat.

It was for that reason, not in order for them to protect me—as I believed erroneously for a long time—that I always stayed close to them, straining toward them, riveted to them, observing their every glance, every word: one second of inattention, of carefree relaxation, of forgetfulness, and their words would fall upon me at the moment when I least expected it, they would jump upon me from behind, or else, all of a sudden, sometimes much later, words of theirs that had penetrated into me without my knowledge, actuated by a mysterious clock-like mechanism, would explode inside me and tear me to bits. I had to catch them all on the wing without allowing anything to pass, all their words, their slightest intonation, and examine them slowly, disconnect them as one would a dangerous contrivance, open them in order to extract from them a turbid, dubious substance with a sickening odor, turn it round and round the better to see it, shake it, keep on feeling it, sniff it . . . And here is the important point, the essential point that should not be lost sight of: it is right here, in this curious fascination, in this need to turn it round and round, to palpate, to sniff, in the sensation, hidden by uneasiness, fear and disgust, while we turn and sniff, of a funny, insipid kind of pleasure, and in the feeling of unacknowledged satisfaction at remaining there glued to them, slimed all over by them, and that it should last for a long time, forever.

They, moreover, make no mistake about it, of that I am certain. She surely feels it, the lady with the unicorn, the little fairy, as she struts there so freely before me. They feel it—and this can be said in their defense—these sly benefactors unbosoming themselves proudly to their young *protégés:* they feel upon them the humid, dog-like gaze, the thirsty leech. Docile, parasitic. Sniffing with voluptuous fear and disgust. Coming to eat out of their hand. Swallowing everything.

I should certainly fool no one, neither her nor myself, if I were stupid enough to shout at her that it was bad luck, my illness, that had made me turn to them, that had forced me to agree to live with them and allow myself to be domesticated by them, kept me from running away. That might take with other people. Those bed-time stories for good little children are all right for others. But they themselves know perfectly well, just as I do, how matters really stand.

They come in brazenly, settle down everywhere, sprawl all over the place, throw their rubbish about, unpack their provisions; there's nothing to watch out for, no grass to keep off of, people can come and go as they please, bring their children and their dogs, entrance is free, I am a public square thrown open to the Sunday crowds, I am a city park on a holiday. No signs. No guards. Nothing with which one need reckon.

"You never do anything else" . . . " 'You' certainly do invent the strangest ideas" . . . " 'You' have a way of staring at people" . . . "You" . . . "You" . . . "You" . . . and we become wizened up, we huddle up against one another, we stick together, pressed close to one another like frightened sparrows.

"You" . . . and we stand at attention in front of him, our anonymous, petrified faces turned towards him at an identical angle: soldiers passing inspection, convicts with shaved heads and striped shirts, lined up for roll-call.

"You" . . . and he transfixes us, thrusts a skewer through first one then the other, a fine spit of roasting chickens, of tender little suckling pigs.

"You" . . . his rapid scratch when, somewhat upset, fascinated by his grouchy, threatening manner, we wriggle eagerly before him, coming closer and closer, with an innocent look, in order to appease, to charm him. "You" . . . his most trusted weapon. His cleverest blow, aimed from far off, prepared well in advance, always a telling one, marvelously unerring and forceful. All his blows amaze me by their accuracy.

The irksome things she forces him to do . . . the evenings out with the family . . . the dinners at a restaurant . . . whether he wants or not . . . there's nothing he hates more . . . Seated opposite them, he watches them . . . two parakeets . . . two hungry magpies . . . their brains weigh less, that's well-known, it's a good idea to keep them shut up in harems, eating sweets, lounging on divans, jabbering among themselves, spinning their idiotic yarns the live-long day . . . a degrading promiscuity . . . their very presence has something debasing about it . . . he stares at them in his hostile manner, he is wearing his crestfallen, sullen expression—he had been in such a gay mood an instant before, but it always comes over him suddenly like that—and I, myself, like the people watching a certain well-known movie, who see Charlie Chaplin's companion in misery turn into an appetizing chicken under Charlie's famished eye, I too, like him, see seated side by side, opposite us, two dolls: the daughter already the image of the mother (he undoubtedly has them in mind—it would not surprise me about him—when he says occasionally in a grating tone that puts my teeth on edge, that young lovers, later on, have only themselves to blame: heaven warned them, but idiots that they were! they didn't want to see, they had only to give a good look at the bride's mother to know what to expect in twenty years), both of them painted, well-groomed, the mother's face cleaned, soaked and ironed out by too frequent visits to beauty-parlors, both bearing, as they should, the distinguishing marks of his power and ability, wearing all the expensive accessories, the mother with her mink stole, the daughter in her lovely summer-weight ermine tippet, pearl necklaces, the daughter's shorter, more modest, as yet but a hope, a timid sign . . . they lean towards each other with collusive smiles . . . the mother, as the daughter grows up, takes more and more with her the attitude of a former school-chum, they go into exasperating school-girl giggles, use little private words, known only to them, on the side—he pretends not to see, but he knows everything—they cook up all their little affairs together . . . walk arm in arm, nosing about in the shop windows, he pays without regard for cost, open-handed, a real doting papa, their friends envy them . . . laying their little schemes together, going crazy over all the rich men's sons, all the scoundrels who flutter round them scenting big money . . . organizing their entertainments, their surprise-parties, their racing parties, building and tearing down their edifices, in order one day, once all the scaffolding and unsightly supports have been removed, to achieve that masterpiece, that perfect work of art, that joy to behold, that target of enchanted, envious eyes, the picture in a smart magazine, the photograph that he will set proudly on his desk, of the young bride amidst a bower of lilies, smiling in her tulle veil . . . They chirp lightheartedly as though nothing had happened—who pays any attention to papa's moods, at his age there's no hope of changing him, he works too hard, lately he has been overworking —they examine the people at the nearby tables, with their hard, glittering bird's eyes . . . that way they have . . . what kind of upbringing has that girl had, anyway . . . but he gave up long ago . . . at one time he still had illusions, when he was young—it had been a terrible disappointment—, he had imagined, to console himself, that it was a matter of training, he had gamboled on all fours in the nursery in order to get her to play hunting in virgin forests, he had built boats and medieval castles, he had given her little tin soldiers . . . But more fool he . . . Merchandise on display—that's all . . . they think of nothing but getting married, all the rest, all the courses, diplomas, expensive lessons, all that is just so much eyewash, a way of passing the time . . . whom do they think they're fooling? They endure without flinching his hostile, icy gaze which should have forced them to huddle up close to each other timorously, all wizened up, faded, withered—and that might calm him—but they feel nothing, perhaps they can no longer escape from this form in which a charm cast by him holds them imprisoned, or else, seized with dizziness and knowing that they are condemned, they themselves, in order to hasten their fate, lay their heads under the blade, or, too sure of themselves and feeling themselves upheld, encouraged by everybody, they intend to defy him, or again, very simply, they indulge in a sort of weak gayety, a sort of sickly excitement, to which they give way occasionally, in spite of themselves, intoxicated as they are by ease, lazy security and frivolity . . . they turn towards me: "Did you see that, look at the table behind you . . . that female with the big hat . . . you can see her in the mirror . . ." I hesitate, hardly, nothing perceptible . . . the slightest movement now on my part, a gesture of recoil to show my disapproval, my disdain—that's what he expects from me, he expects me to stamp the trade-mark on the heavy, hard mold, the iron masks we have just forged for them—and he will keep the masks crammed down savagely over their faces, he will crush their mouths, flatten their noses, they will suffocate, they will wriggle to get away . . . I shall turn aside, ill at ease, ashamed . . . at all costs I must try to stop him, to hold him back, pretend that there's nothing, nothing that isn't quite normal, absolutely natural, turn round without a shade of embarrassment . . . "Where'd you say? That dame with the pointed hat?" . . . smile somewhat absent-mindedly . . . I turn, something prompts me . . . but it is not through a need to protect them against him, that's not it . . . I know what it is . . . I'm more afraid of them than I am of him . . . there is something in them which, for nothing in the world, I should like to set going, something dreadful, implacable, something that will awaken and get under way slowly . . . that threatens him, he doesn't see it, he's going to charge into it heedlessly like the little dog that sticks its nose in a snake's hole . . . I turn, they are encouraging me: "Over there, turn just a little, there, near the window . . . The blonde . . . she doesn't see you." A pact has been concluded, I have accepted their degrading promiscuity, their ignominious comradeship . . . he is watching us: now our fates are joined, the three of us alike, they and I, we're all in the same boat, groveling abjectly . . . our shopping expeditions . . . accomplices searching together, trying to unearth a rare bargain in the junk shops, or at some little second-hand dealer's . . . all that trash that had cost him a fortune, tastes like those of a woman, that *"métier"* . . . call that a *métier* . . . who ever heard of a young man passing his time thinking up all those booby-traps, those wire chairs, so many bird-perches, but those two women will accept anything, the stupidest guy can make them believe what he wants, they call that "an art" . . . and the way they look down on him—that beats all—he's the Boeotian, he doesn't understand anything about "ART" . . . their milch-cow, in reality that's what he is, and nothing else, he knows us, and me too, the young fellow, a pretty product . . . for that matter, it runs in his family, his mother before him never could do anything with her two hands, she couldn't darn a pair of socks, or cook an egg, married badly to that alcoholic who was always half-seas over, but she was so infatuated with him . . . later, as usual, he was the one who had to pay the damage . . . delightful, the nephew, "my nephew," at one time he had been proud of him, he thought something might be made of him, he talked about him to his customers, to his competitors: "my nephew is working for me, he will take my place one day . . ." but what the devil, they're good for nothing the entire family, a lot of nit-wits, ne'er-do-wells . . . All that, and a lot more still, expressed not in so many words, of course, as I am obliged to do now for lack of other means, not with real words like the ones we articulate distinctly out loud or in our thoughts, but suggested rather by certain sorts of very rapid signs that contain all that, summing it up—like a short formula topping a long algebraic construction, that expresses a series of complicated chemical combinations—signs so brief and which slip so quickly through him and through me that I could never succeed in really understanding or seizing them, I can only recover them in bits and snatches and translate them awkwardly by the words these signs represent, fleeting impressions, thoughts, feelings, often forgotten, that have been piling up for years and that now, assembled like a large and powerful army behind its banners, are regrouping, getting under way, about to roll forward . . . I cower, I duck my head, he leans towards us, hate in his eye, hissing . . .

25

" 'You' have a way of staring at people . . ." We remain motionless for a moment, huddled up close to one another, all grey, little sparrows lined up on a wire, a trembling bunch of sickly monkeys, and then, in her, something that had lain dormant—the very thing that had frightened me so, the reason why I had so weakly lined up on her side, against him—something inside her begins to stretch, to deploy, to rise up . . . the envelope in which the charm had enclosed her crackles, splits, now he too is afraid, I know it, a scatterbrained little fox-terrier that has imprudently stuck its nose in a snake's hole—she appears, hard, icy, pitiless, she examines him from an immense distance . . . the lady with the unicorn, the costly statuette, the far-away princess . . . "I didn't take so much as that with me, you hear me, when I went away . . . I left everything, from one day to the next" . . . she was lying on her bed, her cheek in her hand, reading a novel, he was walking up and down, endlessly talking, shouting, everywhere they went he collected crowds with his continual scenes of jealousy, his reproaches, his shouts, he called her every known name, a whore, she was nothing but that, a dirty little whore . . . so that was life together, their life? that was what people called life together! it had been hell from the start, he had always known it from the start, all she wanted was his money . . . why didn't she leave, she could go to the devil, into the gutter . . . where she belonged . . . she needn't count on him to go after her . . . he left, slamming the door, he came back . . . already, on their wedding trip in Syria, when he had caught the fever . . . such cold-hearted-

26

ness, such callousness on the part of a mere girl . . . not an atom of affection or sympathy, less than for the chauffeur, less than for her dog . . . but why doesn't she speak, why doesn't she answer, he came towards her clenching his fists, grabbed her book from her hands, why doesn't she say something . . . she remained unmoved, her face set, her eyes lowered, pretending to read . . . he was sobbing, his head leaning against the door-frame, he was alone, done for, he wouldn't be able to stand it . . . just one word, never an affectionate or fond word, not even his first name the way his mother used to call him . . . but she had never been able to call him by his first name . . . she should say what she wanted, anything she wanted, they had been together ten years, their child . . . everything was ready, the taxi was waiting downstairs, she had passed erect in her traveling suit, with veil lowered and gloves fastened, the chauffeur carrying her valise . . . I felt I wanted to implore her, to protect him, she should forgive him, she shouldn't pay any attention to him, he's so kind, only awkward, nervous, flares up easily . . . She stares at him for a long time without speaking and he looks away. Her lip curls as she turns on him a "look of disdain": "What's got into you, anyway?"

But it's not always like that. Sometimes, despite threatening signs of warning, she is caught unawares: doubtless she has not been alert enough, has remained too attached to her character of the moment, grown too soft, a little too inclined to give way for good to a sort of infantile insouciance, to a somewhat weak-minded cheerfulness, for her to be able to react at once. And that only frightens me all the more. Words that have humiliated us, if at times we havn't the force, rapidity of reflex, cunning and courage needed to retort, are like projectiles that we have not been able, or have neglected, to extract right away from our flesh, they remain imbedded in us, become encysted and risk forming tumors, or abscesses in which, little by little, hatred gathers. He won't lose anything by waiting, that I know. One fine day, at the most unexpected moment for him, and for her too, probably, the hatred that has gathered in her will crop out, it will spurt right into his eyes.

For the moment, she doesn't budge, or hardly. She blushes a bit; we exchange smiles, shrug our shoulders slightly, we are surprised, almost amused, forbearing, we take up good-naturedly where we had left off as though nothing had happened, in voices that are just a bit less self-assured, and taking pains not to look at him: "There, now, she has turned round, did you see that hat? This year's styles . . . unless you're as thin as a rail . . . but for women like that, imagine" . . . innocent little pigs dancing before the very eyes of the big, bad wolf; butterflies that a rustic has tried to seize between two coarse fingers: their wings barely crumpled, they resume their flight.

They walk through meadows, with one step they cross over brooks. Below their caps, the backs of their necks show the same hard sinews. Slung across their right shoulders they wear the same leather strap from which hangs a case containing a silver goblet. Their low-haunched backs move with the same undulating gait. I could follow them to the end of the world. In the restaurant, I can't take my eyes off the man's hands, with their large spatulate nails bordered by a roll of flesh, cutting the meat on the young boy's plate. I follow them to the mineral spring in order to watch them gargle in chorus, inhale together the sulphur vapors, stick the little funnel first in one nostril and then in the other.

I experience real delight as I watch them. In them I rediscover ourselves, I recognize us. This is our picture, our portrait such as a talented artist might have drawn it. They have what is lacking in us, shapeless models that we are, chaos in which a thousand possibilities clash—they have style, a revealing extravagance, simplicity, bold sharpness of feature.

We walk through meadows. With one step we cross over brooks. We trample on violets and daisies, we never stop to look at the hawthorn in bloom, we stare at the hills on the horizon, at the clouds and pine forests, without seeing them, he holds my nose and I swallow while he does the talking, with him you've never finished talking . . . corporations; boards of directors; profit and loss; inflation, deflation, stagnation on the Stock Exchange; war risks; gilt-edged securities; falling markets in Morocco; rise in real-estate values in Argentina; passports; visas; reservations for trains and steamships; dismissing the chauffeur . . . the amount of gasoline stolen from him every month, or the excess mileage he has discovered on his meter; his secretary's carelessness; a typist who has to be replaced—an irreparable loss, a "real pearl," she understood him almost before he spoke; buying apartments, houses; renting places for the summer; sickness, medicines, doctors; livers, lights, kidneys, lungs . . . inside him an endless trickle, it seeps through to the outside, overflows, covers me entirely, covers everything round us—no matter where we are—mountains, rivers, fields, seas, skies and suns, with a layer of soot, of ashes, with a layer of mud.

Sometimes—but it's so unlike me, so little in my line, so remote from the kind of thing I usually do that I can hardly believe I could have taken such a risk, it seems to me that I must have seen somebody else do it or even have dreamed it, while I walked along beside him, swallowing docilely—sometimes in a moment of sudden intrepidity or oblivion, I stop suddenly, and there, right in the middle of the meadow, beside the brook, dilating my nostrils, I make so bold as to breathe in the odor of new-mown hay, look at the distant hills and the pine woods and say . . . "Listen to that . . . those tinkling bells . . . the brook . . . Look over there at the line of those woods . . . that little hut . . ." The respite afforded me by this act of bravura is a very brief one. He turns his head, half-closes his eyes, casts an impatient, furious glance at the little brook, says nothing: a thick, heavy silence that quickly crushes the tinkle of bells and the ripple of the brook. Calling my entire strength into play, I probe his silence. My hearing—as well-trained and sharp as that of a trapper who, laying his ear to the ground, can catch the far-off gallop of horses—detects in it certain disquieting movements. Soon his silence becomes more deafening than the din of the most violent upbraiding and shouting. In my stupid unawareness, in my mad temerity, I have touched upon something very dangerous, something absolutely forbidden; I have committed the greatest offense. I have dared to give him a lesson, I have taunted him. Nature-lover, eh? The little blue flower? Purity? . . . All those dreamers and failures who go walking through meadows breathing in the perfume of flowers, pressing plants and pasting them in an album, chasing after butterflies . . . The countless idiots and good-for-nothings in whose stead people like himself do all the thinking, all the struggling, and they have the nerve—such dirty work as that, I should say not—to scorn the firm, hard world in which real men fight their battles for them, for the entire incompetent, lazy, irritable, fastidious, "esthetic" lot of them . . . he knows them . . . each one a bundle of self-conceit and vanity . . . wearing his wretched little feelings tenderly, gingerly, in a sling . . . and they're the ones who would like to teach him how to live, who want to set him an example of purity and unworldliness, no, really, it's enough to make you die laughing . . .

But I sense, as we walk along side by side in silence, that little by little the uproar inside him is calming down. I venture to take a look at him from the side: it seems to me that he is a bit crestfallen, that he has slumped a little into himself, he has a piteous, destitute, forlorn look that makes me think of an aging woman whose makeup has been removed by brusquely passing a sponge over her face. I am filled with remorse. It was I who had dragged him out of his shell, out of the carapace in which he had been secure, in which he felt everywhere at home, in which he betook himself, unafraid, from one end of the world to the other . . . But it's not only that, that's nothing. I did even worse: it was from me myself that I tore him away. I repulsed and rejected him at the moment when he was trying to hold on to me, to clasp me to him closely, huddled against each other, well protected inside the shelter he had built for himself, and which he never stopped reinforcing, very near, snug and warm, I myself somewhat wedged in, crushed by him . . . I blew it all up at once . . . I suddenly got out from under, and left him alone, naked, all at sea, clumsy, done for . . . a defenseless prey now to the sly threat, the unbearable distress that creeps over him along with the too calm, too soft evening air, the tinkle of little bells and the dubious, rather saccharine odor of the meadow.

I try to make up for it, I should like to be forgiven. I resume our conversation in a slightly uneasy voice, I begin to ask questions . . . "Those stocks, those Moroccan mines you were telling me about . . . how do you explain their having fallen so much lower than they were? . . ." He has to be wheedled, he is sulking a bit, but only as a matter of form: he asks nothing better than to forget, to take up everything again at the same point, as though nothing had happened. Soon he softens entirely, he begins to liven up . . . everything is all right again. The little cyclone, the tiny typhoon, the tempest in a teapot, has calmed down. We start again.

But that, as I said before, is an unusual experience. It's more like a dream, a flight of fancy. For I rarely put a spoke in his wheel like that. I usually do my best to make things easy for him.

I even sometimes take the lead, and, curiously enough, just at those moments when I feel gorged to the point of nausea, when I feel the greatest desire to break away, to flee. I have often wondered what devil eggs me on at those moments . . . Some might say, a love of suffering . . . a morbid need to be humiliated, a vague desire to see that thing that has remained dangerously live under the ashes, finally burst into flame and devour me, or perhaps a childish hope that I might succeed in resembling him, in order to feel at ease with him, in order to be encouraged and accepted, to be, like him, in a safe spot, huddled up to him snugly in his concrete shelter, or else a mad hope of commanding his respect, of beating him with his own weapons, on his own ground? . . . all that at the same time, undoubtedly, then all at once, occasionally, at the most unexpected moments for me, I go up to him, with a begging look, my hand outstretched, and ask him humbly—when I don't really need it and know perfectly what to expect—his opinion, his advice, I tell him stories, I unbosom myself, I confide my secrets, I brag . . . "By the way . . . I wanted to ask you . . . you know that exhibit I took part in with my friend, or rather . . . my associate . . . yes you do, you know . . . that exhibit of work by young artists; I designed a table and a sofa for it . . ." His face is motionless, sagging, his eyes immediately assume the vague, drowsy, bored expression that, at such moments, he feels obliged to wear. I was expecting it, but all the same my voice falters a bit . . . "Well, believe it or not, there's a decorator . . . he's still a young man, not very well known, but very talented, very promising, well, you know, he was very much interested in my work, I don't mean in that alone, everything we do interests him . . . he came to see us . . . he made us a proposal to work with him, to found a sort of association . . . he is better known than we are, in fact, he is already quite a favorite in certain circles . . . We thought that, under certain conditions, that is, by pooling everything . . . We are rather tempted, but we asked to be allowed to think it over . . . naturally we don't want to be done in, so I thought that you . . ." He turns sharply towards me as though he has just waked up and looks at me hard: "Who? What decorator? How's that? What house? Don't know. How much capital has he got? What does he propose exactly? What? I don't understand. On what basis? And what terms? . . ." He doesn't listen to the confused explanation I give him, spluttering the while. He has something else to do. He's too busy getting ready. The opportunity is really a golden one. Eager for sacrifice, reeling already with the heady joy of the martyr, the victim has come voluntarily, quivering and naked, to surrender to his will. No need to hurry. He takes his time. We are alone, shut in together, doors closed, all exits barred. No possible help from the outside. Absolute security. Impunity guaranteed. He takes up his stand firmly right in front of me . . . looks me straight in the eye, his glance points directly at the vulnerable spot, plunges into me like a dart . . . "Listen, my boy . . . since you are the one who has talked to me about it: you know I never mix into things, I gave that up long ago, and you do what you want. But since you are the one who has talked to me about it, I'll be frank. As for that, you know I always say what I think. And I'm not accustomed to doing things in a roundabout way . . . But —if you want to know what I really think, I'll say none of that is worth a tinker's damn. If I had billions to spend, I wouldn't put a sou in a business like that. And shall I tell you why? Because all that, all those fads, all those young geniuses people discover every six months, who are praised to the skies by a little circle of friends and then, two years later, never mentioned again, even their names are forgotten, well, they're just a bunch of wool-gatherers and humbugs . . . They don't understand that much . . . he snaps his fingers . . . not that much, you hear me, about the simplest business matter. They live in a sort of dream world, tinker around a bit here and there, get mutually drunk on one another's compliments, but they just don't know how to work, they haven't even taken the pains to really learn their job, they're satisfied with anything that comes into their heads . . . so-called creations . . . all that is just so much eye-wash, a lot of trash to bowl people over with . . ." I make a weak attempt to disengage myself; but the position I awkwardly assume will only make it more convenient for him to clutch hold of me, to reinforce his grip . . . "You don't think that men like Leneux . . . Because you could have said the same thing about Leneux, or about Tillier, if you had known them when they were getting started . . . —I don't know Tillier, but as regards Leneux, I beg your pardon. Leneux, I do know. At one time I was even pretty well informed about his business, because I bought some stock in it. Leneux is quite another story. He's somebody. A hard worker, he is, and with his head screwed well on his shoulders; he knows what he's about, that I can tell you, he knows his job and he himself works better than any of his workmen. He can drive a nail with the best of them. And, believe me, his stuff lasts. It's sturdy, it's well designed. He has a sense of reality. No wool-gathering about him. And shall I tell you, since we're speaking frankly, since you came to talk it over with me . . . I didn't want to say anything, afterwards you would have said that I had tried to influence you . . . I'm going to tell you something . . . you'll do what you want about it . . . I know people pretty well . . . I haven't seen very much of your boss or, if you prefer it, your associate, but I've been observing him, and I don't believe I'm mistaken. Well, shall I tell you what I think: he and Leneux are just the opposite of each other. I've known lots of people like him . . . and they never amount to much later on . . . he's a conceited little fellow, as touchy as they come . . . I sized him up right away . . . he gets indignant and red in the face, starts twisting about like a school-girl as soon as you dare make the slightest criticism or don't praise his so-called inventions to the skies. I was bold enough to make some sort of innocent joke about those arm-chairs on the electric-chair model that he made for our parlor, and you would have thought that I had bit him. I know people like that well, and remember, my boy, what I tell you: that's not the way to succeed in life. Those fellows consider that things should just fall into their hands like manna from heaven . . . They haven't got the slightest idea what it means to really work, to get bawled out . . . the way I used to get bawled out by my boss when my work wasn't perfect . . . at his age I got red in the face with pleasure when, occasionally—and it wasn't often, I didn't have exhibits at that age, you can be sure of that—I was that thrilled when my boss touched me on the shoulder and said: well, sonny, today's a good day, you can be pleased, what you've done there is not too bad . . . You'll see, you'll remember what I'm saying: with ideas like that, people don't get anywhere. I didn't say a word when you announced you wanted to work with him . . . I didn't say a thing . . . I let people do what they want . . . But you'll see for yourself . . . Life will teach you."

One might legitimately hope, indeed it would be only natural, my instinct for self-preservation, however weak and atrophied, having nevertheless got the upper hand again, that I should react by a fit of real anger, or resentment, a gesture of revolt, of refusal, or else, on the contrary—and this would be just as satisfying—that I should let myself be won over, resign myself, give in . . . But I don't. I continue to abide by the tacit agreement that exists between us, I play the game till the end. Because it's a game between us, nothing more. A sham. A bull-fight minus the kill. If I stopped playing, if I were to take him seriously, as I have seen happen, to my great embarrassment and discomfiture, in the case of certain uninitiated persons, among others, my associate who, one day, after a similar dissertation, innocently proposed to release me from our contract and advised me to go work with someone having more experience, he scowled, he was ill at ease, furious —the game had turned out badly, his opponent had dropped out at the most exciting point—with a crestfallen expression he said, in a changed, toneless, slightly hoarse voice: "Oh! you know, things like that can't be decided in one minute, it's not so simple as all that, we'll have to see about it. We'll see about it later. After we've thought it over, we'll talk about it again."

And people have told me—but if they hadn't told me, I should have guessed it—that he shows his friends clippings he cut out at the time of the exhibit, with photographs of our models . . . "Look, what do you say about my nephew? He's a talented youngster, not bad at all . . . What do you think?"

That, for me, as regards them, is the worst thing: my incapacity to make up my mind about them. Whether to like them once and for all, or to hate them. Put them in the stocks and hang a number round their necks so as to know what they're really like. Everybody (if they didn't, how could people live?) succeeds in doing this, without effort, and with a rapidity and sureness that each time baffles me. People take their stand in front of you, at a proper distance, and look you over: what is he like? What did he say to me? What has he done? Should he be allowed to come closer? Or should he be kept at a distance? Thus their instinct for self-preservation, which is always strong, makes it possible for them to form an opinion and to dare, when it suits them, keep their own distance. Indeed, it is thanks to that, to this instinct for self-preservation, to their self-respect—as they call it—and which I so envy them, that their lines of conduct are so well laid down, so clearly, so purely drawn. I've tried countless times to imitate them. But it's useless. I can't do it. Here, between us, it can't be done.

Her slender, heavily-ringed fingers are holding the menu; with smartly puckered lids and mouth drooping in a captious, fastidious pout, she scans the menu while he, leaning across the table, proffers, offers, himself included, she must order, it's all hers, anything she wants, she has only to say the word, anything whatsoever can be prepared, can be sent for, a sign from her and he will have unrolled before her a flying carpet covered with delicious foods, he snaps his fingers . . . psst! . . . the waiters come running . . . "Is your lobster really good today, unusually good? . . . You see, it couldn't be any fresher, boiled immediately, straight from their beds; believe me, that will whet your appetite, only without mayonnaise, mayonnaise

might be a bit heavy . . . No? You should, you know . . .
Or how about some oysters, perhaps, to start with . . .
Belons? You like those . . . Or clams might be fun . . ." No,
really she's not hungry, no, nothing, none of all that this
evening . . . she turns towards the head-waiter her well-pre-
served, well-groomed, smooth face . . . she hasn't changed
much in the last twenty years, her features have even taken
on a certain nobility, her soft, silky, very transparent skin
still has the same marvelously downy quality, the same
exquisite, fresh smell . . . no, not this evening, just a slice
of ham and a few plain boiled potatoes, that's all she wants
today. At once his excitement subsides. His face falls. If he
could, he would be on the point of dropping into his
grouchy, scowling manner, but instead, he suddenly
straightens up, in the face of adversity we must keep a
stout heart, everything is for the best, the important thing
is for everybody to be happy and satisfied; today the three
of us, she, their daughter and I, are his guests of honor,
his distinguished visitors whom he is entertaining and
showing about, his fond glance pleads for our satisfaction,
our approval . . . "Are you all right? A little bit too near
the passage-way? Not too much of a draft? Fine, fine, that's
good. Everything's fine. Look, did you notice those neon
lights they've put in? That's something new . . . And the
aquarium? Why, that's marvelous." The two women look
politely at the ceiling with absent-minded approval, they
are leaning towards each other, laughing and whispering
. . . What are they saying? . . . he leans in their direction:
"What's that? Where? Who?" They hardly deign to reply

. . . "It's nothing . . . over there . . . you can't see her, she's right behind you. A woman with a big hat . . ." He turns cautiously, and looks . . . he asks nothing better than to do his utmost . . . if they'll only give him a chance, if they'll allow him to come nearer, to join in . . . all he asks is to learn, to understand . . . he is unworthy, that he knows well, he's so awkward, such a boor . . . he feels a bit uneasy, lost, with them everything is so imponderable, so elusive, all in half-tones, subtle, delicate, witty, frightfully fragile . . . And underneath their apparent insouciance, their clever frivolity, are countless hidden traps, hidden dangers . . . in order to avoid these, you must know how to conform to a thousand secret rules which have never been formulated and are impossible to teach, which one should be able to apply at any moment without knowing it, without even a thought . . . a very sensitive mechanism in them—almost nothing will start it swinging, make the needle turn on the graduated circle, less than nothing, a gesture, an intonation, an accent, the line of a hair-cut, of people's clothes . . . the most minute indications are the most important—an eye inside them, which nothing escapes, a pitiless, icy eye, is sizing you up at all times, passing judgement on you . . . a half-smile on their faces, a sly glance, a sudden peal of laughter, and you may be sure that you have been condemned with no possible appeal . . . though he plead, take heed . . . I catch sight of his hand on the point of mopping his plate with his bread, it lays the bread down, picks up a fork . . . she didn't need to flick an eyelash, she didn't even look at him, he felt it

41

right away . . . long, arduous training has schooled him
. . . a current emanating from her, invisible, powerful
waves, like those that guide aeroplanes from a distance,
direct all his movements . . . he bends, straightens up, advances, retreats, fidgets, strains . . . I should like to snatch
him from this charmed circle in which he is caught, in
which I am caught with him, feeling myself, as he does,
no, even more strongly, much more strongly than he does—
as regards all these things I am always more Catholic than
the Pope, more royalist than the King—those invisible
waves emanating from her and weighing upon us, while I
observe, lie in wait, force myself to foresee, to forestall all
her movements, continually on the alert for the effect produced . . . What a relief, what a release it would be, if he
should break the spell, if he should suddenly be trans-
formed and become as he was, seated here in this same spot,
the two women opposite us, two dolls, two jabbering magpies, spouting their nonsense, exchanging their little secrets
under his look of hate, bursting into school-girl giggles
over nothing at all, when he charged at them, head lowered, unmindful of danger, heedless of their sly resentments, their delayed vengeance, when he let fly at us and
flayed us with his hissing, burning "you" . . . I should prefer
that.

But all that is forgotten now, all that is effaced. He has
such moments: at times very little suffices . . . a compli-
ment someone has paid him, a successful business deal, a
smile from the pretty girl at the news-stand, his umbrella
that he thought he had lost and which someone has brought

back, or even nothing in particular—and suddenly everything changes, luck smiles at him . . . for that matter, we make our own luck . . . life can still be beautiful, it depends on us, life is what we make it, a little good will, a little good humor, and things come out all right . . . people pass their time making a stupid mess of their lives when happiness is there right within reach . . . he's impatient to get home, he hurries, quick, he must straighten it all out right away, everything can be patched up, nothing is ever entirely lost, he runs up the stairs, whistling . . . people are right, you can say what you want, it's wonderful, in reality, that's the only thing that matters, a home, a wife, a daughter, despite all the cares, all the friction—who has none? . . . Oh! he knows what he's like, he's not very good-natured, he must not always be too easy to get along with, not a mean bone in him, certainly, but awfully nervous, flares up easily—he races up the stairs two steps at a time, he gets out his key . . . she's there, she's waiting for him in her room, making herself ready, surely . . . a pink, silky nest, and she too, pink and silky, sweet-smelling, just a little bit faded, but that makes her all the more touching, perishable, fragile and sweet, he longs to protect her, to coddle her, he loves her, in reality, that's what it is, he has always loved her, nothing else has ever really mattered, it's strange all the same, it's wonderful, one can really say that, after so many years, still the same impatience, still the same excitement . . . he almost runs as he crosses the vestibule . . .

She, as soon as he comes in, as soon as she hears—she

recognizes them right away, she has known them for a long time—that voice, that tone that he has in his moments of emotion, that childish, defenseless, naïve, caressing tone, and that limp, muggy voice, it seems to her—I know it, I feel it each time just as she does—that right away everything inside her bristles like fur on a cat's back. At first, you don't understand very well what it is you feel when you're near him in those moments: a certain embarrassment . . . a revulsion . . . that coaxing, damp, limp intonation creeps into you, tries to get at you in your most secret, best guarded spots, it's a lack of decency, a criminal lack of respect, an attempt at rape . . . One has the feeling of being the tool of his pleasure, his plaything . . . He doesn't give a hoot what others might feel . . . in fact, he doesn't see the people about him, he doesn't look at them . . . you might die of sorrow, pine away beside him, without his seeing it . . . people are nothing but puppets, dolls, subject to the whims of the spoilt, stupid, frivolous child that he is . . . he fancies that it suffices for him to shout "I quit," that in the twinkle of an eye he can change rôles, play something else, wipe out, as with a sponge, with that muggy voice of his, what he has engraved in her, and in me, the indelible marks left by his scratches, his bites, his bursts of hatred that burn and disfigure, vitriol. With a hardly perceptible movement (but which he perceives right away: it's as though a cold breath, a cold pale irradiation, emanated from her, from the somewhat too neutral tone in which she answers, when he asks where they're going . . . "I don't know, wherever you want." . . . from her silence

. . . from the gesture with which she lifts her coat as she gets into the car ahead of him . . .), she brushes him aside, keeps him at a distance, she sets a gap between them that he tries to bridge, she spreads out an icy desert that he seeks to cross at all costs, he grows restless, over-active, tense, the dance begins. The rôles—without either he or she being able to change them—have been cast between them for the evening.

No matter what pains I take to open and close my door as silently as possible, and go stealing through the corridor, her hearing, which is as practiced as that of prisoners in their cells, picks up immediately, and recognizes, the faintest noise about her in the house. Ensconced in her bedroom, she supervises, keeps watch. Sometimes I believe that I am safe, I have succeeded in passing beyond the most dangerous spot, the great open space of the vestibule where the floor-boards always crack loudest, and am about to turn the latch of the main door beyond which I can begin to decamp, when all at once I feel in my back, running up my spine like a mild, electric discharge that makes me jump, the expected sound of her voice: "Are you going out already? Did you finish your rest? I've got something to say to you . . . Only five minutes . . . I must speak to you . . ." I splutter a vague excuse, unconvinced however, just as a matter of form . . . My time—and they know it— is not what it is with other people, well fenced in, guarded by solid partitionings against which they would injure themselves like thieves who tried to climb walls bristling with bits of broken glass. My time has no walls, no spikes. My time is a passage-way open to the four winds . . . I splutter that I wanted to take advantage of the sunshine, but she says that the sun has gone in, that it would be better to wait a while, to avoid sharp changes of temperature, I'll be less apt to catch cold, there's no hurry . . . And I give in right away. I never do resist. Relieved, in fact, despite my mild impulses towards escape, and the rage, the revulsion, that her voice had aroused in me at the moment, glad to slip back on to my natural slope, to drop back into what, for us here, is the normal state of affairs. If she were to play me the trick of allowing me to escape several times, without trying to catch me, I know well—and so does she—that I should soon be back again, under one pretext or another, knocking at her door. As I follow her, it is rather pleasant to feel once more the sensation of slight dizziness, of very slight nausea, such as precedes a fainting spell, that I always experience when I let myself go like that, when I let myself drift, tossed about, at the mercy of their movements, those minute movements that always make them fidget in one spot; while I float, inert and limp, borne away, then back again, by the weak ebb and flow, like greyish carrion dancing on the surface of the warm waters that border on tideless seas.

We settle down in her room, in our usual spot, I on one corner of her easy-chair, she opposite me, on the edge of the couch. She points to the wall with a movement of her head: "Do you hear that? They've been there, shut up in her room for hours, that makes over two hours that that girl has been there . . . You saw yourself, we had hardly left the table when she arrived. Entire days are spent like that, doing nothing, listening to jazz, babbling away . . . What anybody can talk about with a little parrot like that, I'd like to know . . . Yesterday, I couldn't stand it any longer, they had been listening to jazz all afternoon . . . I went in . . . there they were sprawled out on their chairs . . . the disorder . . . I'll spare you . . . dirty dishes on all the furniture . . . the floors covered with cigarette butts . . . reading *Votre Beauté* . . . she saw perfectly well that I was furious, but don't think that made them move, on the contrary . . . it's enough for her to realize that I'm put out by something, for her to do it on purpose . . . I know that I make a mistake to mix into what she does, it doesn't do any good, but that's easier said than done . . . the fact is that, for some time now, the situation has been getting out of hand . . . she's no longer interested in anything, she's stopped reading . . . she used at least to like concerts, from time to time she would go to a picture exhibit . . ." Her voice is tapering away to a fine thread that hardly issues from her swelling throat; on the other side of the wall something heavy is also swelling and pulling, a heavy flabby existence, grafted onto hers, living its own life with the sly, invincible obstinacy of a morbid excrescence, like a proliferating tumor; one can hear, coming from there, pitiless, piercing, peals of laughter and loud voices, the clink of tea-cups and spoons, that, at times, make her shudder and grow silent: brief twinges . . . it has to be felt, palpated, examined well from every side, pressed the way we keep feeling and pressing a sore spot, reassuring ourselves, irritating it, and the more we press, the more it swells . . . "For instance, I remember, already last year, when there was that exhibit . . . those Flemish painters . . . I couldn't stand it any longer, it was about to close, it had been on for two months, I had already been to see it several times . . . you know how I adore painting. I'll grant you, our children are not necessarily like us, but just the same . . . she didn't set foot there a single time . . . I had decided not to say a word, what's the use, but I couldn't help it, I made so bold as to suggest in a sort of indifferent way . . . as if it went without saying . . . because you have to be as sly as a fox now to make her do the slightest thing . . . I suggested that she could go with me if that amused her . . . I wanted to see them once more, they're so marvelous, aren't they, you never get tired of looking at them . . . well, you should have seen her expression . . . her face hardened . . . you know how she can look . . . she muttered that she couldn't go, that somebody was expecting her, it was that little nit-wit, an ignoramus who's not interested in anything, who has no conversation . . . when I think . . ." her voice is becoming hoarse, tapering off more and more to a very fine thread . . . "when I think of what we didn't do . . . you know your uncle . . . he always did what I wanted about things like that, he kept saying that it was no use, that it was a waste of both time and money, but you know how he is, he never haggled about things, nothing was too good, the smartest private schools, the best teachers . . . I hoped she would make some friends, that's so important . . . there were Malut's daughter, a charming girl, Roland Despré's two girls, in other words, the very best social background, she could have chosen any number, but of course, she had to hook up with the most vulgar and the most stupid . . . The other day, really that gave me a shock, you'll never guess what she reads . . . I went into her room to straighten up a bit, I took advantage of her being out—she gets up at impossible hours, the maid complains, she can't get anything done—well, do you know what I found? piles of detective stories, all kinds of horrible things, Delly's insipid novels . . . of course that girl lends her all that, she adores that, naturally, what can you expect her to like, in the environment she lives in? you should see her parents . . . Oh! and do you know what I found under a pile of idiotic books . . . your book, the one you gave her . . . you remember, you racked your brain before her birthday to know what to give her . . . Apollinaire's poems in that charming edition you had found on the quays . . . well, my dear, you needn't have taken such trouble, she hadn't opened it, the pages weren't even cut." . . . Several birds with one stone, several motions at a time, that's what she's doing at this moment, that's what they always do: while she feels about for the sore spot on herself and presses and scratches it, she comes close to me, rubs up against me, caresses me, flatters me. In the same way that the patient, during a painful operation, or a laborious extraction, finds

49

comfort in holding tight to the strong, healthy arm of the nurse, she squeezed my sturdy arm—all of my own weaknesses, which she knows so well, all the savage carving in which, on other occasions, she had indulged herself on me, are effaced, forgotten—we are on the same side, amongst honest folk, energetic and refined, we understand each other almost without a word, we speak the same language, let's up and at the common enemy . . . But I am seized with loathing, a desire to tear her from me, I refuse the alliance, I don't want to play her game . . . a little dignity, what the devil, a little decency . . . my tone is irritated, coldly distrustful: "Oh, there I think you're going a bit far, you're just getting yourself worked up, aren't you?" . . . her display of suffering, her weakness and dependence impel me to be insolent . . . "She's not so soft as all that . . . Remember how proud you were when she passed her exams . . . She must have worked just the same . . ." She laughs with a metallic, false sort of laughter . . . "Work? I was proud? Are you joking?" . . . She lowers her voice a bit: "Those exams, now I'm going to tell you how she passed them, but that you won't tell to anybody, eh? you promise me? it must remain just between ourselves." I recognize now, by my excitement, by the sudden flush of warmth that stirs in me, that this was just what I had wanted, this as well, at the same time (I too always kill two birds with one stone): to make her betray, make her deliver the girl into my hands. Plead false in order to find out the truth . . . Find out . . . always this morbid curiosity, this necessity to know what they're hiding, to take a peep behind their scenery, to obtain confirmation of what I scent, what I surmise . . . She leans towards me, her voice is softening, moistened by the saccharine delight of betrayal . . . I'm going to tell you how she passed them, those exams . . . it was because we paid the price, with private lessons, we spent a fortune, she had to be coached in everything, you'll laugh, in natural science, in history, and with the best teachers . . . she had French lessons with a University Professor . . . in fact, it was thanks to him that she passed those exams, she had the good luck to happen on a subject he had made her work on one month before the examination, he had planned it all for her, he had masticated all the ideas for her, otherwise, you may be sure . . . she hadn't done a thing for three years, always at the foot of her class . . . she was no longer interested in anything . . ." She remains silent a moment, looking into space . . . "And when I think . . . What a gifted child she used to be . . . so bright, interested in everything . . . And a hard worker . . . Everybody paid me compliments about her . . ." Back up a bit, that's what she's trying to do now . . . she has felt in me a movement of satisfaction: I must not, after all, feel too much at ease . . . not impute to her . . . she has nothing to do with it, on the contrary . . . good blood will tell . . . the original soil was a rich one, unusual ability . . . the secret language is so clear, the words written with invisible ink are so legible, that she would not need to insist if at the same time she were not impelled by a desire to scratch herself harder, to make the wound bleed, to palpate, press the sore spot, to lift, pull, tear off . . . "It's very simple . . . she was bright in everything . . . marvelous memory . . . at three she recited several La Fontaine fables by heart. When she was twelve or thirteen years old, I had to go and take the books away from her at eleven o'clock at night. As for sports . . . Swimming . . . She skated beautifully . . . Her teacher told me that she would be a second Sonja Henie . . ."

Those were happy days. The tables turned. At that time, the flow of nourishment from one to the other, had been in the opposite direction. She had been the parasite, the flabby excrescence attached to the other, from which it drew its sustenance. Settled down, as one often sees them . . . seated at the edge of tennis courts, beside swimming pools or skating-rinks, cosily huddled up to themselves in a sort of comfortable motionlessness, a delightful security, their avid gaze clinging to the child's every movement, their mouth gaping complacently while they become penetrated with the vivifying irradiations released by the achievement, in sweat, anxiety and joy, of a successfully accomplished gesture.

But let the awaited satisfaction be lacking, let the child grow frightened, give up, or fail, and all their unemployed energies will find vent in explosions of hate, blows and shouts, the child is suddenly confronted with a shrew whose face is disfigured by resentment and rage, a famished beast, avid for carnage . . . "Oh, I can tell you that she has changed considerably . . . at present she's a gawk and a dough-ball. Little by little she has let everything drop, tennis, swimming, in fact, she has even changed physically . . . she's too fat, she no longer has any muscles, any resilience . . . you've noticed her martyred look when she has to get up from a chair . . . you hardly dare ask her to hand you an ashtray . . . but there's just one thing she can always find strength for, oh, she's never too tired for that, and that is, to look at herself in the mirror, she spends hours at it, she could have become a world champion, got the highest University degrees, if she had spent a quarter of the time at it that she passes examining herself . . . it makes me positively sick; one of these days I'm going to break all the mirrors in the house . . . And to do what, I ask you, to spend the entire day shut up with that idiotic girl . . . I'm going to tell you something . . ." she lowers her voice . . . "if you think I don't know . . . they're interested in one thing only . . . young men . . . how to please the boys . . . popularity . . . it's understandable that a young girl should want to look well, but this is something quite different . . . I was tidying her room one day and I found a little notebook" . . . their rapid, ferreting hands . . . they collect rotting refuse in the bottom of kitchen sinks, feel about in greasy water, unfold dubious linen, soiled diapers, no repugnance, no shame, stops them, it's their rôle here below, their mission, always to be rummaging, to scrub dark recesses, to clean them all, things, souls, bodies, to scrape, to mend, to knead, to prune . . . "That day, I assure you, I got a shock. I suspected it, but I didn't think things had reached that point: it's a real obsession. That's all they think about . . . am I as pretty as I should be? . . . did so-and-so like me? . . . what did he think? . . . then endless beauty hints, you would think she was a middle-aged woman afraid of growing old, recipes for making eye-lashes grow, for having a slender nose, for acquiring charm and smartness . . . poor child, the trouble is that it all takes place here . . ." she points to her forehead . . . "in her mind . . . whenever she has to make an effort, or go out, it's finished, there's nobody left, as soon as a young man comes near her, pftt, she wants to run away, she's afraid of him . . ."

Astonishing, really—I can never admire it enough—the prescience, the extraordinary clairvoyance that, without our knowing it, govern certain of our movements: all that, all of what she is divulging, all of what she is passing on to me, and more, much more still, something subtler, more complicated, I had guessed it, perceived it, all at once, and not only I—there would be nothing so astonishing about that: I have known them pretty intimately and for a pretty long time, it could have been accumulating in me little by little without my noticing it, and then crop up all of a sudden, in one lump—not only I, a friend of mine who hardly knows them—although to tell the truth, things like that are often more clearly perceptible at a distance and to a less accustomed eye—had also perceived it, we had seen the whole thing all at once, without speaking of it, even, . . . now I realize it . . . it all comes back to me, the entire scene, the tiny tragi-comedy, that day, on the stairs . . . when we passed them . . . the two little girl-friends, very much the school-chum type, all timid and wriggly: a single gesture had revealed the whole thing to me, that furtive gesture with which one of them, when she saw us, had immediately smoothed the roll of hair on her neck, or even less than that, nothing perceptible to the naked eye, nothing that can be described, just a vibration that went through them, a certain unsteadiness, a weak titillation . . . something had stirred faintly, something avid and frightened . . . we had sensed, emanating from them, a sweetish effluvium, an insipid odor . . . and, in the same way that a doctor who smells a sore or notices a pale red blotch, makes his diagnosis right away . . . no, that's not true either, we didn't have time to think anything, we didn't diagnose anything, what suddenly rose up in us, without our knowing very well why, may be compared rather to the gluttonous rage of a tiger who feels his prey palpitating under his paw, all soft and already resigned, or else, one might better compare the effect upon us of the effluvia they gave off to that which the sweet stench of carrion has on vultures, we dived right at them, my friend first, being quicker, more skillful—I'm far from it, but I followed him immediately, I shared in the feast—he looked at them smiling, the words must have come to him naturally, he certainly didn't hunt about for them, there were only too many to choose from: "Tell me, that friend of yours I met with you, what ever became of her? You know whom I mean . . . a tall, blonde girl . . . you remember . . . he turns towards me: a marvelous girl, very slender, with sort of slits for eyes . . . We thought she was so nice . . ." It seems to me that I heard, while they answered with a pitiful, constrained little smile, having collapsed all at once from the prick, as though deflated, grown suddenly limp and crumpled: "Oh, yes . . . I know whom you mean . . . Andrée . . . yes, we see her from time to time . . . yes, indeed, she is very nice . . . she's at the Sorbonne this year, working for a degree in English . . ." it seems to me that I must have perceived, escaping from them like gases from a hole in the belly of a dead animal—the faint whistle made by putrid exhalations . . .

What I experience now resembles satisfaction, the excitement of a scientist who sees his hasty hypothesis confirmed by experiment. I should like to understand it better, study the process more closely . . . "That's very interesting, what you just said, that idea that, with them, everything takes place here (I point to my forehead). I had noticed it too . . . It is as though they were not really living . . . as though they were living in a novel . . . a slightly old-fashioned novel . . . they themselves have something old-fashioned, something antiquated about them . . . young ladies of the old school . . . they don't belong in our time . . . it's very curious . . ." I must make amends. I made a mistake to speak with that slightly disgusted superiority of the good housewife's ferreting hands, cleaning dark corners, palpating the hole in kitchen sinks—it wasn't that, at least not quite that, it's always a mistake to plunge headfirst like that, in a single direction, it doesn't take long to see that you have to retrace your steps—there is in her expression, while she answers me with just a touch of bitterness, a look of earnestness, of noble resignation, detachment. Like the scientist who agrees to sacrifice his own body to the progress of science, rising above her own suffering, she consents to help me in my quest: "Yes, as you say, it's curious. The other girl, I know nothing about, but in any case, as regards my daughter, you have judged rightly: she is outmoded, she's a girl of a century ago. At her age, on the contrary, one ought to be rather in the *avant garde,* it seems to me, ahead of one's time, one feels like smashing everything, breaking through old limitations . . . When I was that age . . ." She reflects a moment, she is hesitating . . . "You know what I'm going to say . . . sometimes I wonder if it's not because of me . . . if it's not my fault, indirectly . . . she knows that I've had a rather brilliant life, that I've been rather sought after . . . I wonder if, in her case, it's not a desire to resemble me . . . that often happens, doesn't it? . . ." I interrupt her impatiently . . . "Yes, it's very possible, even probable, but that's of no importance, that's not exactly where the question lies" . . . This is not the moment to allow ourselves to wander off, we're hot, we're about to touch the point, I feel it, whence came that strange smell . . . "It seems to me that what matters especially, is what you just said, that it all takes place in her mind . . . she has no real desires of her own, no real impulses, the whole thing is simmered without heat . . . She's satisfied with ready-made images, that's why she's always trying to imitate someone . . . that's why . . . now I understand what it was that I sensed vaguely without ever having quite explained it . . . that's why, with young people her own age, young men especially . . . I can confess this to you: even with me . . . there's something wrong, one feels no fervor in her, if you understand what I mean, no sparkle . . . no real temperament that attracts people . . . towards which they are drawn . . . On the contrary, one feels something cold, a bit sluggish . . ." I've gone as far as I could: the gangrened limb is almost severed: I dare not go further. Her turn now. She gathers her strength together, she's really suffering, I can see that, but we must be courageous . . . "yes . . . that is undoubtedly it" . . . the words are coming with difficulty . . . "you are certainly right . . . that's it . . . a certain lifelessness, that's the whole thing . . . no strong instincts . . . no temperament . . . nothing but sterile harping on the same thing . . ." She collects all her strength, in order to make one final effort: "asthenic, really, that's what she is . . . what she has become. I've known it, in fact, for a long time." The tie is cut, the painful ablation is over. The sick limb is nothing now but a flabby mass of gory tissue lying apart from the body.

At this point, someone more naïve than I am, less experienced, convinced of her courage, believing that he was relieving her entirely and feeling himself relieved, unburdened at last, would not have failed to add: "However, she's like that. You'll have to resign yourself. At her age, you won't be able to change her." But, as my uncle says, "I know with whom I have to deal." I know that I've already let myself go much too far. It's always dangerous to take a direct part in this last phase of the operation. This is the moment to be careful. I try to get out of it, to back up . . . "Oh, there I think you overstate a bit . . . A certain lack of vitality, perhaps . . . that, yes . . . but between that and saying that she is asthenic . . . let's not exaggerate things. We have all passed through periods more or less like that . . . I believe that it's largely a matter of age . . ." Too late. Badly played. She gives me a cutting, sidelong glance of hate, she has assumed her coldly polite voice, her society tone: "Oh, well . . . that's that . . . Believe me, don't ever have any children . . . And what about yourself . . . I'm impossible . . . I talk to you about nothing but my troubles . . . what have you been up to lately? How are your plans coming along?" She hardly listens to my reply. Once more she's all ears. She's on the look-out. And should the door of the next room be heard to open, or there be a step in the hall, she would jump up right away, all agog, slightly ill at ease . . . "Excuse me . . . I must go . . . I think I had better go . . ."

It is astonishing to see with what rapidity, with what invincible force of attraction, they come together, become re-welded. Two hours later, I meet them in the hall, coming in gaily, their arms filled with parcels, their pointed laughter fused into one peal . . . you would never believe that they are mother and daughter, people say sentimentally, you would think they were two sisters, or two friends . . . I am ready to bet—there's little risk that I'll lose—that the alliance between them has been revived at my expense. This time, no doubt about it, I am the designated prey that the mother, in order to calm her own resentment, or her remorse, has fed to her child. As they trot about, arm in arm, stopping to inspect the shop windows, or seated side by side, their little notebooks and pencils in hand, watching the latest fashion shows, they lean towards each other: "You know, at times he makes me anxious . . . Really . . . To-day we had a little talk, I asked him what he expected to do, how his plans were coming on . . . he began to splutter and seemed quite bewildered . . . When you consider how old he is . . . Just think . . . After all, can you imagine a man like your father, at his age . . ."

Nothing more commonplace, when all is said and done —I recognize that—nothing more usual, than entertainment of this kind. Everybody, more or less, shares with us the need we feel, from time to time—and even rather frequently—to throw a bone to gnaw on at this person or the other, in order to cheat our own hunger, a rattle to chew on, in order to calm our dull irritation, our itching. Moralists and satirists have often described it, often joked about it, psychologists have not neglected the study of what they call the need for disparagement: the remedy used most frequently, according to them, by those who suffer, who seek relief, from an inferiority complex, the supreme tonic for depressed persons. Only, compared to our games, these current and, on the whole, rather harmless pastimes, are as polite parlor games to the blood-letting games of the arena. It is rare that one or the other of us doesn't come out of them—and especially myself, I believe—if not maimed for life, at least considerably battered. And yet I am always amazed to see how, like certain women for whom a provident nature allows them to forget the pangs of child-birth, we never fail, still panting and with our wounds freshly dressed, to seize upon the first opportunity offered us to start over again.

With him, often, when I begin, in order to allay my apprehensions, I let myself believe that I have yielded to pity: he is so exasperated, it is so painful, so embarrassing to feel—as I did that time when we were walking, he and I, side by side, in the meadow—how distressed, dependent and shaky he is, to see his eternally unappeased disquiet, his hungry dog look—that I throw this to him to soothe him. But from that moment on, somewhere further down inside me, I realize one thing: he is the master. He gives the orders. I pretend to believe that I give in to him, the way one gives in to a sick child's whims, or to the supplicating eyes of a dog. But the dog, in this case, is myself. With my eyes glued to him, I watch, I obey. As soon as he throws a pebble, or merely outlines the gesture of throwing, right away, like a well-trained dog, off I go, I hunt, I dig, I unearth, with infallible flair I find, I retrieve. I am both skillful and prompt. Remarkably disciplined. Long training has sharpened all my senses. The slightest little thing sets me on the alert, makes me prick up my ears: a sudden change, hardly perceptible, indefinable, in the nature of his silence, in which it seems to me that something—like a snow-ball—is revolving upon itself and increasing in size, or else, that a hollow, a void, is forming . . . I couldn't say very well what it is . . . or all of a sudden it's his eyes that become set and heavy . . . and right away, I leap up, so cleverly, so quickly, that it seems to me I make almost no effort, and with an innocent look, that's the look you must have, I retrieve . . . "Do you know whom I ran across?" He doesn't move. I assume a tantalizing, playful air . . . "Guess . . ." He makes a gesture of impatience. "I haven't the slightest idea, I tell you. How should I know?—Somebody who liked you a lot . . ." He shrugs his shoulders and turns in his chair, he is wearing his inscrutable, contemptuous expression . . . I wag my tail . . . "Try and guess . . . You don't know? Do you give up? . . . Those people who were at our table in Aix-les-Bains. You remember them? . . . The Z's . . .—What Z's . . .?" He is looking at me: there is in his eyes the hate-filled repulsion for me and for them, that I know so well . . . "Oh, that old ass?" It seems to me that, in spite of myself, I make a slight movement of recoil, and that guarded gesture that we make in order to wipe from our face the tiny drop of saliva that the person we're talking to has let fly at us. I give a nod of dissent . . . "Oh, he's a fool, if you like. But he hasn't done too badly . . . They've just bought a house on the Riviera . . . He told me his business was going very well . . . he said that he would not forget his conversations with you . . . that you have retained a youthfulness and spirit . . ." His expression of loathing becomes more marked . . . "He asked me if he could see you . . ." He gives a start: "See me! Ah! that's the last straw . . . Now you know perfectly well that I don't want to see those people. You know I think they're bores . . ." I defend myself weakly: a pretence of defense that only succeeds in getting him excited . . . "No, I don't know; you went out with them, you played bridge and went on walks together . . . He insisted . . . I told him that you were very busy, that he should telephone . . ." He straightens up, fairly hissing . . . "I played bridge with them . . . That's a good one . . . that's a fine one . . . a fine reason for seeing people again . . . just anybody . . . the first people that come along . . . because I talked to them a bit in a hotel, when I was bored to death . . . What does he want out of me anyway? I have a horror of people you meet in summer resorts who try to see you again . . . who want to get to know people," he sneers as he pronounces the words "know people" between quotes. "It's not for my personal charm that he wants to see me again, that's not like him. I know his kind. He had already put out a feeler, in fact. He wants to interest me in his business deals . . . He's got lots of schemes afoot . . ." he all but quivers . . . "But you did that on purpose, that's not possible . . . In fact, it was you . . . but for you, I would never have gone near them, I would have avoided them like the pest. You were the one who introduced them to me . . . You make a specialty of hooking up with people like that . . . Only, my boy, I beg of you, don't bring them into my house. I want people to leave me damned well alone. Tell them I've gone away, or died, or whatever you want, but I'll have none of them, none of that, thank you . . . that would be the last straw . . ." He is silent for a moment . . . I have only to wait without budging. He's got it now, he's not going to let it drop, it's too choice a morsel . . . He's thinking it over, he smiles to himself—a little secret, contemptuous smile . . . "And is she there too?" I pretend not to understand: "Who?—Who? why, that old fright . . . that scarecrow . . . His wife . . . What a sight she was! It's not possible, she must not have changed, she's always been like that. She must have been good and rich for him to play along . . . And what a pretty dance he must lead her . . . Oh! I bet he makes her pay for it . . . At times I was embarrassed, he was so caddish . . . Honey-bunch . . ." His laugh scorches me . . . "Honey-bunch . . . that suited her . . . By the way, come to think of it, and the daughter, what ever became of her, she had a funny name too, didn't she? . . . Zézette? . . . Zouzou? . . . What was it they called her? She was quite a card too . . ." At last we've got somewhere. This is it. He's got it. In fact, from the first he had sensed it, smelt something, he knew it was there, but he took his time, he was saving it for dessert. I too, I knew from the first, without putting it into words—I didn't even have time to think—I'm so quick to discover what he needs and bring it to him—I knew that it was a prime cut I had gone and got for him, a choice morsel, a real marrow-bone, and that this was the marrow: a tender, rich, succulent piece, an exquisite treat, he has it within reach of his teeth, he's going to bite into it . . . But to be quite frank, despite all the cruel disappointments I have had as a result of too numerous experiences, I continue to doubt, up till the last moment. I still maintain one hope: the same confused hope I must have had when I was choosing the piece, the same absurd confidence that he would behave decently and generously, that he would not, after all, permit himself to take advantage . . . and, at the same time, I was impelled by curiosity—I feel it now, too—the irresistible curiosity that exerts itself on me to my own detriment, it's as though I were seized with dizziness, I want to see how far they will go, if they will let themselves really be tempted, if what I foresee, dread, expect, desire, is going to happen; a need, too, to defy them. I remind myself of a clown I saw in I forget which circus, whose act consisted of holding his face up close to the other clown, who threatened to slap him, and saying: "All right, try it, go ahead." And the other one, every time, "went ahead." This time, he too, as usual, "goes ahead." He even adds subtleties of his own invention. He is no longer talking to me, but to someone else—he always does this when he has the good fortune to have someone else present—to his wife or his daughter; he suddenly pretends to ignore me: and thus, with a clever movement, he floors me, gags me, and forces me to witness, without flinching, what is to come . . . "Oh! she too was something of a card, she gave great promise, she did. Not so ugly as her mother . . . she'll go a long way, a sharp little thing, a real sly one, I watched her closely, underneath that look she has as if butter wouldn't melt in her mouth, she never loses her head, she knows what she's doing . . ." He grows silent a moment, apparently thinking over what he has just said, then nods and smiles to himself: a means he uses to give to his judgments, which he hurls over my head like that, a semblance of objective proof, of evidence. And yet I am still in doubt, he seems so innocent, so unaware . . . I am perhaps accusing him mistakenly, I am so suspicious, they often tell me that, my mind is so perverted, I am so touchy, it's not absolutely certain that he quite realizes . . . he has perhaps forgotten, it is so unlike him to remember things like that, the gentle summer night, the tepid lapping of the water, our stifled laughter, our whispers, her smooth, warm elbow in the hollow of my hand as I helped her jump from the boat . . . she turns her head to one side, I stroke her hair ever so lightly . . . goodnight . . . I'll see you to-morrow . . . to-morrow . . . above all, not make any noise . . . I slink down the hall . . . he opens his door, sticks his head out: "That you? You know what time it is?—Yes, I know . . . I went for a little boat-ride . . . it's such a lovely night . . .—For a little boat-ride? But I've told you already that you're not allowed to take the boat out at night. And besides, listen . . ." he lowers his voice . . . "I wanted to speak to you . . . I don't want any fuss . . . I beg of you, don't amuse yourself taking that girl boating at night. I'll have none of that, no night serenading . . . Those parents of hers act as though they were furious . . . for several days now they've looked mad about something . . . yes they have, I know what I'm saying."

Formerly, when I was more naïve, and still very awkward, sometimes, at such moments as these, when he held me floored at his mercy like this, I would occasionally make a struggle—I couldn't help it—, rise up in protest, still hoping madly that he had forgotten, that it would suffice to remind him, seeking to find out at any cost, to force him to lay his cards on the table . . . I became indignant: "Oh, please now, uncle, none of that . . . That's not nice of you. You know very well that I was crazy about Zézette . . . You made enough fun of it . . . have you really forgotten that?" Then he finally turned towards me, he was looking at me with amazement: "What's the matter with you, anyway? Am I supposed to remember all your affairs, all your infatuations? You must be crazy . . . Can you beat it, he demands to be treated with consideration and respect. Great romantic love . . . I have profaned his feelings . . . you have to watch every word you say . . . everybody around here is so delicate, so sensitive, they all have to be handled with gloves, soon you won't be able to talk about any-thing . . ." irritated, but in reality embarrassed, abashed, a bit ashamed, and I embarrassed right away, ashamed for him, for myself, already regretting my outburst, quite ready to believe in his innocence, in my own guilt . . . No, now I don't make a single move. I'm going to wait until the banquet is over. I allow him—in fact I am no longer as daring or as fearless as I used to be—I allow him to devour the juicy morsel quietly. He eats with shameless relish, playing around, enjoying himself: he still doesn't address me directly . . . "What was his name, anyway, that little so-and-so? that guy . . . you know perfectly well . . . that papa's boy who always drove around in his racing car . . . His father owned factories in Tunisia, or somewhere or other . . . I always saw her hanging around with him, making eyes at him . . . Oh! she'll paddle her canoe all right. As for that, she was well trained by her mother whose one idea was to marry her off . . . that won't be hard, she will undoubtedly make a good match, they needn't worry. She was not the kind to do something rash. She knows what she's about . . ."

He can frisk about at his ease, stuff himself until he can't eat any more. With me, as I said before, they have nothing to fear: I don't even succeed in getting really mad at them, much less in hating them. And even, I must admit, while these games, these fights between us are in progress, I have the curious sensation of being torn between them and me, of always having one foot in each camp. What's more, if I had to choose, I believe I should be more inclined to take their side against myself. It's that assurance they have, their innocence (true or false—no matter: if it's acting it's so well done that it has become second nature, they themselves mistake it), it is that innocent way they have that inspires my respect, and puts me to confusion. Always, even when I feel their teeth about to sink delicately into me, I am prepared to blame everything on myself. I'm ashamed (that's why I hide them so successfully) of my wincings, my little starts of pain. It seems to me when I wince that I am the guilty one; I am the black sheep, the noisome creature who—should I dare complain to them— would make all good people turn aside with loathing: they would refuse to look at my wounds, all the pretended bites, the slurs, the blows beneath the belt, that no one else receives, or collects, about which no one ever speaks, or cares, concerning which it has never occurred to anyone to teach anybody how to ward them off; I who fish in troubled waters, who disturb calm waters by my reflection in them, by my very breath; who see in the air the invisible trajectory of Lord knows what stones that nobody has thrown at me, and who bring back what nobody expects; I who am always rousing what would like to remain dormant, who excite, incite, heed, plead, I the impure.

*I*t was not by chance that I met Martereau. I don't believe in accidental meetings (of course I only mean those that count). We make a mistake to think that we're going to stumble against people haphazardly. I always have the feeling that we are the ones who make them spring forth: they appear at a given spot as though made to measure, to order, and they correspond exactly (often we don't realize this until much later) to needs in us, to desires that are at times unavowed or unconscious. I'll admit, however, that it is more reasonable, more satisfactory, to say simply that, having sought them doubtless a long time without knowing it, we end up one day by finding them: there's a shoe, they say, for every foot.

I've always been searching for Martereau. His image—now I realize it—has always haunted me, under various aspects. I gazed at it with nostalgia. He was the distant mother-country from which, for mysterious reasons, I had been banished; the home port, the peaceful haven, to which I had lost the way; the land on which I could never go ashore, tossed as I was on a rough sea, drifting constantly with the changing currents.

Even as a young child, I used to watch him with admiration and envy, hiding in my corner, huddled up to them in their warmth, dismembering their every word; it was he who imitated a locomotive's whistle far from their presence, on the foot-walks, who sailed his little boats, built mills in brooks, kept a close and watchful eye on the spot where his paper aeroplanes were going to land, examined each pebble to see whether it was silex or shale; he who had the power, without lifting a finger, to make them keep their distance, to inspire respect; an occasional silent slap, a short exclamation when he tore his clothes, strayed too far afield, forgot the time; whereas the people about me sprawled belly upward, exposed themselves, proposed themselves, bit me, coaxed me, fell out with me, suddenly left, in order to frighten me, enveloped me, in order to smother me, to bend me to their will, in ponderous silence; Martereau, from whom there emanated a mysterious fluid that kept their words at a distance and made them bounce far from him, like the little balls that dance on the crest of fountains.

No need of heroic measures for him, of *"sorties"* with all sails set, of sly or violent counter-attacks (every movement provokes them, excites them, the slightest gesture leaves you dangerously exposed); he doesn't need to move. His motionlessness, in fact, supports them. His hardness makes them hard.

Later, I took pleasure, in my day-dreaming, in making him assume other aspects. I liked to imagine him blooming under other skies. I discovered for him and for me, for the nostalgia that he aroused in me, richer soils, more propitious climates.

Holland, in particular, fascinated me: a little Dutch town with tidy, sleepy little streets, bordered by identical houses of dark brick. He was seated at his window (a single pane of sparkling glass) behind rows of green plants, tulips and petunias, a middle-aged man, slightly bald, a bit heavy—I preferred him like that—seated near the window in his easy chair, motionless, smoking his pipe. On the walls about him, a few pictures: a young village girl, a rough sea-scape, sunset in a fishing port. The surrounding furnishings were neither old nor handsome: the most ordinary furnishings, of standard make, chosen without misgivings or effort, the objects of loving care; their comfortable, simple ugliness had a sort of homey charm. It was the twilight hour and his wife, who was visible through the half-open door, busy in her white-tiled kitchen, was about to come in to light the hanging lamp and set the table. In the half shadow, could be seen shining in front of the fireplace, orange-tinted arabesques traced by the incandescent serpentine of the gas heater. Also, I was about to forget this —and why should I deprive myself of it—a pot-bellied copper tea-kettle was "singing" away on the stove.

I, of course, was on the outside, watching him from my hiding place under the porch. Exactly like a ragged child gazing at an enormous Christmas pudding in a lighted shop-window.

But for both of us England was a blessed land. In England he was a magnificent jointed doll, with a smiling, pleasantly tinted face, that wore a different suit for each hour of the day, and lived in a white marble palace: a sumptuous plaything held up to the wonder-struck gaze of an entire people. Over there I was part of the fervent crowds that waited for hours to catch a glimpse of his motionless, smiling countenance behind the windows of the long, shining limousine that bore his coat-of-arms; to see him appear on the balcony, bowing his head in our direction, waving slowly. An entire picture-book suited to my taste sustained my day-dreams, assuaged my hunger. On every table, in every shop-window I could gaze at the lovely bright-coloured pictures that showed him, silhouetted against the ocean, on the bridge of a dreadnought, his white-gloved hand held close to his Admiral's cap; or else in a General's uniform, motionless and erect, astride his horse, while the regiments filed past him in perfect order; at the bedside of the wounded; shaking hands with a working-man; but above all, and best of all, in his own home, in the intimacy of the family circle, seated by the fire opposite his wife, whose expression is also frozen in an unalterable smile, before an ivory-encrusted table on which playing cards are spread out, a card in his raised hand, watching attentively, with eyes lowered, playing solitaire; bending over his wife who is seated at the piano, turning the pages, while she plays his favorite pieces for him; walking with his children, blond haired cherubs, dressed in white, on the foot-paths of the estate; feeding sugar to ponies; patting the neck of his favorite setter; a heroic dummy passing through all the ages under our very eyes, at an admirably steady, firm, even pace: as a baby in long, lace-trimmed clothes, on his grandmother's knee; as the mischievous child and prince charming; the warrior at the front; the young officer holding the hand of his betrothed; the happy father bouncing his first-born on his knee; the son with bared head and slow of gait leading his father's funeral procession; finally, he himself on his death-bed, his face hardly more impassive, still pleasantly made-up, almost smiling . . .

Precious casket, luxurious jewel-case lined with immaculate satin—not an awkward rumple, not a wrinkle where the slightest bit of dust might settle—in which are displayed to the joy of all eyes, fitting exactly into the compartments that are intended for them, enormous precious stones, diamonds of the first water, beautifully cut and polished, hard, pure, unalterable.

Meanwhile, Martereau was there, right nearby; one had only to stretch out ones hand. Martereau in the flesh, a hundred times better than the finest playthings and the most sumptuous caskets. Martereau, whom I had known for a long time.

And thus it often happens, when fate is kind, when the reality we have always hoped and longed for is there at hand, that we do not recognize it at first. It was only little by little, with wear, that Martereau revealed himself. And then, perhaps I myself had never been for long, in his presence, in that indispensable state of receptivity that makes it possible for his charm to produce its effect. More than once, when I caught sight of him, it so happened that I tried to avoid him, to flee him. It seemed to me that the placid gaze of his benign eyes would do to me what a clumsy patching-up, or stitches taken too soon, do to a wound that is still running: underneath, it continues to run, it decomposes, it stinks. Beneath his clear, kindly gaze, which got me flustered, I felt I wanted to hide my eyes, and especially my lips over which, in my bad moments, something dubious, something shameful, quivers and plays; when I can, I always manage to put my hand negligently over my lips, which take forever to find the right position. No, for everything to go well when I see him, like Christians in a state of grace, I must be well prepared, I must feel more or less steady. Then, as soon as I see him, with no effort, docilely, I go straight up to him, my hand outstretched. His hearty, cordial hand-shake, his tap on my shoulder: "Well, how goes it, young fellow?" have an immediate effect on me. This is the laying on of hands, exorcism, the sign of the cross, that causes the evil One to flee. All at once, as though by enchantment, they disappear, all the crawlings, tremblings and shudderings, all the blemishes and wounds left on me by their unhealthy contact, their ambiguous caresses, their bites. Everything grows smooth, hardens, assumes clear outlines, an aspect that is well-cleaned, orderly and shining. The bad dream, the spell, vanish: I see clearly, like everybody else, I know where I am and who I am. "How goes it, young fellow?" Underneath these words, in back of his eyes, cleaving to them closely, without the slightest crack through which anything whatsoever that was suspicious might seep, nothing but sincere solicitude, the frankest sort of good-heartedness: "And how's the health? Well, by Jove, he looks as if he were getting better, put on some weight . . . that's a good remedy, eh? letting Auntie spoil you a bit, with all those good things she gives you to eat? I can tell you, he's being well taken care of . . ." I acquiesce, I smile: "Oh! as for that, certainly.—Now don't laugh, because at your age it's serious, you can't play with things like that: good food, rest, for illnesses like that, they're everything. When I was young, they gave me up, I was spitting blood, and the doctors had no hope of saving me. They wanted to send me to Tunisia, to God knows where else . . . Well, do you know where I went? To Normandy, to my grandmother's . . . And I slept like a log and ate like a cormorant. I said: the microbes won't eat me, I'm going to eat them. And look at me now, I'm still here. And no bragging, I can still hold my own. There aren't many young men who can match up to me. Only, you hear me? No nonsense.

You'll have to stick to your quiet life and be very careful. But you are reasonable, I'm sure."

Reasonable—true enough. That's what I am. I do take care of myself. It's because of my health that I am here, for obvious reasons of health, on the advice of my doctors that I live this sort of muffled, slow-motion existence, that I accepted their hospitality. It is this semi-activity which I am obliged to accept, this "mother of all vice," that keeps alive in me my idle musings and gives me that sensitiveness—abetted by my physical weakness—of a hysterical woman, as well as a morbid sense of guilt. Reasonable, nevertheless, I am, I know it, living my day to day existence like the next one, without ever doing anything reckless, or losing my bearings, ever. Never have I been able to make a real scene, break some object, "smash everything," renounce what quite evidently—I know it as well as Martereau—is to my interest. All the rest, the contacts, spells, caresses, bites, dizziness, repugnance, shivering, strange attractions—are but flourishes, ornaments, garlands, vine-leaves, which, for diversion, my idle fingers wind about this strong, straight, smooth, round stick that all can see: the most normal, most reasonable sort of behavior, the surest and healthiest instinct for self-preservation.

And they know it here, in our home, that's certain. They know too, like Martereau, what matters, what alone is important. My aunt knows it very well, when she orders my piece of broiled meat, bakes my favourite cake, pours out my glass of port before lunch in order to whet my appetite. "You're very lucky, they're so anxious the minute you aren't well, or lose weight: it's touching to see. That's because they like you so much, they're so fond of you." At once—and Martereau, too, feels the way my words clothe my sentiment like a perfectly fitted sheath, without a fold, without the slightest wrinkle—I reply: "I know that. I too, Monsieur Martereau, I am very fond of them." I have the impression that we are as far down as we can go, in the treasure chamber: there where, as in the armored cellars of the Bank of France, where they keep the gold that guarantees and gives value to our currency, are to be found the deep, the real sentiments (all the rest here between us: so much counterfeit money that is nowhere negotiable, paper bills that children make for fun, frivolous, puerile forms of amusement, the whims of spoiled children, crack-brained notions, shimmerings, reflected images), the deep perfectly simple sentiments that give value and significance to the only things that count: our acts. "Yes, your uncle has often told me that you were like a son to him. In fact, the other day I had to console him. He was worrying a bit about your future. He would have liked to see you succeed in life the way he has done. He would have liked to push you; he said how sorry he was that you hadn't continued to work with him a while. He's afraid you haven't found your real vocation, that interior decorating doesn't quite suit you. He's afraid you're wasting your time. I told him: just let him alone. All these young people must be left to shift for themselves. Understand me, he didn't say no, he agreed with me. I told him: You'll see, when his health is better, and he'll be in better spirits, he'll regain confidence in himself, he'll feel more like hard work. At present, he's just taking it easy, doing what amuses him, tinkering round a bit, not tiring himself, his health comes first. But you'll see, that'll straighten itself out. As time passes, and we grow older, problems solve themselves. I myself, as sure as you see me here today, I went through the same thing when I was young: I used to daydream and write poems, stretched out on my bed the live-long day, I did. And now, look at me."

I look at him. I never tire of looking at him: he is for me the most marvelous, the most calming of sights, and the most stimulating there is. His slightest movement fascinates me. All of his most insignificant gestures, like the quite simple, unique, perfect line of a fine drawing, seem to me to contain him at every instant, to express him entirely: as when, preceding me through the vestibule of his house, his upper body leaning forward, he wipes his feet slowly and carefully on the mat in front of the concierge's *loge*, taps softly on the glass with his folded forefinger, pokes his head through the half-opened door and asks: "Is there any mail?"; or when he goes up the stairs, feels in his pocket, takes out his key, turns it gently in the lock, opens the door for me. I can't take my eyes off his heavy fingers as they pull open the zipper of his tobacco pouch, take out a pinch of tobacco, shake it gently, stuff it into his pipe, press it, tap on it. It seems to me that everything about me, even perhaps about him at times, everything that trembles a bit, quakes, or quavers, comes like iron filings lifted by a powerful magnet, to settle there, in the quiet, precise motions of his thick fingers. Time itself is caught, imprisoned in the fine network woven by his gestures. Certainty and security have their dwelling-place here.

When I'm at his house I feel like a child who's been brought up in the slums, amidst blows and bellowing, as he takes his seat in Sunday school, listens to the teacher, sings hymns with the others, leafs through holy books, gazes at sacred pictures: I look at the yellowed, old photographs on the mantle-piece: the one of Martereau's mother, an old lady with white hair, in a lace bonnet, seated in a big armchair, holding a drinking baby-chick. "My mother used to give them hot wine, Martereau explained to me. The sickliest ones were always brought to her and she poured hot wine in their beaks to give them strength. After forty years of marriage." Martereau added, "my father used to say about my mother: 'She didn't bring me a sou of dowry, and she was not what you might call a beauty, but—and I've said it for forty years—I won first prize when I married her.' " Reverently I turn the heavy gilt-edged pages of the purple-plush album with its large steel buckle; my enchantment always surprises Martereau, it amuses him, flatters him doubtless a bit, too, he pores over the book with me, repeats what I never tire of hearing: "Ah! this one you know: that's my wife and myself in the country, in her parents' garden, before we became engaged. What a ninny I was . . . I came to see her every day for six months without daring to propose . . . That's us in Corsica, on our wedding-trip . . . she was frightened to death on the steep paths, her dress got caught in the briars, the donkeys re-

fused to budge, look at her, she was in a tight corner . . ."
Mme. Martereau smiles, the fine, clearly drawn wrinkles
that line her close-grained skin form an aureole about the
corners of her eyes, Martereau has his arm about her
shoulder, they look at each other, smiling. Martereau
turns towards me: "You see, young man, it runs in the
family, I must have inherited it from my father . . . since
that trip to Corsica, twenty-five years have passed, so they
have, and we shall soon celebrate our silver wedding anniversary; well! for me nothing has changed, and I could
wish for only one thing, believe me, to begin all over again,
follow the same road together, from the start. It's gone too
fast, that's the only thing I regret." He alone, Martereau,
is able to achieve that, without effort, unintentionally, to
get me to look at him the way I do now, while he stands
there in front of me, leaning against the fireplace, his
arm round his wife's shoulders, without my feeling like
looking elsewhere, without the appearance on my face of
that constrained little smile, falsely credulous and moved,
a bit embarrassed, that makes your lips twitch in such cases,
in spite of yourself, when people take up their stand in
front of you—one click and it'll be over, don't move—and
want you to look at them.

But Martereau wants nothing, he seeks to arouse neither
envy nor admiration. It doesn't occur to him to want to
give people a lesson, contented and peaceable as he is.

They are there in front of me like rivers, or trees, or
fields: spread out with the same noble lack of shame, the
same indifference.

Their sentiments—and this is what I admire so much about them—have the burning glow, the transparency and malleability of white-hot steel . . . For six months he didn't dare propose and during the year of their engagement, he hardly dared (the chaperone her parents had given them was quite useless), he hardly dared touch the fingers of his betrothed when they went walking—they had been to St. Cloud, to Versailles—so strong was his love for her, so great was his respect for her. Like white-hot steel their sentiments flowed readily into prepared molds, they became hard, heavy objects, very sturdy, smooth to the touch, without a rough spot, faultless . . . We turn the pages of the album: there they both are again, she in a white apron, her sleeves rolled up, they are laughing as each one holds the handle of a soup pot from which emerges the bald head of their first-born . . . "My husband absolutely insisted on having him photographed in a soup pot: it held him entirely, he was so comical; look at the face he's making." Martereau smiles indulgently, remains silent: embarrassment, delicate emotion, tenderness repressed, as is meet, in a manly way; he turns the page: "Look, here he has changed considerably, this time he has out-grown the stew-pan, here he is as a Spahi . . ." Just here I try to turn the page more quickly so as not to upset him, but he holds me back: "That's my father on his death-bed. He died a perfectly natural death; he passed out of old age at eighty-nine surrounded by his children and grandchildren and great-grandchildren. At eighty, he said to me: "Is it possible, I'll swear I must be getting old, I'm getting hard of hearing." We laugh softly. Everything is for the best. A tamed death comes like a familiar animal to receive our friendly pats, to eat out of our hand. I turn the page: he bursts out laughing: "Ah! that one, was she a sour-puss! Cousin Matilda. She died young; she took the veil at twenty-four, there was nothing anybody could do to stop her. I hated her when I was little, she could get me so mad . . . And here, what do you say to this, you don't recognize me? That's me in my sea-dog outfit. On the *Stormy Petrel*: that was my fishing-boat. Yes, sir, I was great at fishing, and not only for compliments. It was marvelous: both sails and motor. Look, here I am coming back with my six hundred mackerel: six hundred, I'm not lying to you. That happens in those parts, in Brittany. All you need is to come across a shoal of them: they were as close together as sardines in a can, if you get me. You only had to drop your hook in and help yourself. One every second, the time it took to make the movement: and up it came! My wife counted them one by one." I turn the pages, relaxed and content, filled with quiet cheerfulness . . . "Ah! that one, there, is not so funny, that was just after my accident. Here is my wife with our second son on the stoop of our house, just before we moved . . ." Of course, things haven't always been rosy, there were some hard knocks, death, sickness, periods of bad luck, honest-to-goodness troubles that can be shown in broad day-light, that everybody understands, with which everybody sympathizes, troubles that are like big thick, heavy, blocks with clear outlines,

clearly drawn . . . clear and clean, in one block, like Martereau himself. Worthy of him. Made to his measure.

I know of course that there's no use in exaggerating
things, that I must be careful not to let myself be carried
away by the need he awakens in me for perfection, for
absoluteness. Of course, too, he is perhaps not exactly as he
seems to me at this moment, in my presence he probably
improves his line very slightly, he perhaps gives himself
a tiny finishing touch in order to become identical with the
picture of him that I see, and which covers him so perfectly. Then, he has other aspects—copies of other pictures
that are quite as clear: high-tempered like all men . . . his
wife smiles her affectionate, indulgent smile, when he says,
as he looks at her mischievously, that he is what might be
called an angel of patience. She nods her head: "An angel,
ah, that you certainly are. Only, hot-headed: that's what he
is. Not a mean bone in his body, but he flares up. Not with
her, of course, but it seizes him all of a sudden, you can't
stop him. One day it took hold of him with one of the
foremen—at the time when he was in the stone-mason's
contracting business—there was a rascal in whom he had
every confidence; he had caught him stealing and the
fellow, in addition, dared to stand up to him; he shook
him so hard he frightened me, I assure you, I thought he
was going to choke him. But an hour later, it was finished:
he had forgotten about it, and was ready to forgive."

Other aspects still, so reserved and pure of line, that even
his wife may know nothing about them, or wisely pretend
to ignore them. A bit flighty, even, in his odd moments,

who knows, and who would be surprised that as handsome a man as he is should have had a few passing fancies; his wife has never seemed to suspect anything, he has never told her anything about it, he loves her, she knows that very well, so why make a fuss, why dramatize, with women you never know how things will turn out, although his own wife would probably have understood and forgiven him, but when all is said and done, you can never tell, you risk ruining your life for nothing, for things that, in reality, are quite unimportant, all men are like that, "roosters," as their doctor said—an excellent general practitioner, a jolly good fellow, that one, ah! he's had his fun in life, all right—roosters, with only rare exceptions, but those exceptions, their cases should be examined more closely: there's always something about those fellows, believe me, said the nice doctor, something about them that's out of kilter.

Suddenly we feel a draft: a safety valve opens, a rush of air sweeps up all our repressed energy. Generally it is he, my uncle, who feels this most strongly.

For a long time he had let himself be coaxed every time his wife broached the subject, he had grumbled . . . "Another one of her ideas, one of her fads . . . What would we do with a country place? You know perfectly well that we'll never go there . . . I know you, once it's bought, and we've sunk a fortune into fixing it up, you won't care about it any more, you won't want to hear about it even . . . It'll be re-sold the way we did the place in the south, and we'll lose any amount on it . . ." And then, one day, as she says, "it gets him": "Suppose we go there? Why, right away! Let's go now. There's not a moment to lose if what that swindling agent of yours writes is true." He's assumed that excited, brisk tone of his . . . "It's perhaps a rare bargain, who knows? one that won't wait." He gives me a tap on the shoulder: "Come on, let's go, you can very well excuse yourself, it's not important, you can do that to-morrow . . . That's nothing, you can send a message . . . Well, then, if it's too late, just don't let them know, it can't be helped . . . they'll wait for you a little while, it won't kill them, they'll understand that something kept you from coming . . . what difference does all that make, come on, let's hurry." I can't resist an agreeable and, at the same time, painful, slightly ambiguous sensation of dizzi-ness, resembling what drug addicts must feel when they are about to take their drug: there will be a break in time, a delightful suspense . . . already a feeling of happy anticipa-tion, of joy, lifts and bears us along, we speed ahead . . . "Hurry up, let's not waste any time, take some warm things and something to eat, and you, get the car, I'm going to telephone to the agent."

Between us, a truce is signed. We are brothers-in-arms ready to share the same adventures, to brave the same dangers . . . "Be sure you are warmly enough dressed, he calls out to me, the weather is not good. Put something really warm on, take my heavy sweater if you want, it's windy. Don't forget that in the country, it's two or three degrees colder than here. Take some blankets for the car; the carriage rug isn't enough."

As always, that good-natured, excited manner of his makes her withdraw right away, play the rôle of kill-joy. She shivers, wraps her fur coat round her, goes to the window: "It's completely ridiculous, really, to go to the country in weather like this. It's going to rain cats and dogs. We wait for months and then suddenly you'd think a fire had broken out. It'll be delightful, won't it: we'll be wading in mud, everything will seem awful to us." But he hangs on, he's bent on going—I recognize, because I feel it myself, his gnawing hunger, how impossible it is now for him to resist his impulse, to let all the tentacles in him, which were straining ready to seize their prey, collapse and hang limply in space—"no, really, it's nothing . . . it's just a shower, it'll pass over, it may even be that it's not raining out there . . . and besides, you are wrong, you know, it's better, on the contrary, to see it in its worst light, that way, at least, we'll know what to expect. Come on, everything's ready, let's not waste any time, the days are short at present," he takes me by the arm, and drags me along, "Let's go, come on, let's hurry, she'll follow." We wait for her in the vestibule; he grows impatient; "For God's sake, what's the matter now, what's she up to now, your aunt? It's always like that with women, they never know what they want. She takes an age to get ready, you'd think we were leaving for six months. Go and see, please, tell her it will be dark when we get there, if this keeps on. I bet she's in the kitchen gabbing, doing Lord knows what. It's incredible, always when we're just about to leave . . ." I find her standing motionless in the middle of her room. "Well?

aren't you coming? Come on, I beg of you, uncle is getting impatient." Suddenly she takes off her hat, throws it on the bed and with a look of relief, shakes her short hair, "No, I'm positively not going. It's too idiotic with this weather, no, go on without me; if it's attractive I'll go to see it later. You can tell by yourselves. Really, today I don't feel like it, the weather's not good enough, and besides, I'm tired." She takes off her coat in a decided manner. "No, don't insist. Really, I'd rather stay home."

At the same time that I am admiring her poise and strength, I experience, within myself, the icy stirring of something that I know well . . . a sort of distress and bewilderment. He, as soon as he catches sight of me, before I even have the time to splutter . . . "No, she positively is not coming, she says for us to go on without her: the weather's too bad, she feels tired," it seems to me that he grows pale, that everything about him loses color, grows white, like a piece of fabric dipped in sulphur, his voice is toneless, deflated: "All right, so what shall we do? Shall we go?" We pick up the covers from the seat in the entrance hall, limply take up our umbrellas, go weak-kneedly down the stairs, as light and translucent as ghosts. Our distant objective also wavers, grows indistinct. We walk along, driven in spite of ourselves, towards a dreary, useless fate. As we get into the car he turns towards me, a look of hate beneath his puckered lids: "At least I hope you didn't forget the map? You always forget everything." I can't wait: "Oh! that's true, what am I thinking about? I'll be back right away, I'll only take a minute," I dash up the stairs,

I hurry, she's stretched out on her bed reading, in that "Woman Reading" pose that she always affects, one cheek resting on her hand, I beg her, "Come on, make an effort, let's go, you're spoiling everything, without you it's not worth while going . . ." She stretches herself, gives a groan: "Oh! why?—You know perfectly well . . ." I take hold of her arm and pull her up, laughing, I know that with her you must not attack directly, or try to appeal to her better nature, to her emotions, but indirectly, with casual lightness, above all without speaking of him, but of myself, of us, in a playful, cheerful manner: "Come on, I'm going to kidnap you, we're going to have fun, we'll eat a bite in some little country inn, it'll be nice and warm, there'll be a big stove burning, we'll drink the kind of little white wine you like, and then we'll go take a look at the place, perhaps it's marvelous, you never know, we'll make plans for fixing it up," I put her coat on her shoulders, she pulls away: "Just a minute, you big loon, I haven't got my shoes on.—All right, hurry up, I'm going on down, we'll wait for you in the car, but above all don't change your mind; that I would never forgive you." I run up to him, I'm beaming: "She's coming, she's coming with us, she was afraid of the bad weather but she's made up her mind, she'll be right down." He is suffused by an immense joy, an immense relief that he tries not to show, in order to save his face, he shrugs his shoulders exasperatedly, he grumbles: "Ah! really, it's incredible, with all that we'll never get off, one needs iron nerves to stand you two." All distress has vanished, the threat is averted, she's coming down, she's on her way down, life is coming down to us, she takes her place beside us in the car, she nods her head indulgently, smiles . . . "Really, what a crazy thing to do, look at this weather. And here . . ." She points to a parcel on her knees . . . a feeling of warmth spreads through us, of joyful security, of exquisite mellowness, a sucking babe who feels his mother's breast between his famished lips experiences no greater appeasement . . . "And here, of course, are the sandwiches: naturally, you had left them on the seat in the hall."

We tuck the covers about our legs, he leans over and touches the chauffeur on the shoulder: "You can go ahead now." He sits well back in the car, slips his arm through the strap, gives a grunt of satisfaction, "Well, Westward, ho! Off we go!" The delights that I had foreseen start, we drive through puddles of water, sheltered from the rain and the wind, packed in warmly in our water-tight box. At last there is a respite, an exquisite suspense, a hollow forms to receive us, a bend in the stream of time, a shelter, a cozy nest in which we are all snuggled together, while outside, all round us, people move and hustle about, leap over gutters, go into houses, come out of shops and cafés, run after buses, so many twigs swept along with the current. Relieved, indifferent, filled with a gayety that is as light as an empty shell, we watch them smilingly, we gambol joyously about . . . "Look at that fatty over there . . . watch out, she's going to get soaked, boom! there she goes, I saw it coming. And that tiny little fellow, there, with his big bag, a regular ant," ants, slight pressure on the accelerator sends them running, a skid makes them swerve from their path, we laugh as we grab hold of the doors, adventure lies ahead, we are free, light-hearted, skipping along.

We slow up in a dismal little burgh, set amidst wide, flat fields. "It's that way, after you leave the village: a big wall on the right. You stop there." She looks out of the car window with an annoyed pout. She alone has the courage to say out loud: "What do you think? This doesn't look like a very exciting place, does it?" We don't want to see it, we dare not think it, the mutilation would be too savage, too cruel . . . that of a tree whose branches are cut in spring, when the sap is rising, no, no, all is not lost, we must examine it more closely, hope is still permissible . . . he encourages her: "Wait, you haven't seen anything, wait before you start lamenting, the agent said again when I called him that it was a very nice place. You can't see anything from here, it may be a little palace . . . you will turn it into a Petit Trianon . . . You have to ring here: the agent said that the caretaker had the key." I ring. Nobody answers. "Let's wait a while longer. Ring harder. He may be at the far end of the garden, the agent assured me that the caretaker was always there, that there would always be somebody. Perhaps we should ring the bell at that little house there, next door." There they know nothing, but for heaven's sake, where on earth is he? a certain impatience, not to say anxiety, seizes hold of us, this is incredible, we didn't come fifty kilometers in the rain for nothing, we knock as hard as we can, we race about, I cross farmyards, heedless of barking dogs, of geese that come lowering at me, leaping over puddles, muddying my trousers, "the caretaker, the caretaker of the house, where is he? we've asked everywhere . . . Did you go to the bistro, or to his daughter's, to the farm next door?—Yes, but nobody knows where he is. We were told that he was always in, otherwise, you can imagine . . . we would never have come fifty kilometers in the rain . . . Wait a moment, I have an idea . . ." There are soft highlights in the oilcloth on the table; the stove radiates warmth; she holds our destiny in her hands, her words foretell heaven's favor, the wheel of fortune is turning; I suddenly fall in love with the big Henry II sideboard, with the wooden shoes she puts on, the loosely crocheted shawl she pulls round her shoulders . . . "Wait for me here, I'll be back, I think I know, he must be at the Mayor's, he told me he had to get him to sign a paper for him . . ." People are kind, it's a mistake to run down peasants, these people are obliging and kind, this is real nobility, disinterested generosity, to go dashing about in the rain like that . . . To live here, near them, always; come and sit for a while here every day; hear the stove crackle, rest my hand on this oilcloth, remain here near her, near the dog, the cat, see the ball of wool roll along the freshly washed pink-tiled floor, life is kind, life is good . . . here she comes back again, she's nodding yes with her head, luck has smiled at us, fate's kiss is upon us . . . "I found him, he had gone to see the Mayor, he's coming, he'll wait for you in front of the house. Mercy! what awful weather!—Thank you, thank you very much, you've saved our lives, imagine, to have driven fifty kilometers in the rain for nothing . . ." I am seized with a need for sympathy, for communion, for fraternity between us, which she shares, to which she responds . . . "Oh! we've got all the rain we need, it's worse than in early November . . . after such a summer, it's not surprising, it was to be expected . . . Naturally, in Paris nobody pays any attention to it, but out here it's an awful mess, nothing but mud . . . Well, we can't order the weather to suit us, can we?—Ah! no, that's true, unfortunately we can't order it to suit us . . .—It's like everything else, isn't it?—I should say so, yes, indeed . . . well, good-bye, and thank you, no, don't bother, everything's all right, thank you."

Waiting at the door, while the caretaker puts the key in the lock, my uncle fairly quivers with impatience; a minute more and the child in him, given full rein, would make him jump and clap his hands . . . "Now! let's see . . . he pushes me by the elbow . . . you're the great connoisseur —for once he is even generous in his delight and excitement—you're the future great decorator, keep your eye open, you hear, and your good one, at that."

A bit gloomy perhaps, the house, and the grounds a bit dark, in this rainy weather especially, but there's a certain charm in the simple, stately forms of these old grey-stone walls, in the undulations of the moss-covered tiled roof . . . Just what we need, what we were looking for, what I had long been wishing for . . . anything can happen here . . . we should only have to let ourselves go, flow gently into the mold and assume form. Firm, simple outlines. I shall sit in the sun on the lower steps of these old stairs, with their smooth, worn edges, they will come down armed with baskets and pruning shears, they will bend solicitously over the rose-bushes, we'll watch my uncle as he strolls about the lawn, comes to a halt, breathes in the smells, gazes about him . . . I fondle the old iron handrail. "They're lovely, aren't they, these old handrails?" In him there's an immediate recoil, a movement of retraction, of withdrawal . . . A blunder on my part, a false step, his good-natured mood had made me forget for a moment to be on my guard . . . he examines suspiciously a few cracks in the façade, points out to the caretaker the saltpetre on the walls of the vestibule, the loose paper hanging down: "Tell me, what's this, it's very damp here, the walls are oozing with moisture. Look at that." The caretaker reassures him: "Oh! no, Sir. Don't worry about that, the house is perfectly sound, it has a good exposure and the walls are very thick . . . that's because it hasn't been heated for a long time." This is undoubtedly one of his good days. That was just a little passing reaction. He wants nothing better than to let himself go. "There's no denying, it's not so bad . . ." He gives a nod of approval when the caretaker makes us admire the beautiful hardwood floors, their fine inlay, the woodwork: "If you had to build that today. The labor alone, at present, you can imagine . . ."

We go through great big rooms with high windows and vast fireplaces, we walk down wide halls, go up and down stairs . . . Doors open, then still more doors giving on to other rooms, ladies' boudoirs, smoking-rooms, closets, secret cupboards . . . We spread ourselves, we launch out in every direction, we grow in size, we blossom forth with suppressed needs, unsatisfied desires, whims, dreams . . . this is the ideal spot . . . "for you . . . just what you wanted . . . Look at that, wouldnt that make a magnificent studio . . . there's even a separate entrance . . ."

It was doubtless the odor of dampness and mildew in this big abandoned house, in these rather dilapidated rooms . . . a sort of vague mustiness . . . cold left-overs from other people's lives . . . that began to creep over me while I was launching out and blossoming forth, nodding delightedly at each new surprise, something was seeping in slowly . . . disturbing emanations. They close in upon us, we've gone too far, we're caught, surrounded, there just in front of the window of my "studio," that larch is already taking liberties, its hooked, black fingers are digging into me . . . those disheveled shrubs at the end of the field are inserting themselves into me, they press upon me, affix their seal upon me, they are going to mark me, I shall bear them engraved in me: an indelible gash, a scar . . . Break loose, flee . . . I am seized with a sudden fury, I take a leap in order to extricate myself . . . "A studio? . . . Oh! you know me, I don't think I'll stay here very much, don't consider me . . .—What do you mean, not consider you! I like that . . ." not that, of course, they wouldn't let me do it, no cowardly deserting, no unfair dropping out, it's too late, we're together, united in the same adventure, abandoned to the same fate, they pull me, crush me, hurt me . . . "I like that, that's something new . . . On the contrary, you are the one who'll be here the most, I hope, on account of your health . . . It's principally for you, all that. You need the country more than we do . . ."

The caretaker is still leading us on. It's getting dark and colder. She shivers . . . "Brr, I'm beginning to freeze . . ." My uncle looks out the window at the mist . . . "What's that over there, at the other end of the meadow, a lake? a pond? Ah! a pond . . . that's fine . . . he laughs derisively . . . now you can give water parties, everything's all set . . ." His acid jet penetrates us, pursues its course inside her, inside me, corroding our sensitive tissues . . . She laughs her pointed laughter . . . "Indeed . . . huh, and you, during that time, you'll be dreaming all alone in the moonlight, on the terrace, huh, . . ." Shut in here all together, caught together in the same trap . . . The emanations envelop us, we are clasping one another, scratching one another . . . we must tear ourselves from it right away, escape to the out-of-doors, into the open air . . . the caretaker wants to show us the workings of the luggage lift, of the dumb-waiter, he wants us to go down to the basement to inspect the kitchens, the wine-cellars. Impossible. We must leave. Night is coming on. Behind the windows, all round us, like a dark, hostile sea, flat wind-swept country, fields as far as one can see, and we here, lost, having come nobody knows why . . . we must make an effort, break the spell, there's still time, we just went a little too far for prudence, we carried the joke too far . . . out there the lifeboat is waiting for us, we'll be saved,

97

all this—the house with its cracked façade, the big darkish rooms, the larch with its hooked fingers, the disheveled shrubs—all of that will drift out of sight, disappear forever, fade away . . . "No, no, we haven't time, we must go back, it's getting dark, it's not a good thing to drive at night in weather like this, we've seen about everything . . . thank you . . . We'll think it over . . . Come back to see it again when we've more time . . . Thank you, don't bother to come with us . . . We'll find our way . . ." At the end of the walk the cheering lights of the car serve to guide us . . . quick, climb into our nice warm little upholstered casket, the car door shuts behind us, we are saved, rescued, we are secure . . . the hot-water bottle, our carriage rugs . . . At last. How good we feel! Quick, back to Paris . . . Go ahead . . . Once we're well settled among our cushions, we look at each other, we look at my uncle . . . For a moment our fate is in the balance . . . He's going to take us savagely by the scruff of the neck, turn our heads and force us sadistically to look—the mere thought makes us bristle with repulsion—in front of us, behind us, all about us, an abyss, a frightful white void . . . I can hear him now . . . "Well, you must be satisfied . . . another afternoon lost, wasted, for nothing; you've always got your ideas, your plans . . . For months you've been pestering me about this . . . What would you expect me to do in a hole like that? I'd be ten times better off in a hotel anywhere, but it's always you, what you want . . . 'I must have a house of my own, the country, studios, parties . . .' a lot of parasites who can't afford hotels and will come and live off you . . . But you've just got to have it, imagine, the whats-hisnames bought a darling little place for nothing . . . I know those little dream-spots, the amount of trouble they can give, what they can cost . . .but that keeps you occupied . . ." However, not at all, our luck turns, he leans back against the cushions, there's a mischievous childlike gayety in his eyes, his cheeks are charmingly wrinkled with naïve kindliness, he looks first at one, then at the other, bursts out laughing . . . "Well, so what do you think of it? Are you tempted? . . . the . . . the . . . He is choking with laughter . . . the foot-scrapers . . . did you notice his look of importance when he said: 'In front of each door there's . . .' he has difficulty pronouncing the words . . . we are seized with schoolboy giggles—Yes, yes, we had noticed it . . . foot-scrapers . . . he did say that: 'And in front of each door you have a good foot-scraper'—Imagine, that's really a unique bargain . . . that ought to make us decide right away . . . if nothing else . . . foot-scrapers! . . . And the pond . . . when I asked him if there were any mosquitoes . . . 'Oh! mosquitoes, not really, no.' . . . But I saw screens at the windows? . . . 'That is to say, Madame had that idea in her head . . . so she had a few put in . . .' She had that idea in her head . . . that's wonderful! . . . She had visions . . . You remember . . ." We laugh so hard we cry . . . tears are rolling down our cheeks . . . "in the Camargue . . . the night we spent in that village . . . with you seated on a chair . . ."—"Yes . . . yes . . ." I should say we do remember, it's one of our choicest morsels, one that we serve up as a treat from time to time when we feel we want to be well shaken, heated up, delightfully purified—as one is by the scalding steam and healthy flogging of a good turkish bath—by these explosions of good hearty laughter . . . "when you spent the night on a stool watching for them . . . your face, that morning . . . You remember . . . how you caught them . . . whack! . . . whack! . . . your groans . . ." We split our sides laughing . . . "Oh! Oh! I can't bear it . . . stop . . ."—"She had that idea in her head . . . That may be why she wanted to sell the place . . . They're a nightmare, mosquitoes . . . Can't you just see it now, when we'd be taking a breath of air on the terrace in the evening . . . whack! . . . and again, whack! . . . Ah! these agencies . . . They're all alike . . . what a lot of cheats . . ." Having barely escaped from a common enemy, from the same furtive threat, free, light-hearted, letting the overflow of our spirits scatter joyfully about, snuggled up warmly to one another, we roll along . . . we're already in the immediate suburbs, the air between the rows of houses is softer, now we see the first lamp-posts, traffic-policemen, passers-by, pedestrian crossings, red lights . . . "Let's not go right home . . . How about dinner at a restaurant?"

Delightful greenhouse tepidity, discreetly subdued pink lights, shimmerings, gentle clinking, a mild hum . . .

Relaxed, indifferent, listless, we float along . . . We become serious and attentive again only for the moment needed to study the menu . . . "It made me as hungry as a wolf, that little adventure did . . . Not you? Why yes, of course, everybody's hungry. Nothing like the country to give you an appetite . . . Now . . . let's see . . . What's good today? What shall we take?"

Martereau, needless to say, doesn't worm his way in through secret doors. He's not one of those at whose unspoken command I hasten to retrieve and fawningly lay my find at their feet. No, Martereau enters here in all dignity and all honor, by the front door. Out of good, avowable motives. I mention his name without fear—or almost. He might well, my uncle, as he always does, just as soon as I mention someone's name, pucker his eyelids and pretend not to hear . . . "Who's that? Who? Martereau? . . . To do what? What an idea . . . What makes you think I should ask him?" But it will be easy to call him to order . . . "Oh! as far as I am concerned, you know, what I say about him . . . I just thought that Martereau could give us some good advice, that's all. I think he knows the ropes. In fact, it was you, wasn't it, who told me that at one time he was head of a stone-mason's contracting business . . . He's a man you can be sure of, with plenty of common sense. But do as you want. I haven't breathed a word to him about anything connected with country places. I wanted to speak to you about it, first."

I know perfectly that just here my motives are not so simple, so pure as all that. They never are with them. Again this time it's my uncle who provokes my reactions. I want to charm him, to make an impression on him, to show him my credentials . . . prove to him that I'm with him, like him, like he pretends to be, on the right side, in the world of real men, not in the one in which I and my friends "your associate, as you call him," tremble shamefully, no, in the world where are to be found standing steadily on their two feet, with their heads screwed well on their shoulders, the people you can be sure of, with common sense, industrious, unassuming, bound up in their work; the world in which, with all deference to me, he himself has always lived and worked hard, he had to, money didn't grow on trees, did it, Monsieur Martereau? People like us, we know that . . . But, ah! these young men, they're so impatient, they would like everything to fall like manna from heaven without their having to lift a finger . . . Martereau agrees with a frank, amused smile, Martereau is with him, on his side . . . Seated a bit apart from them, I fold my hands in my lap, I look at them, I too nod and smile, everything is fine, I am satisfied . . . they are my handiwork, this is my handiwork, bringing together these good people who get along so well, who speak the same language . . . the child of divorced parents who sees them finally together must feel this same delight . . . together, in what is secure, what is normal . . . I am with them, like them, their bond of union . . . we understand one another . . . those little taps that my uncle gives me in passing are nothing, just tickling—Martereau is there —harmless jests, the kind of innocent teasing that mature persons go in for with young people . . . Martereau nods with an indulgent smile . . . "Ah! sure enough, the younger generations, ah! life will teach them . . . They will learn, don't worry . . ." Everything's cozy. I feel like stretching, out of sheer well-being. I'm about to doze off here beside them, fall asleep, like a happy child.

But I believe that I'm about to mistake my wishes for reality, I'm rambling off . . . Martereau himself is not strong enough to sustain us when we're together, my uncle and I.

I know quite well that if I were not there, everything would be different, there would exist between them the unbroken calm I dream of, complete understanding. Martereau would quite naturally make him stand on his feet.

I am the spoil-sport between them. I am the catalyzer. I am continuously prey to uncontrollable reactions. I'm afraid, I'm ashamed, I'm trembling, I can't take my eyes off them, I keep watching in order to prevent, to stop something that can start up at any moment. I look first at one then at the other, trying with the fascinated attention with which spectators at a tennis tournament follow the ball, to follow the outline of their words: of his words, especially . . . will they bounce back again with this stroke and rebound against Martereau, or else, this time, as the result of too violent a hit, aren't they going to penetrate. become embedded . . .

And yet, however closely I look, I am unable to catch the slightest tremor in Martereau, nothing, not a wrinkle. Impassible, smiling, as hard and pure as could be desired, delightfully innocent, Martereau watches us, amused, while we dance our usual St. Vitus dance, which nothing can stop . . .

Cling to my uncle as tightly as possible—above all, no side movement which might permit him to think that I am keeping my distance, observing him from above, and from afar, securely settled down beside Martereau—entwine him closely in order to calm him, to contain him, that's what I must do now, it is what I do: a smile on my face, a look of approval, I nod proudly, I make such an effort that I feel myself being proud of him, I really do admire him, there are plenty of reasons for doing so, in fact, even my aunt, who is watching the three of us silently, gives a slight nod of assent, Martereau too approves, understands: Drudged? He, my uncle? Worked all his life? He certainly has, and how! Who doesn't know that? Without ever counting on anybody . . . and he'd been darned right, it had succeeded . . . Life must have been hard for him in those days . . . up at six winter and summer . . . "At seven o'clock I was on the job . . . You, Monsieur Martereau, you may remember that. No, even you were too young at that time, that was still before the Millerand decrees . . . we had a twelve hour day . . . Oh! there was no question of vacations or leave with pay, everybody worked hard, from the top to the bottom of the ladder, France was not what it is today. I was a young engineer, graduated, I can say without boasting, with a grade that was not too bad, from Civil Engineering School . . ." I sense in advance each word that he is about to speak, I feel like preceding him I am so aware of what we are heading for, but I still have a little hope . . . I nod, interestedly, I turn an appreciative, confident gaze upon him . . . not a second, I know it, does that eye of his, forever on the watch, leave me . . . "Yes, I had some pretty good training, what I was taught was real solid learning, no nonsense, you can believe me . . ." No, no, who would dare to doubt it . . . He smiles an acid smile . . . no "amusing little dodges" . . . It seems to me that my aunt gives a faint stir . . . Martereau, still motionless— hardly a glance in my direction, or not even, it must just have seemed so to me—approves respectfully: "I should say so, I know."—"I had a very good position, rather high up for a young engineer, just out of school . . . well, every blessed day I had to get there before the bell rang for the workmen. Ha! they make me laugh, all of them, with their workmen's paradises, their utopias . . . Show me the engineers in Soviet Russia who would have to do that.

But we thought that was natural, we liked our work, we liked to see things done well . . . And then I myself, I must say that I was crazy about research work . . ." Research work . . . There we have it finally, that's it. It's almost a relief . . . we're about to take a gentle turn . . . "But you, Monsieur Martereau, perhaps you never experienced that. Each man has his own *métier*, hasn't he, his own bent . . ." I make a faint movement, just a slight waver in the direction of Martereau, this time I feel like clinging to Martereau, to protect him, but I know that with the slightest gesture I'd be lost; in the same way that a soldier under bombardment must combat the impulse to leave his foxhole, I have to force myself not to budge: I mustn't give any sign of sympathizing with Martereau, I must stay glued to my uncle, stick close to him . . . we branch aside now, we're off . . . "Ah! when you begin to grow old, my dear Monsieur Martereau . . ." I smile warmly, eyeing him fondly . . . "when you think over your entire life . . . that happens to me sometimes at night, when I can't sleep . . . I look back on my life from the beginning . . . well, when all is said and done, it's the only thing that counted in life, as far as I am concerned, the interest I had for what I was doing, my curiosity . . . always to be looking for something new, to experiment . . . there's nothing like it . . . for me a job you choose just to earn money, that's beyond me, I never could have done it, I would have rather died of hunger . . . there are people—and, mark my words, educated people, intelligent people—who can't stay put . . . they change their jobs the way they do their shirts . . ."

Martereau doesn't budge and my uncle looks so innocent that I begin, as usual, to doubt . . . as usual, in spite of the evidence, I should like to persuade myself that he doesn't think of it, that he's forgotten, that I'm wrong . . . and yet it was he—I'm not dreaming—who told me, it was he, I'm certain of it, who said to me: "He's tried his hand at everything, our friend Martereau has, construction, masonry . . . Twenty years ago he was an insurance agent, then he had a little electric appliance business, or heating apparatus, I forget which, it didn't go, either . . . he's always come out pretty badly from everything he's undertaken . . ." No, he must know that he's got us this time, Martereau and me, we're shackled, bound hand and foot, we are lying helpless at his mercy . . . "The secret, you see, of all those people who can't stay in one place, the secret of those people, is that it's not the breath of their nostrils . . . what they're after, is to get ahead in life, as they say today, make money . . . You know, if I had written a book like Ford on how to become successful, I should have said that it consisted in being interested in something, in one thing, no matter what, but the same thing, all your life long: in the thing itself and in nothing else. Keep hammering on the same nail. There's nothing like it. I always say that to young people: hammer on the same nail . . . there you've got the secret. As for money, it'll come one day—later . . . more than you need. For years, and not so long ago at that, I only took two evenings off a week—my wife can tell you, she reproached me enough with it—two evenings out, you understand me, all the other evenings, I was at my desk, grinding away . . . I would re-make a plan fifty times, I would read up on things, I was investigating . . ."

That's his force. The force of all his kind, as I said before. They feel that nothing will ever happen to them. They are certain of their impunity. Well protected. Sheltered behind their words. Nobody could succeed in getting a hold on the smooth ramparts of their speeches and accede to them there where they crouch in their cowardly way, spying on us, from where, safe behind their ramparts, they sprinkle us with pitch and boiling oil. It amuses me when I see my aunt, who forces herself (the way I myself used to do) to hurdle the rampart and get at him, to my fright, to my joy. Not at the moment of course, that would be too risky, it would be certain to fail; but afterwards, gently (it's that mania they have of inspecting every nook and cranny in order to remove all impurities, to try to remove all the spots; she would brave all blows, urged on as she is by this instinct—their duty, that's what they call it) . . . I'm amused, although I'm a bit afraid, when with her obstinacy of an ant recommencing work that has been destroyed, she takes him on—at first, insidiously, even gently, for the occasion . . . "You know, dear, yesterday with Martereau, I wonder if you were right . . ." He gives a start, immediately on his guard, turns aside . . . "So what, with Martereau . . ." She advances a bit: "I don't know, myself, it's perhaps just an idea, but I was a little uncomfortable, I wonder if you didn't make a mistake . . ." He becomes suddenly brutish: "A mistake? A mistake with Martereau? What are you driving at? What's the matter now?" She fidgets and

recoils, a bit frightened, but the temptation is too great . . .
"You know, when you were talking to Martereau . . . you
had forgotten, perhaps . . . when you talked about people
who are always changing their jobs . . ." He gives her an
astonished, furious look . . . "People who change their jobs?
So what? What's the connection?—But you're the one who
told me he hadn't succeeded very well, that he was a jack-
of-all-trades . . .—I said that? Me? First of all, I never said
it, I know nothing about him, what he did or didn't do,
and what's more, I don't care a rap, I never even thought
about it, nor did he . . ." She's still wriggling, fawning,
but she nevertheless advances a bit further—her sense of
duty impels her, the need to accomplish her mission—
"Oh! yes he did, that's just it, I'm sure he must have noticed
it . . . it seemed to me that he winced a bit . . . I felt
uncomfortable . . ." He laughs with the kind of laughter
about which we say—and the description is a good one—
that it makes our spines shiver, he's about to blow his jet of
corrosion at us . . . He fairly hisses . . . "Indeed! it seemed to
you . . . you saw that, did you . . . you saw that . . . You
always see everything, you people do . . . everything that
nobody else sees. You think that Martereau is like you, a
sensitive plant . . . thin-skinned . . . Well, I can tell you,
he didn't think a thing, he didn't notice anything, he's
not a woman, not one of these over-excited little fellows
. . ." She puckers her lips and nods as though in doubt,
on her face there is an expression of obstinacy as well as
of apprehension . . . Then he straightens up, he stares right
at her, and while I wait, already shrivelled up—he pounces:

"And what's more, shall I say something? Well, believe it or not, I don't give a damn about your Martereau, about what he thinks or doesn't think, or what all of you think, nobody can give me any lessons—he's shouting—I say what I feel like to people, I've succeeded pretty well like that up till now, I don't need advice from anybody, let me alone, just let me damned well alone, will you . . ." Cockroaches, loathsome vermin crawling in damp darkness amidst foul odors, that's what we are, she and I, as his foot hunts us down and crushes us; the nauseous liquid that spurts from us makes him sick to his stomach. Martereau too, if he saw us, would be sickened. He would be against us, with him: Why, certainly, he hadn't noticed anything . . . What an idea . . . What won't people imagine . . . They would be together, on the right side, the side of strong, healthy men, we're not silly women, are we? as your uncle so rightly said, we're not hyper-sensitive, complicated little milk-sops. As far as he, Martereau, is concerned, it's true. If she saw him "wince," she saw nothing but her own reflection, our despicable, paltry image. Martereau doesn't "wince." That's not his way: he has none of those rapid, hidden, slightly shameful movements that one curbs immediately. Even the pendulum in me that right away starts trembling and vibrating in unison, revealed none. If I become excited in his presence, it's the result of a movement that comes from me; in any case, without receiving the slightest impulse from him. Not a shadow flits across him. Not even the most imperceptible tremor as he observes us with an amused smile. But "observes" is not the

111

right term. Martereau doesn't observe. In the same way that his thick, clever fingers gently grip his pipe or his fish-hook, his mind clings closely to the outlines of words: familiar, reassuring outlines. Words are not for him what they are for me—thin protective capsules that enclose noxious germs—but hard, solid objects, from one casting, it's useless to open them up, make cross-sections, examine them, we should find nothing. But if there is anything to which I might compare these words that Martereau absorbs with his indulgent, amused smile, it would be rather to a coin as it falls into the slot of an automatic distributing machine, then continues on the way laid out for it between the edges of a straight, smooth groove until it falls at the intended spot: it suffices to pull the handle, and a trigger releases the box of candy or the matches. "Believe me, you must hammer on the same nail . . ." there's nothing inside, not a single noxious germ or deadly bacillus, it's just a simple piece of nickel, it glides through him and drops, I can pull the handle: "What do you think about that, Monsieur Martereau, about what my uncle was saying?—Why nothing, what should I think about it, I myself am something of a jack-of-all-trades, you know, but it's an arguable point of view, it has succeeded with a good many people, with your uncle, to begin with . . ." Tasteless food, insipid candies—we must be satisfied with them. It would be useless to pull the handle, nothing else would come out.

I know all that perfectly well, but I've got to be absolutely sure, I've got to be persuaded that nothing happened, that there was really nothing, that Martereau made not the slightest movement, that there was not the faintest tremor in his most remote recess, that it was I, once more, who trembled, God knows why . . . tempests in a tea-pot are my great specialty . . . This time again, I can't stand it. As soon as Martereau gets up to leave, I rise—I feel right away that my uncle is on his guard, he scents treason, but it can't be helped, I've nothing more to lose now: "I'm coming too, Monsieur Martereau, I'll go a little way with you, walk a bit in the air . . ." My uncle's eyes narrow: what he had sensed would happen, dreaded and sought to avert, to nip in the bud, what I so feared to let him see— a connivance between Martereau and me, a fondness on my part, an admiration for Martereau, based, and he feels this perfectly well, we know each other so well, on my hostility towards him—finally becomes evident . . . Martereau accepts innocently . . . "Yes, do come along, why not . . . only put something warm on, so you won't catch cold, it's chilly . . ." My uncle shakes his hand jovially, in front of him he controls himself, he makes the best of things, but he knows everything, he even knows perhaps what's going to happen, what I'm going to try to do, he foresees it with the hateful clairvoyance that he has some-times: it's always from hatred that he derives his perspica-city . . . "Well, good-bye, Monsieur Martereau, I was glad to see you again, don't forget us . . . you must come again soon . . . You know me, I live like a hermit, I go out so little, but you must come again, it does us good to recall the old days . . . And, besides, eh? don't forget, think of us if you come across a bargain, you'd be doing us a great favour . . ." He leans on the handrail . . . "And you there, watch out that you don't catch cold.—No, no, don't worry, I'll be back in ten minutes, it's just to stretch my legs a bit . . . I'll sleep all the better."

We walk down the stairs in silence. I'm impatient, I can scarcely contain myself, I would like to skip the preliminary stages and reach my goal right away, but I don't know how to go about it, I hesitate. We're hardly out of the house, however, before Martereau himself, without meaning to, helps me out: "My, but he's funny, your uncle; what a character, a strange man. He must have known how to make his way in life, he's got plenty of nerve . . . I bet he lets nobody tread on his toes . . ." I agree, smiling . . . "Oh! that he doesn't, I don't believe so . . . Not he." But to my great disappointment, Martereau veers aside right away . . . "Does he still work very hard? I thought he had more or less retired from business . . . But I get the impression that he's still very active . . ." I assent absent-mindedly and he looks at me somewhat surprised: I sense that there's not a moment more to lose, I take the plunge, it seems to me that I have leapt over the void . . . "Listen, Monsieur Martereau, I should like to ask you . . ." it's a mistake to approach him like that directly, too solemnly, I've begun awkwardly, but it's too late . . . "frankly . . . my uncle— it's idiotic to ask you this—but what impression does he give you?—What impression?—I mean, when you said: " 'he's strange,' what did you mean by that? . . ." I've taken the hurdle, landing, as best I can, on the far side, I catch

hold in order to climb up on the other bank, I hang on
. . . "Well, do you know that as long as I've been living
with him, I don't yet understand him very well, I'm still
not accustomed" . . . I'm crawling, I pull myself up by the
force of my arms, underneath my feet is the void . . .
"Listen, Monsieur Martereau . . ." I feel dizzy . . . I would
like to let go of everything, let myself drop into space . . .
a temptation like that which a sadist must feel when faced
with the purity and confident seriousness of a child . . .
"listen, this will doubtless surprise you, seem queer to
you, but with you I'm going to be frank, I'm going to say
what I really think . . ." He turns towards me and looks at
me attentively. His calm face with its simple, noble lines
seems to me to be grave and almost a little concerned. At
the cost of great effort, I make a final recovery and pull
myself up, this time to safety, rather far from the edge
. . . "what I really mean is this . . . Sometimes my uncle
gives me the impression of being misanthropic, he's a bit
severe with people, his own early years were hard, he had
quite a struggle, and it hasn't made him very forbearing
. . . But in reality, there's not a mean bone in him . . .
He's unsociable, but when he takes a liking to somebody
. . ." I'm settled now in a place of safety, disporting myself
in all security under his reassured gaze . . . "You, for instance, he likes you very much, he's told me that many
times: 'Ah! I like to talk to Monsieur Martereau.' You
should come to see him more often. Your visits do him
good." Martereau nods, smiles, stretches out his hand: "Ah!
yes, he told you that? But I too like very much to see him,

115

he's very interesting, I like to talk to him. He has retained all the fire of youth. That's very rare. And with that, he has experience.—Fine, well, good-bye, Monsieur Martereau, I'll tell him that you'll come again soon, he'll be glad.—Tell him to come and see me too, eh; informally, as between neighbors. And if I hear about a house, I'll let him know, but just now good bargains are rare." I leave him, relieved, I feel reassured, purified. I'm on the right path. Everything is in order. Without having to lift a finger, Martereau has set everything straight.

"What is it made of, the house?" Sitting opposite them on the little folding seat, I ask this timidly, as the three of us, Martereau, my uncle and I drive along between little gardens and separate houses in the nearby suburbs. Martereau turns on me the somewhat surprised gaze of his large, clear eyes. "The house? Why, it's made of mill-stone . . . That's what I was just explaining to your uncle: otherwise, it wouldn't be at that price, you can imagine. You should see what almost any one of these little houses can cost. Undoubtedly, it's the best type of construction we have today. Absolutely reliable. However, you'll see yours, that is, the one I'm speaking of: it's a fine house, a real villa." I sense my uncle's delight, how he's licking his chops. He turns to Martereau: "Ah! but you don't seem to realize, my dear Martereau, that you have just dealt this young man a deadly blow. Because mill-stone happens to be our pet aversion. My wife is going to let out a howl, it's the very height of abomination. What they want is something old: an old chateau, never mind if it's a bit run down— or a thatched cottage . . . Above all it must be poetic . . . you didn't know that?" Martereau smiles and fixes his surprised gaze a little more intently on me . . . "Well, what did mill-stone ever do to you? It's not bad looking. You get quite accustomed to it. And I assure you that when you live in it, it's marvelous. Sturdy. Never gives any trouble. No dampness." I blush and turn my eyes towards the car window. It's unjust to make me pay like this for my former erring ways. I accept mill-stone. I'm looking forward to it. May it sparkle in the sun with all its ochres, all its gold-dust. May there be a china cat on the roof, with its back up, or on the circular lawn, with its tail up; may the box shrubs be trimmed to look like birds, and may the two parrots cut for air-holes in the shutters be looking at each other. I ask nothing better. Nevertheless, when the car stops, I say: "Already?" I just let that slip. Perhaps it was a need to annoy my uncle a bit, or the impossibility for me to quit entirely the character that he absolutely insists I must play, or a sense of duty: after all, I am not here merely for my own personal satisfaction, but also as my aunt's emissary, delegated by her as an observer: "A villa quite near Paris . . . What an idea . . I wouldn't go if they paid me a fortune. But you go, do, I beg of you. You can tell me what it looks like. Your uncle can do the rashest things. He's quite capable of buying it." Martereau, who is on the point of getting out, with one hand on the half-open car door, turns and looks at me severely: "Now, let's get this straight. Your uncle told me he wanted to be within easy access of Paris, otherwise I should not have spoken to you about it. Here, we are within twenty-five minutes by the clock of the Gare St. Lazare. The owner goes to Paris every day. Real country is all very fine . . ." My uncle lays a hand on his arm . . . "Of course, of course. But you don't have to explain that to me. I hate out-of-the-way holes. No desire to go bury myself in the dead country. I want to be right nearby. We haven't got a dozen cars in the family." We proceed, the three of us, I flanked by them, along the gravel walk under the pom-pom rose arbors. We mount the several degrees of the cement terrace. I fall back a bit. I turn around. It's a lovely day. The first sunshine of the very first Spring days. Tufts of lavender, yellow, white primroses huddle innocently against the cement edge of the terrace. A Japanese cherry-tree silhouettes the tender freshness of its pink petals against the roughly austere surface of the garden wall. This Spring shut up in a cage, held on leash, has something reassuring and at the same time, moving about it. I'd like to stay here. Sit on this bench in front of the house. Listen to the shy chirping of the birds . . . My uncle is becoming impatient: "Well, what are you doing? Looking at the view? Come and look at this: it's interesting. It's really in very good condition. Not so much as a wall-plug to be put in. No disagreeable surprises in store for us. Martereau tells me that there are almost no repairs to be made; a few trifles: a few pieces of slate to be replaced on the roof, a gutter-pipe, a little papering, perhaps. That's all. And look at these rooms: they're light, they're gay, not like those damp old holes of yours. And come and see the bathrooms. Hot water everywhere. The house is entirely oil-heated. Let's go look at the burner: they say it's marvelous." We linger in the big clean, brilliantly lighted cellar, examining the furnace, reading what's written on the various levers: you feel tempted to turn them; it's quite true the system is marvelous, a child could take care of it. In ten minutes the entire house is warm. Martereau being the strongest of us three, is the first to tear himself away from these delights. We must go. When we come out we find him waiting for us near the car, with the owner of the house: "So what do you think of it?" My uncle does all he can to hide his satisfaction, his excitement: "Well, it doesn't seem bad. We'll have to see. We'll have to think about it." I know that if he followed his inclination, he would settle the matter right away; he has a horror of hesitating, of putting things off till later on; he's as impatient as a child with a new toy. I must admit that, for a brief moment, I share his impatience, his excitement. The only thing is—and we neither of us forget it—there's my aunt.

Loud voices, a shout, a slammed door are almost always the premonitory signs of her silence. Silence is her surest method, the most perfect procedure, amongst all those she uses, to train him. As for him, he knows quite well, when he goes out pulling the door to behind him to make it slam as hard as he can (at that moment, nothing could keep him from giving her this slap which she is expecting with every strained nerve), he knows that, without fail, with the icy, calmly deferred determination of a sadist, she will inflict his punishment upon him.

Only in this way, at the cost of inflexible determination, long, unrelaxed patience and immense, incessant efforts, has she succeeded, more or less, in teaching him, as she says, to behave himself: he knows now that he must remain standing behind his chair until she comes and is seated at table; that he must excuse himself when he is called to the telephone during meals, and I always feel sorry for him at those moments when, in the manner of a trained dog, or a dressed-up monkey, he turns towards her, as he lays his napkin on the table, and says: "Excuse me." Once silence has been applied, it is maintained with the regularity and inevitability of a well-organized penitentiary system. The culprit is subjected to it for a period that she estimates according to the seriousness of the offence committed and the signs of suffering and repentance she discerns in him.

Few people can stand this torture by silence for long. Certain of them, when it drags on, being incapable of holding out, feeling they have nothing more to lose, and being seized with a desperate need for self-destruction, or else risking all to win all, hoping in that way to force the other person to fly off the handle, make a big scene, break valuable objects, go into a rage, shout. As for him, having been schooled by long training, he usually accepts it with resignation: he settles down in this silence like an old offender who, each time that he's brought back, immediately drops into his prison habits. At first, in fact, he himself doesn't feel at all like talking—they can all go to hell, he's fed up—his rage is fermenting. At meals, where the method holds full sway, he eats opposite her in silence, concentrating dismally on his plate, scowling, with puckered lids and lips drawn into a sulky pout that we know well; or raising his head from time to time, looks straight in front of him with a fierce, fixed stare. Their daughter and I, caught between this look and hers, which is icy, remote, pretend to be disporting ourselves innocently, light-heartedly. In such cases, however, our mimicry is a bit unnatural. Under difficult circumstances like these, we are rather indifferent actors, being too preoccupied, doubtless, by our desire to follow, from the viewpoint of experienced connoisseurs, the various ups and downs of the skillful struggle in which they are now engaged. But there exists between them a system of compensation: that of vessels connected by "U" tubes. When the level lowers in one, you'll see it rise right away in the other. As he becomes more and more depressed, she becomes at once cheerful and full of life, chats with us, shows off. He then becomes gloomier and gloomier and doesn't lift his eyes again from his plate except to ask us, his daughter and me, hoarsely and briefly, to pass him the mustard or the bread, especially when they're right within her reach and, normally, he would make his request to her. Occasionally, it's he—but very rarely, in such cases he is much the weaker of the two—who, one fine day, comes into the dining room, lively as anything, rubbing his hands together, and gives me a pinch on the arm: "Boy, what weather! I skidded twice. On the Pont de Grenelle we all but made a complete about face." She immediately assumes her set expression, one eye-brow, the left one, arched high, which gives her the look of a cruel Indian. She now resorts to drastic measures and sets what I call her pumping system into action: her silence becomes denser, more ponderous, it attracts us more strongly, our words are caught up by it, our words flutter an instant between us, hollow, inconsistent, they whirl about for a moment, then, being diverted from their course and unable to reach their goal, they crash down somewhere inside her—a little formless spurt—caught up by her silence. She sees this perfectly and derives intense pleasure from our vain efforts. Little by little, we lose heart: our voices sound more and more off-key. Our words having now grown frailer and frailer, lighter and lighter, are whisked away immediately, we scarcely hear them. Finally we stop talking. All that remains in the emptiness, occupying it entirely, spreading out in every direction, is her silence. Then, after a moment, when she has quite relished her victory (it seems to me that, after we have finally given up, I hear her sigh of satisfaction, her shout of triumph), after a few seconds spent in conscious delight, she begins to grow frisky: her daughter and I, as a result of our collusion with him, are banished; but when one of the maids comes in, she starts smiling at her, pays her compliments: "The temperature of your wine is just right this time, it is really perfect, you're becoming quite a wine butler." The maid, although she surely knows this subtle strategy as well as we do, allows herself to be taken in, the way one always lets oneself be taken in by the most fulsome compliments, she blushes, very pleased. Indeed, the maids are often a great help to us. In the painful moments during which all four of us say nothing, they permit us to stretch ourselves a bit, to take a breath of air; they force us to make an effort in order to save face. When one of them comes in, we start talking to her right away . . . My aunt especially: one of her greatest concerns—and it's also one of her weaknesses—is that the servants should notice nothing: a vulnerable trait with her which occasionally, when he's driven into a corner, he uses to advantage, by starting to talk louder and louder, when they both know that they can be overheard, in order to intimidate her, to frighten her, and force her, for a moment at least, under the threat of an intolerable humiliation, to give in to him.

This time she's held her own for a long time. The matter at stake is worth it: that awful suburban house that he persists in wanting to buy, and then, above all, the necessity to punish him severely for his outburst of fury, his rudeness, the entire house had resounded with his shouting.

With him, once the usual first phase is over—threatening silence, angry looks, sour remarks addressed to us, to his daughter and to me, and which, we all know, are aimed at her—his strength diminishes visibly. It's been evident for some time now, that he would like to patch it up: during the last few days, he has been making timid, touching efforts to edge in sidewise on the conversations she has with us at every meal, growing proportionately more sprightly and full of life as his level lowers. She could afford now, and she knows it, to do whatever she wanted: he's as weak and toothless as could be desired; the silliest remarks, in which are displayed the most shameful signs of her femininity, of that sort of frivolous stupidity that usually enrages him, he listens to without flinching, with a sort of emotion, a hidden nostalgia.

She adores that exquisite moment when she receives the reward for her strength of character, for her endurance . . . that's what comes of having held her own. As in the old days, when he used to come to her parents' house, a rather timid man who remained seated with the grown people and never stopped watching her from afar, without showing it, but she felt it, it seemed to her that invisible threads coming from him lifted her up, directed her movements, made her spring about, lithe and light—a young goat—on the terrace steps, laughingly shake her curly head, play catch with her sisters, free, elusive, a butterfly, a firefly . . . now that she had set between her and him the vast impassable spaces of her silence, without needing to turn her eyes in his direction, she again felt his gaze which, like dust-covered foliage washed by a heavy thunder-shower, had recovered its former freshness. As in the old days, invisible threads lifted her up: she leaned her curly head towards her daughter, she laughed her youthful laughter—girl-friend or elder sister . . . everyone said it . . . and she far and away the better looking, a young bird, a bee flitting about among the flowers, gathering honey . . . "Darling, you should have seen, at Jacques Barelli's, there were some little Scotch wool jackets . . . one adorable one . . . but as for the price . . ." You could feel him marking time impatiently, he would have liked to break loose, run to her, stretch out his hands . . . "What is the price? But what does that matter? That's ridiculous. Go ahead, buy them. I'll make you a present of them. Get several, if they are that pretty." It was touching to see him making every effort, sidling up, trying his best—but he was held firmly in place—to come as near as possible to her, he looked at his daughter—"He's all the rage, Barelli, just now? Are his things nice? Do you like them?" His daughter, ill-at-ease, splutters: "Oh! yes, certainly . . ." while her mother's icy, somewhat surprised look pitilessly forces him to retreat.

I believe that I know their secret code so well, I am so accustomed to deciphering the real meaning of their re-actions, that, with them, I put no trust in appearances. Occasionally, perhaps, not enough. My excessive mistrust must even at times lead me astray. Today, the abrupt change in his attitude, the way, all of a sudden, after sev-eral days of shy attempts at reconciliation, each time re-jected, he has now taken on the look of a lonely, broken old man, of an abandoned Samson, appears to me to be merely a new means—all the others having failed—of dislodging her from her position. It even seems to me that this is a means that I've seen him use before, I forget on what occasion. The bitter-sweet remarks that she addresses to him by way of us, her carefree, sprightly manner, her laughter, all roll off him without his seeming to notice them: he's a big, motionless animal, with a thick hide. A pachyderm with ponderous, drooping lids, nobly wrinkled. He drums on the table without listening to our chatter, with a fixed stare, his mind elsewhere. I feel that she, too, a bit surprised, is studying him—mistrustful and at the same time, slightly anxious. Finally, at the dessert course, interrupting us all of a sudden, sweeping aside our frivolous chatter with one gesture, he leans towards his daughter and towards me: "Listen to me, children. I must speak to you. I'm a bit worried about something just now. Nothing serious . . ." (just what is needed to lure her, the quiet, restrained tone, the manly desire to be considerate of her, not to take easy advantage of the situation), "I must go away for a few days. I think everything will turn out all right, but I must go in person. So, my little girl, I'm going to ask you to do something for me. You'll understand with no difficulty what it is about."

I see his manoeuvre right away . . . Their daughter—his most powerful weapon, pitch, boiling oil, which he usually pours hissing with hatred over his enemies—is now his white flag . . . Their daughter who gives all its destructive force to his "you" . . . "Ah! you never do anything else . . . Oh! you, you've always got a lot of ideas . . . That's all you ever think about: a lot of piffle . . ." Their daughter, an

essential ingredient in the manufacture of his vitriol . . .
Put on the same level, snubbed, labeled, ashamed and
blushing in their ridiculous nudity, anonymous slaves
chained one to the other, cattle led pell-mell to market; as
different from him in their resemblance to each other,
their helplessness, their stupidity, as animals are from
men . . .

People can make fun of me if they want, his "you"—and
he knows it right away, without even having time to think
about it, and we all know it—his "you" means all that
and more still: "You," low creatures whose very contact is
degrading, "you," all the stupidity in the world, "you," all
the concessions that have been forced upon him, all the obstacles, all the shackles that have impeded his flight, the
impurities that have besmirched his soul, that made him
lose his youthful freshness and eagerness, forget the dreams
that, in his madness, in his joy—his sole joy, the only
real joy—he had caressed when he had walked along singing, alone, under starry skies, his knapsack over his shoulder, sleeping in barns, Lord of creation, bard, prophet,
conqueror, long ago when he was twenty . . . His "you"
says all that to them. The "you" marks the moments when,
nevertheless, he pulls himself together, repulses them in
order to catch his breath, calls them to order—sometimes
they go a bit far—forces them to keep their distance. We
know all that—not in so many words, of course, but in a
far quicker, subtler, more complex, obvious way. We know
other things, too, seated there all attention, the four of
us, round the table: his confident, fond manner, almost

a bit humble, the muggy intonations of his voice when he pronounces, as though he were coddling them, wheedling them between his tongue and his palate, the words: girlie, my little girl, the "you" gives them their entire value, sets them off, provides a back-drop for them. Against it his present fond attitude stands out. His "you" forms a tragic accompaniment, ponderous and harsh, to the sweet, somewhat mushy melody of these words. Or, to make still another comparison, underneath the words little girl, drawn out so fondly, the "you" is the secret letter written in invisible ink. Being experts, we make it appear right away, enormous, over-spreading everything: which explains doubtless, the embarrassment, the slight loathing, the desire I've mentioned already, and which we feel right away, when he indulges in his fond outpourings, to brush him aside, to snub him . . .

He leans across the table, an affectionate light in his eyes . . . "Listen, little girl, listen carefully, and you'll understand . . ." She blushes, smiles a contracted little smile, inside her, one of the substances that go to compose the "you", escapes and rises in light bubbles . . . "Oh! you know me, if it's something complicated . . . financial questions . . . I never have understood anything about them . . ." He makes an impatient gesture with his hand to stop her. She's obstructing his manoeuvre. She's about to put a spoke in his wheel. Exasperating, inert and limp, incapable of getting out of it cleverly, of freeing herself right away from this form, from this ludicrous mask with which he himself—but it was nothing, a game, a whim, a passing reaction caused by edgy nerves, when he snubbed her: "What do you understand about it anyway? What do you know about it? You only repeat what you hear other people say . . . Did you read that in *Vogue?*"—with which he himself had rigged her up . . . She's doing it on purpose now, to go him one better, to appear stupider than she is, in order to get her revenge, to flout him, to remind him of what he would like to wipe out, to forget . . . But already, her mother, he feels it as I do—there's not a reaction in one of us here that the others don't notice right away— divides in two, doubles up, turns in order to see the danger, to look it right in the face, right at him, at me . . . She wants to see through our eyes (all by herself, the expression that her daughter is wearing now, she wouldn't see it —without us, she wouldn't see anything—or even if she did see it, she would pay no attention to it, would attach no importance to it, in fact, she doesn't care: the tie be- tween them is too strong, the fusion is too great . . . It's just to divert herself a bit, to amuse herself, tickle herself, scratch herself, exasperate herself, to rub up against me a bit, that she comes and talks to me about her daughter, complains . . . in order for me to reassure her, to tell her that it's nothing . . . the way she starts back right away when I clumsily agree with her . . . and the way the two of them unite against me: two broken pieces re-welded to- gether) . . . In order to avert the peril, her mother immedi- ately transports herself inside us, inside the enemy camp, and sees with our eyes what we see: a silly, simpering little nitwit, a little goody-goody . . . . she would like to inter-

vene, we feel it, she puffs up her feathers, grows excited,
she wants to protect her daughter, to set her straight again,
the way she did on "Prize Day," when she examined her
with an anxious eye before she went up on the stage to
recite her poem (that look they have then: at first restless,
ferreting, then suddenly staring, moist, shining—I know
of nothing to equal it in intensity except the look of a dog
stalking its prey), when she inspected her from head to
foot, gave a quick pat to an out-of-place curl, smoothed a
pleat . . . How often I've seen him take fiendish delight in
provoking, in increasing this emotion in her, sensing how
she followed, trembling, the contemptuous, hostile, hateful look he turned on their daughter, taking pleasure, as
soon as he was sure she was watching him, in intensifying
the load of his hostility, hatred and contempt when the
girl started to simper . . . "Haiphong, let's see, where is
that? in China or in Japan? S.F.I.O.,* what's that?" or
when she simply made the exasperating gesture—it's one
of her mannerisms, a mania—of cautiously smoothing the
hair coiled on the back of her head between her rounded
fingers . . . "A fine product . . . you can be proud . . . you've
done well . . ." His mean look said that to her . . . Now
he could be satisfied: he has scored a hit against the enemy,
who is abandoning his positions, but he doesn't want to
defeat the enemy, he knows that revenge would follow,
that's not the type of victory he's after, he wants a peace
pact concluded in forgiveness and forgetting . . . "No, not
at all, dearie, what are you talking about, that's ridiculous

* Initials denoting the French Socialist Party.

. . . You'll understand very well . . . you can understand this
as well as I can, all you need to do is to try." He turns
towards me: "You know, if she wanted to, that girl . . .
you'd be surprised . . . I was struck by it when I helped
her with her algebra—whenever she took the trouble, she
understood almost intuitively. For that matter, she comes
by it honestly . . . she's exactly like my mother . . . Look,
when she raises her eyebrows like that, she's the spitting
image of my mother. And she was a cracker-jack, your
grandmother was, believe me. After my father died, she
managed his business all alone: a little bit of a woman no
bigger than that. And she brought us all up. In fact, during
his lifetime, my father consulted her about everything.
Today, they're not so rare, women like her, I've met some
in business who were remarkable, real bosses. As for you,
my little girl, if you wanted to, if you ever had to, I'm sure
you would get along marvelously well . . ." He's passing
the sponge, wiping off the thick layer of varnish, the dirt,
the dark coating . . . underneath, the picture appears with
pristine colors, the cheeks become rosy, the eyes shine . . .
his flesh, his blood, his hope for the future . . . for whom
do we work, for whom do we build, if not for our children,
he looks at her . . . radiant youth . . . his wife's mischievous
smile, her bright eyes . . . how often people have said to
him: she looks intelligent, your daughter does, but we demand so much of our children, we never have sufficient
confidence in them, and they need it so . . . a little back-
ing, a little affection and they would blossom out . . . "Listen, dearie, I'm going to explain it to you . . ." His eyes

leave her now and look directly in front of him: a keen, precise gaze that pierces to the heart of the invisible object he's staring at, an earnest, clear gaze; all mugginess has gone from his voice, all trace of "you" has disappeared; we listen to him attentively; we respect his clear-sightedness, his masculinity—always efficient, energetic, quick in serious moments, we admire him for this, and he knows it . . . "listen, it's very simple, it's this . . . I'm worried about certain money matters . . . nothing serious . . . they'll straighten out . . . but I must go away for a few days, and I have a sum of money here that I prefer not to keep for reasons of taxation . . . I should like to invest it to advantage . . . I'm thinking of you and your future . . . but you understand I don't want the treasury to come sticking its nose in it, they fleece us enough as it is, if things keep on like that, it won't be worth while working at all . . . and so, dearie, I'm going to entrust it to you . . ." he turns towards me . . . "I want you both to go to see Martereau—you can even go alone, if you want to; no, it's better for you to go together—and take the money to him. I've spoken to him on the subject, he knows what it's all about, you have only to say to him: Here, my father wants to buy the house . . ." he makes a movement with his hand as though to stop us . . . "not to live in, there's no question of that, I don't care a rap about that, it's simply as an investment, I'll probably sell it again soon, but momentarily, it's an excellent investment. Martereau, you understand, will purchase it in his name with the money you are going to take him—I've spoken to him about it, he has agreed: for him, it presents no difficulty; he can justify this money easily in the eyes of the Treasury . . . whereas, just now, it would be very awkward for me to have to declare it. So dearie, now that you've understood it all . . . go to see him today . . . I shall count on you . . ." Her mother looks at her, her mouth half-opened, her eyes shining . . . she is holding on to herself not to answer for her . . . Of course, of course she'll go . . . she's a good little girl, reliable, eager to help, she can be counted on in difficult moments, despite her appearance of a spoiled child . . . Reliable and responsible, like herself . . . All that ridiculous play-acting, all that biting and sulking are effaced; all three of them united; a single block; there's nothing in the world stronger than that, sealed by so many years; all the rest is nothing, so much dust, it's swept away, we are breathing purified, vivifying air, he feels the excitement—exquisite—of moments of crisis . . . like a few years ago, when he had feared he was bankrupt . . . her warmth, her sudden gentleness . . . she had taken it very courageously, a good helpmeet, she had really been a sport, she had stuck by him, encouraged him . . . they had drunk coffee in the kitchen, she had made him laugh, it would be amusing, really, to live the life of people of small means, she was quite lively, active, almost affectionate, they had felt happy . . . and now, while she approves in silence, he feels once more this same current that comes from her, sustaining and carrying him along . . . they are not yet on speaking terms but he knows that hostilities are over, she nods gentle approval, gives her daughter an encouraging look, when he says to her in a tone of calm, firm mildness that inspires respect: "Well, now, do you understand everything? I'm going to give you the parcel; I'm taking the train for Brussels in a little while, I've a lot of things to do still. It would be better if you took it this evening, my mind will be more at rest.— Why, of course, I'll go today." She looks at me: "We'll go together, eh? are you coming with me? I'm delighted to go to see Monsieur Martereau, he's so nice. In fact, I've got a crush on Monsieur Martereau . . ." while her parents watch her fondly, she blossoms out, shakes her feathers . . . Her mother, who feels that they can both enjoy themselves now and let themselves go, watches her with an almost bewildered, ecstatic look, the result of her excessive maternal passion, of her pride . . . I myself am so pleased, that I listen with emotion . . . it's a moving thing, all the same, a young girl in her fresh naïveté . . . "Really, it's true, what I'm saying, don't you think so Mama, he must have been marvelous, Monsieur Martereau . . ." Her mother looks at her smiling, she nods her head with a movement that means: aren't you a silly goose . . . Just listen to her . . . Encouraged, the girl wags a saucy finger: "I adore Monsieur Martereau . . ." For a moment I fear—she's going too far, just the same—that everything will come tumbling down, the entire clever construction, something seems to have stirred in the father, a ghost glided past; however, what am I thinking of, there can be no question of it, he's listening, looking fondly at his wife who is nodding her head like certain music-lovers who beat time when they hear their favorite pieces . . . "But listen, Mama, don't you agree with me, frankly. . . ." Her mother's eyes are devouring her . . . isn't she pretty, isn't she sweet, cute as a fox . . . what a smile, what dimples, just as soon as she's in a good humor . . . her father laughs: "Ha! good old Martereau! he'd be darned surprised if he heard that, he probably doesn't imagine himself as a Lothario . . . But be that as it may, since it gives you such pleasure, so much the better, you'll go to see him today . . . I can't say whether he's an Apollo or not, but in any case, he's a very decent fellow, he can be relied upon." Victory is his, the fortress has surrendered, on the ramparts they're hoisting the white flag. His wife rises: "Go ahead, darling, and don't forget anything, remember all your father has told you; above all, be careful not to lose the money." She turns to me: "I think it would be better, just the same, if you went too . . ."

It's over. A permanent peace pact is going to be signed. Now it's only a question of formalities. A suitable moment must be chosen. In our presence, a certain embarrassment holds them back, but as soon as we'll be gone, they'll start talking again as though nothing had happened, a wee bit contracted to begin with, their voices not very well placed (they never have things out: he won't stand for them, explanations, reconciliations, and long ago she was obliged to forego satisfaction of the need for these stimulants which, from the very first—except on rare occasions—he pitilessly refused to furnish her). And yet, she has often said this to me, human relations are like that . . . why not recognize one's mistakes frankly, talk them over, the way it's usually done among civilized people, among cultivated people? . . . This, for her, is what has been most lacking, "but for him, those things are so much Chinese, and that's what a woman, believe me, and remember that later on, can least forgive . . ." be that as it may, it's become a habit now; just the same, it will be delightful, the impression of meeting again entirely refreshed, purified as though after a long absence, so much has happened during those few days, so many minute events, small cares, these worries of his . . . by the way, she got a letter from her brother—it had come just at the right moment, couldn't have been better timed—goodness knows what stupid things he's done now, his business is going badly, in other words, the usual thing . . . and he will feel flattered, cheered up, by this contrast that she has always tacitly underlined, he knows it, between her brother and himself, he being so energetic, such a hard worker: a man. Oh, as for that, he can be relied upon. Strong. Generous . . . "Have you got his letter? Give it to me, I'll see what can be done. I'll attend to it. . ."

We get up from the table, their daughter and I, they should be left alone. We too feel soothed, lighter, borne on joyful wing . . . "Shall we go now to see Martereau? All right, let's go now, we can always try, perhaps he'll be at home."

As we walk along side by side, carrying the valuable parcel, good little Red Riding Hoods going to see their grandmother, I feel delightfully adjusted, in order: a precision instrument that's just been cleaned, well dusted, oiled and wound up. This state, I have noticed, brings good luck; everything goes well; the wheels round us, with which we interlock without friction, begin to turn harmoniously. We find Martereau at home. He comes to the door himself, in his house-slippers, his spectacles pushed up from his eyes, resting on the thick stubble of his gray hair. Immediately cordial, with no effort, as he always is, glad to see us . . . "Well, well, what a surprise . . . What fair wind . . . Do come in . . . My wife has gone to do an errand, she won't be long . . . You've caught me with my slippers on in the middle of the afternoon, that never used to happen to me, but it's a matter of age, it can't be helped, a touch of gout . . . But do sit down, sit down . . . that makes you smile, doesn't it, Mademoiselle, the infirmities of old age, gout . . . You don't know what that means . . . Ah! it's not pleasant to grow old . . . But you, yourselves, how are you? And that health of yours? Fine, all's to the good . . . And your parents? I saw your father the other day, younger than ever, in excellent form . . . Well, what have you got to tell me that's nice? What's new?" I look at my cousin . . . the honor is hers . . . She blushes and fidgets a bit, speaking in her sprightly, high-pitched, clear voice, very young-girlish, she even lisps slightly, the way certain actresses do when they play youthful roles . . . "Well, it's this, Monsieur Martereau. It's Papa who sent us to see you. We've come to talk business with you . . ." Martereau raises his eyebrows, opens his eyes wide with astonishment and nods comically, as though much impressed . . . "Business? You've come to talk business with me?—Yes, we have, just imagine . . . But it's true . . . Papa couldn't come himself, he's

137

obliged to go away for a few days, so he asked me, that is, he told us . . . In fact, you know about it. He spoke to you on the subject . . . It has to do with that house . . . You know, the villa you advised him to buy . . ." Martereau raises his hand: "Oh, 'advised' . . . if you want. Your father asked me to let him know if I heard of anything . . ." She interrupts him: "Yes, yes, naturally . . . I mean that you agreed it was a good buy . . .—Oh! as for that, the house is in very good condition. It's well built. It's worth the price.—Exactly. So then, Papa thought it would be a good investment. Only, he's worried about certain matters just now, he told you . . . so he sent us to ask a great favour of you . . . he told us that he had mentioned it to you the other day and that you had agreed, that you were willing to buy the house in your name so that he wouldn't have to declare it to the income tax office . . . But you surely understand it all better than I do . . . So, here . . . he gave us the money . . ." Martereau listens attentively. He nods gravely: "Yes, I did tell him that: it's an agreement. If he decides to take it, I'll do that for him, I promised to help him out." I take the heavy envelope tied up with a string out of my inside jacket pocket and hand it to him. His thick, deft fingers skillfully untie the knot, take out the packets of bills . . . "As a matter of form . . . you don't mind?" . . . count them rapidly. We remain silent. The only sound to be heard is the crackle of the paper . . . "That's right: two million, eight hundred thousand francs." He gathers the packets together, gives them a tap to even them up, puts them back in the envelope, re-ties the string around them. He turns his revolving chair towards his desk. Takes out his key-ring. Chooses a key. Opens the drawer, puts the parcel in it. His rather fleshy hand, with its thick smooth skin, turns the key cautiously and firmly in the lock, plunges the key-ring into his trousers' pocket. He turns to face us: "Very well. I'll tell my wife, so that she will know that there's some money belonging to you in there: you never know what can happen. Tell your uncle I'll start on it tomorrow. I'll telephone the owner this evening.— Thank you. Thank you very much . . ." We look at each other . . . "Well, that's that . . . We won't disturb you any longer . . . I think it's time to go now . . .—Already? Oh, do stay a little while, you're in no hurry . . . My wife should be back any moment . . . She'll make you a cup of tea . . ." But we stand up. "Thank you, but I think we ought to go home. They're expecting us . . ." Outside, on the landing, while we're saying good-bye, my cousin—it's a gesture she frequently makes, out of timidity, doubtless, in order to hide her embarrassment—rubs her hand across her forehead. Martereau smiles mischievously: "You've got a migraine, have you? it's as tiring as all that, business? . . ." She laughs: "Oh! no, it's not that, it's nothing. I've just a slight headache, it'll go away in the open air . . ." Martereau lifts his right forefinger: "Do you know this old song? They used to sing it to me when I was little . . ." And standing there on the landing, wagging his raised forefinger, nodding his head in rhythm, he sings softly: *I've got a headache, you'll never guess why. My grandmother switched me, and she made me cry* . . . All three of us laugh in chorus while he shakes our hands . . . "Well, we'll see you soon, good-bye, my best to your mother and father." He closes the door, and we hurry down the stairs. My cousin's laugh, a bit off-key, badly poised, doesn't exactly fit into the place inside us, into the space all ready to receive it that the little ditty had dug for it. A final chord, anticipated and necessary, but not very cleverly struck.

*I*t was to be expected (I've already said that we function like vessels connected by "U" tubes), it was enough for him when he came into the house—he had been gone for nearly six weeks—it was enough, when he set foot in the entrance, for him to see how lively and excited we were, our retriever dog's shining eyes, (sometimes it seems to me that he senses it, before he even sees us, that the air displaced by our mounting joy weighs upon him) for his level immediately to become lower: he throws out to us in passing a quick, cold: "Everything all right?" and goes straight to his study where he shuts himself in.

But we're not discouraged by little things like that. The

most excruciatingly painful experiences will not keep us in such moments, when our own level is so high, from acting like normal persons: everything's fine and we're on the right side, the side he's on too, thank heavens, except for occasional rare moments. On the side of what's reliable. The side of what's true.

As soon as we hear him open his door, we dash off. Of the two of us, his daughter is the more excited. "You know, Papa, you'll be pleased, everything went off very well, Monsieur Martereau accepted right away, as he had promised you he would. We gave him the money and he said that he would get in touch with the owner the next day. You should go to see him." He turns on us a hard, penetrating look: "The owner? What owner? Oh! yes, of the house. You gave him the money?" He is speaking to me, to show, according to all accepted rules of the game, that she is unworthy: "Did you ask him for a receipt?"

The cards that have just been dealt him are so good, his luck is so great, that I might almost be tempted to rejoice for him. But above all, I admire him. I admire the unerringness of his blows. "I know, as he says, with whom I have to deal." A brief acquaintance, a quick diagram, a few broad lines . . . are enough for him. He's a good workman who, in order to do good work, does not need very complicated tools. Now, all at once, he has discovered in us the point, the joint into which he has inserted the fuse of the infernal machine that will reduce us to a powder. But which infernal machine? Why, the most every-day, the most ordinary implement, the one that every man of parts uses on all occasions, without dreaming of doing the slight-est harm: a simple, perfectly natural question.

How weak and awkward I feel beside him. I keep pal-pating, searching him, inspecting his every cranny, I spy upon him with the anxious attention of a sick person watching for symptoms of his ailment. I feel his slightest reaction in advance. I foresaw the backward start he would give as soon as he saw us approaching with arms out-stretched to embrace him . . . how he would recoil sniffing, with his back up . . . he has a horror of being cajoled like that, of that sort of nun-like cheeriness . . . "Come along now, everything's for the best, enjoy yourselves, go on, be happy, there now, smile a bit, give us a nice little smile . . ." People are trying to set him straight again, teach him how to behave, they keep watching him in an underhanded way: he feels the repugnant contact of soft little suckers clinging to him and palpating him, he would like to tear them from him. It was easy for me to foresee the path that would be left in him by the words: "You know, Monsieur Martereau was so nice, he accepted right away, just as he had promised you he would." I heard the seething they produced in him as they went on their course, the little hiss of limestone being corroded by acid: Ah! indeed, he accepted . . . What an honor . . . What a favor . . . that was too kind . . . So they imagine I need that little guy . . . I don't need anybody, I've never had to owe anybody any-thing . . . It's their fault if I got embarked on this whole business, it was to please them . . . worn out finally by having their houses and their Martereau dinned into my ears: he's the latest infatuation, the newest fad . . . they swear by him, they coo like pigeons at the first moron that comes along . . . I could give them the moon, but nothing's ever good enough . . . they consider that perfectly natural; whereas Martereau has only to lift his little finger, everybody weeps with emotion, with gratitude . . . Sensitive souls . . . Delicate feelings . . . I'll show them a thing or two, I'll bring them down to earth again . . .

I knew all that. I could have described in advance, better than he himself could, the chemical process by which his words: "And the receipt?", like the gas that a chemist prepares to collect in a test tube, had escaped. But I didn't make a move to avert, to hinder the process, as usual, docile, timorous, I didn't interfere, never daring to trust myself, to give freedom of the city to my presentiments. And she, his daughter, is like me: I hate her, in fact, for that reason. We are both, she and I, like the people who, when they see sea monsters, ectoplasms or table-turning with their own eyes, shake their heads, nevertheless, and say: "If that existed, everybody would know about it. There would have been reports on the subject to the Academy of Science." No one has ever told her, no one anywhere has ever proclaimed, that certain questions should not elicit "quite naturally" certain replies, that when you're asked why you didn't demand a receipt, in certain cases you should never, under any circumstances, reply, as she is doing now, her wide-open eyes expressing astonishment which, from her standpoint, is only just, only normal: "But you didn't tell me you wanted one." Above all, not add: "I thought you had complete confidence in Monsieur Martereau, that perhaps it wouldn't be very tactful, very nice . . ." I experience a sort of satisfaction, a sort of relief, when the inevitable reaction occurs. These words, like the faint sound that sets an avalanche in motion, immediately start the enormous, suspended mass on its way: "Ha! I'm the one, it's me—he is taking his time, dragging out his words—naturally . . . I was wrong . . . I'm always wrong . . . it's my fault, all the stupid things you do . . . I don't think you're dumb enough . . . I don't consider you retarded enough to warn you that you don't hand over two million eight hundred thousand francs directly like that to a 'gentleman' . . . No, really, it's outrageous . . ." He smirks: "It wouldn't be nice . . . you have every confidence . . ." To begin with, I have no confidence in anybody, and then, even if it had been my own brother, how can I tell what might happen to him . . . But you two, you don't give a hoot . . . You can afford the luxury of being generous . . ." He suddenly grows silent and stares in front of him, frowning as though he were trying to examine closely something at a distance, something that only he sees—this always makes a great impression on me, rouses my apprehensions—his voice has a brassy sound, he's talking through his nose, apparently to an intelligent, sensible man—they're alone, as one man to another—to someone who understands, who knows . . . "But he, Martereau, that's very surprising . . . he's no little greenhorn, he wasn't born yesterday, he knows what he's doing, just the same, he knows perfectly well that they're not done, things like that, he knew very well, he did, what he was doing . . ."

It's not an illusion, not an imagined reminiscence; no, I have experienced exactly this before, I recognize the sensation: this up-rooting, this rending, everything trembles, cracks, gapes open . . . I feel as though I were split in two, an icy blast rushes into me . . . What he has just said, his nasal, assured tone, have touched my weak spot, re-opened an old cut that was never well knit together, that sense of rending that, long ago, when I was little, their pointed laughter gave me, the words they whispered to one another so I shouldn't hear, but I did hear, seated beside them in the kitchen, waiting for them to finish serving my parents and take me to bed . . . I tried my best to hear, to understand, to look the threat, the danger, directly in the face. They pointed to the platter brought back from the table: "Do look at what she's left us, you should have seen her picking over the pieces. Nothing seemed too little for us. Look at it: it's all gristle and bones." And their waggish laughter: "Oh! believe me . . . you've nothing to fear here. There's no risk of putting on weight. With her, at least, you're sure to keep your shape . . ."

A stronger person than I am, would have held his own, would have become hardened, compact, but I was so soft, so malleable, so little was needed, one little scratch of the surgeon's knife sufficed . . . I began to open up limply with horror and delectation . . . further still, as far as it could go, I let an icy wind enter into me . . . everything was wavering . . . breaking up . . . my mother's look at table, as she examined the pieces on the platter, insisting: "Don't you want some more, take some, there's plenty left for the kitchen . . ." I must experience this suffering to its very depths . . . Everything in me becomes unsteady and opens up . . . I feel cold . . . Martereau's gesture when he turned the key in the lock . . . His big, pudgy fingers as they pulled out the key . . . His look when he turned towards us.

See Martereau again right away: his nice smile, the placid, direct gaze of his big, limpid eyes, his firm handshake, his good hearty voice . . . "Well, well, so it's you? What fair wind? . . . And how's everything? What's new? What are you up to?" Everything will fall into place immediately, reassume shape, it was nothing, what was it, anyway? A bad dream, crazy notions, tell me, what's the matter with him now, my little dickey-bird, my great big silly boy . . . She's seated on the edge of my bed with me snuggled up close to her . . . the silky softness of her very fine skin, more silky than silk itself, her fingers on my neck, on my forehead . . . Why, how warm you are . . . I cling close to her, I close my eyes, I feel drowsy, I breathe in the delicious odor that is hers alone, mine alone, my secret, I discovered it, I invented it, the odor of certainty, of security . . .

Not a second to be lost . . . I dash up the stairs two steps at a time, I don't wait for the elevator, I'll get there more quickly on foot . . . three flights, the door to the left: I ring the bell.

Nobody. Not the slightest sound behind the closed door. Silence all about. I sit down on the steps. I keep watch . . .

There now, is the soft sound of the elevator gate, the live throb of mounting hope, I stand up, I press my face against the bars of the shaft, I try to see . . . a bump, a start: something inside me has come undone and is hanging down. Then the faint, sickening, sliding sound of the gate being pulled to on the floor below. I sit down. I listen . . . And it starts all over again . . .

I must leave, give up. I must prepare myself to endure what I dread so much, the painful sensation, in the place left empty by the enormous swelling of desire, of hope— as in the place of an amputated limb—of dull twinges, shooting pains.

Now is the dangerous moment when all kinds of disquieting things happen. They occur always at those moments when I let go my hold, when everything starts falling to pieces. It's at these times that I see them loom up. They always appear at a given point when I am floating along like that in fragments, adrift. I admire that sure scent of theirs; the way they smell at a distance in me, perhaps without realizing it, an odor of decomposition, the vague stench of carrion, and turn aside. I'm afraid of their eyes which observe me furtively at the instant when I am not looking at them, afraid of their sly movements. A feeling of anguish, almost of panic, seizes hold of me when I see them cross the street pretending to be busy, preoccupied, in order not to arouse my suspicions; or else when, caught unprepared, seeking a refuge, they take their stand a few feet away from me before a shop window and make a pretense of examining the things in it, their entire will to resist, their entire effort of defense, gathered in their thick backs, that have become hardened like shells; or again, when they've had the misfortune to see me too late, when I'm too near—no possibility of flight, no refuge at hand, they're obliged to have recourse to desperate, very bold means—and they keep on walking straight ahead, their faces expressionless, inscrutable, eyes staring, in the manner of a sleep-walker advancing along the edge of a roof, surrounding themselves with a bewitched circle into which I am unable to enter.

When I saw Martereau appear, I nevertheless gave a sudden start of hope, a brief impulse, at once repressed. Martereau was coming towards me between the lines of a pedestrian crossing, his dark felt hat on the back of his head, in his arms a large parcel; his face wore an inscrutable expression, his eyes had an empty stare; it seemed to me that either to accost him or to touch him would make him fall over backwards. At the instant when we passed each other, my eyes riveted to him and the ghost of a smile on my face, I made a slight movement in his direction, I couldn't help it: his face became even more petrified, lost all expression whatsoever—the empty face of a doll—and his eyes, at the moment when he passed close to me, stirred very slightly, turned away at an infinitesimal angle, while I sensed how, with all his collected force, he repulsed me.

Now to keep cool. A stout heart. A clear head. Try to be sincere. Useless to sham, it's not true: I'm not so surprised as all that. There's not a single reaction that others have, however unexpected it may appear to be, which really catches us unawares. Not a reaction which hasn't already been roughly outlined and which we hadn't perceived, without admitting it. This reaction of Martereau's, that is so surprising in him, so unlike him, this same reaction that frightens me so, I recognize it, I've seen it before, it comes back to me like a forgotten flavor, like a vague odor that I might have had a whiff of without taking particular notice of it . . . it was that day when Martereau came to see us, when I admired him so much, compact and hard as he was, as motionless as could be wished—a perfectly smooth ball. The jets of scalding steam that my uncle sprinkled him with didn't leave the slightest trace, there was not a spot of tarnish or dampness on his gleaming polish. Martereau was standing in the parlor doorway, on the point of leaving: "Well, it's high time for me to turn in, I always go to bed early, early to bed, early to rise . . ." and my uncle had slapped him on the shoulder with that protective familiarity that always makes me so ill at ease—I feel a warm flush, I grow red, get upset—a nice big, condescending slap . . . "Oh! you, I bet, my dear Martereau, no need to ask you if you're a good sleeper . . . You must surely sleep well, you must not know what it is to lie awake, lucky devil that you are," and he had laughed that indefinable laughter of his, admiring and contemptuous: a robust fellow, good old Martereau . . . and Martereau had nodded, he had had a nice good-natured smile: "Oh! that depends, occasionally I too am unable to sleep, when I'm worried or very anxious about things, but I must say, it's very rare . . . Usually, I can't complain, I sleep well . . ." His eyes had retained all their limpidity, he hadn't seemed to flinch, but I had sensed the way he shrank from that nice big friendly slap: a very slight gesture of recoil, a hardly perceptible movement, the kind we perceive frequently without the help of any sort of exterior sign, without the help of a single word, a single look; it's as though an invisible wave emanated from the other person and ran through you, a vibration in the other that you record like a very sensitive apparatus, is transmitted to you, you vibrate in unison, sometimes even more intensely . . . I had repeated within myself the movement he had outlined in order to withdraw, I had felt his annoyance, his repugnance, I had seen what he saw: that portrait of himself . . . ah! good old Martereau, nothing nervous about that fellow, nothing on his mind, not the least bit complicated, nothing deep about him, no need to wrack your brain . . . A good old nag, sturdy and easy-going . . . He would have liked to slap the hand that held this crude mask crammed down on his face, but he had restrained himself, he had fallen in with the game . . .

A while ago, when he saw me—I recognize it, I'm sure of it, it was the same reaction, only strong this time, very clear, very expansive . . . with me, he let himself go, being tired as he was, in a hurry to reach home with that large parcel in his arms—he didn't have the strength . . . this time a lot was needed . . . It's that, I see it, I've got it, I feel that I'm going to be able to separate, to isolate the most noxious element of this poisoned mixture that I have just imbibed. I know what made me so afraid, it was not because, like everybody else, he had had that movement of recoil, which they all have at those moments—and yet I should have thought that he was stronger—he noticed me from a distance, when I didn't see him, he felt something limp, prehensile, floating, borne towards him on the current, flabby tentacles ready to reach out suddenly towards him, all their cups opening avidly to cling to him, to suck . . . he shriveled up, grew hard . . . no, that is not what pained me so, I know what it is: it's peculiar to him, Martereau: he felt, like that time when we watched him saying good-bye in the parlor doorway, that, as soon as I had seen him, he would have to don his childish masquerade in order to give me pleasure, recompose and serve me right away what I was expecting, begging for: the kindly smile, the frank expression, the ease of gesture, the sincere hand-shake, that do me so much good, and set me on my feet so quickly . . . he always sees me so weak-kneed, each time he has to make that effort, in order to get me on my feet again and force me to remain like that . . .

That's it, I've got it: he watches me, manoeuvres me . . . I'm the doll, the puppet . . . He knew when I passed close to him what to do to keep me from approaching him . . .

He knows that, with me, so little is needed, I'm so malleable, a slight impulse suffices, a breath, to keep me at the desired distance . . . he reads me like an open book, he too knows with whom he's dealing . . . one more little try, this time I think I've really got it . . . that day in the parlor doorway, while he was lending himself to that childish game, there was about him a sort of secret satisfaction, an enjoyment known only to him, the same he must feel now that he has forced me to pass him by without coming near him . . . He certainly made a fool of me . . . he got the best of me . . . The sly satisfaction in the cautious motions of his big pudgy fingers as they put the package away in the drawer, turned the key in the lock . . . "Well, that's done . . ." the way he turned and looked at us almost fondly, while we were frisking there before him: tender little suckling-pigs in the lair of the big bad wolf . . .

You sense this same relief when, after not feeling very well, after a period of uncertain, disquieting symptoms, suddenly a high fever breaks out and the eruption appears. So it wasn't just hypochondria, an imaginary ailment, you really are sick, with an honest-to-goodness disease that's easily diagnosed, well-known, respected, you have the right to stay in bed, to be taken care of, to call the doctor . . . I go into the first café I come to, quick, I'm in a hurry . . . a coin for the telephone, please . . . where is the booth? where? under the staircase? Thanks, I see . . . "Hello . . . that you Uncle? . . . yes, it's me.—Hello . . . what's happened to you? Where are you? What's the matter?—Say, listen. I went to see Martereau. He was out.—All right, so what . . .—So, well, I just met him on the street. He couldn't have helped seeing me, he saw me perfectly, and he had the nerve to pass a foot away from me pretending he didn't see me. I was about to speak to him, when he looked the other way. It's clear he wanted to avoid me. I'm beginning to think you were right. I'm worried by what happened about that receipt . . .—Listen, son, you're crazy. He didn't see you, that's all, or else he was in a hurry. You always go from one extreme to the other. Before, he was a saint, now he's a crook, why not a murderer? Nobody can say a thing to you, you take everything literally. I was put out about that receipt because I like things to be done right, for people to have their two feet on the ground, whereas you're always in the clouds . . . But don't worry, I know, I know people. As it happens, he just called me. The house has been bought for a little less even than I had expected: he arranged the matter of the transfer duties. He'll also take care of the repairs, that's something he knows about. You'd do better not to waste your time on such nonsense."

The joy, the exquisite relief of waking. I am on good, firm earth again, surrounded by familiar objects. The universe is once more a well-oiled machine, the closely interlocking wheels of which glide smoothly into one another and turn in an identical rhythm. The glum cashier of a while back, when I pass in front of her again, answers my smile with a smile, and nods graciously. What friend, what enemy, seeing me now, would do otherwise than to cross the street immediately to come and shake me by the hand? The concierge seated in front of the door tells me without my asking her—but I don't have to ask her, I know it—that Monsieur Martereau is in, he just returned. I ring the bell and there he is, I hear him coming, the door opens and there is his nice, cordial smile, his vigorous hand-shake: "Well! so it's you? I telephoned your house only a little while ago. Come in, I just got back, and my wife too, she just came back. You were lucky to find us in . . ."

It's doubtless because of my excessive joy, my overflowing spirits, that I feel impelled to engage in a little sport, to play with fire, I am so sure of myself, so deft, I could manipulate, with no fear, the most breakable objects, the most dangerous contrivances . . . "You know, Monsieur Martereau . . ." but I run no risks, what I want is to amuse myself, now that I'm settled in a safe spot on the bank, to reconstitute the dramatic event, recall those frightful moments—the effect of contrast is so delightful—when I felt myself drifting along, borne away by the current . . . "you know, I saw you a little while ago on the street . . .—You saw me? When was that?—Why, just a few moments ago, you were carrying a large parcel, you were walking two feet away from me . . ." He steps back the better to see me and looks at me in a surprised manner: "But why didn't you speak to me?—To be quite frank, I thought you didn't want to see me! . . ." I want so much to be reassured, cajoled . . . why, are you quite mad, see here, what sort of an idea is that, what won't he think up next this crazy loon, this silly boy, I snuggle up to him, wriggling with anticipated pleasure . . . "it seemed to me that you saw me quite well and that you looked elsewhere just when I looked at you . . ." Smiling, he touches my shoulder: "Now tell me, my young friend, do you get like this often? I knew that you were inclined to be a bit whimsical, eh, from time to time . . . but it never occurred to me that it was as serious as that." Relieved, gratified, I laugh, I continue to amuse myself a bit longer . . . "Ah! the fact is, you don't know me . . .—Well, I'm beginning to believe that I don't. Come along, let's go in here, this way," he pushed me ahead of him, "come and talk to my wife . . . Look, I'm bringing you something of a card, we don't really know him, would you believe it, he's a highly complicated person . . ." he taps his forehead with his forefinger . . ." a screw loose, he's got it into his head that I don't want to see him any more, that I pass him by without speaking to him . . . There now, you'd do better to look at this, look, if that's not a beauty . . ." his wife quickly tears off the last remaining serpentine of paper from around the chromium railing of a new stove standing in the middle of the kitchen . . . "We were unpacking it, it just came this morning . . ." Madame Martereau shakes my hand absent-mindedly and turns towards the stove with a look in which her entire being would appear to be concentrated, it is so attracted by it: with this look she clings to the object entirely, there's not so much as an inch of her that isn't sticking close to it. Martereau looks at her. "Well? Is it all right? Do you like it? What do you think of it?" She shakes herself as though to wake herself up . . . "Yes . . . I don't know why, but they seem funny to me, these enameled stoves do . . . I was so used to the other one . . ." Martereau nods, smiles . . . "Ts . . . ts . . . women are all alike: she absolutely had to have a new stove, she was killing herself with the old one, and now that she's got a new one, she misses the other . . ." Madame Martereau raises in our direction an expression of guilt: "Oh, no, I don't want to say anything, of course this one is better . . . with the other one it took me two hours to shine the brass . . . In fact, when I had finished I always used to walk over there . . ." she takes two steps backwards and stands near the door . . . "I had to stand there in order to look at it, to be sure that the brass railing was well polished . . . but recently, I must be getting old . . . it must be a good two years since I looked at it: now, as soon as I've finished, good-bye, that much less drudgery; I like this one just as well and it won't need so much care . . . only, it can't be helped, you do grow attached to things, all the same . . ." Martereau puts his arm about her shoulders, presses a kiss on her hair, hugs her to him . . . "There now, the other one isn't lost, you'll be using it again out there . . . You know we're going to live in your house . . . I told your uncle that a little while ago: certain repairs must be made right away . . . We thought, my wife and I, that it would be more convenient to be on the spot in order to supervise the work, it will be less tiring than going back and forth. We should like to be of use, the only thing is that we're growing old, my wife is right, we can no longer do what we would have done some years ago . . . Do you know what this stove is? It's the present I gave her for our silver wedding anniversary . . . Yes, indeed, that's what it is. It's exactly twenty-five years ago today since I slipped this ring on her finger."

They stand there both of them before me, their backs against the door. He has his arm around his wife's shoulders, she is leaning against him affectionately. A handsome couple: she a little smaller, rather slight, he tall and strong, complexion still clear, nice, well-marked wrinkles, thick, gray hair. They look right into each other's eyes, the way lovers on colored postcards do, he with his head leaning towards her, she with her face lifted towards him . . .

Silence. Time to contemplate. I feel ill at ease, slightly abashed, I would like to look elsewhere, but I don't dare.

No one stirs when they assume their pose like that, the engaged couple in the midst of the family circle; the bride and groom before a group of friends; the happy father seated facing the audience, his first-born standing between his knees; old couples. They stand there before you, heavy and motionless. They are planted there like flags, they unfurl proudly in front of you, like banners.

And while they are contemplating each other, turned one towards the other, inside them an avid, cunning eye is spying on you. They feel that they are very strong: no matter how hard you try to break away from the wily, obstinate pressure they're exerting upon you, to make an effort to look elsewhere, you won't be able to escape them. They know that the entire universe sustains them and that an invincible force emanating from them compels you to look at them with moved approbation, with admiration, even—and this quickens their sense of triumph, their secret and somewhat sadistic relish—with a twinge of envy.

But certain of the rare persons to whom I have ventured, with extreme prudence, however, to mention these things, which ordinarily no one touches upon, even in thought, have asserted that I was wrong. The strong people, they assured me, are not the ones you think. In this instance, the weak people are the ones who stiffen up like that under your very eyes, as though they were playing statues, in a posture of felicitous love. They are the ones to whom it seems all the time that a pitiless, mocking eye in you is observing them. They're ashamed, they're afraid, docile and timorous as they are, to feel that it can't fail to see, this reproving eye, how different they are from the model of perfection deposited in each one of us and prescribed by the entire universe. They do their best to deceive you by offering you as lifelike an imitation as possible: a bit forced, but is it their fault? a bit stiff and flat, as copies are . . . Perhaps they strive to deceive themselves, and they hope that by insisting they will end by catching in this mold made to contain it, a real live feeling and, along with it, the freedom, the fantasy, the secret, shy tremor, of life itself.

This, these compassionate, clear-sighted persons went on to explain to me, is what makes sensitive souls like yourself feel ill at ease and abashed in their presence. It's their shame that you are ashamed of. It's merely out of human respect, out of pity, that you contemplate them with admiration and envy, to make believe above all, even to yourself, that you notice nothing, that you're taken in.

Madame Martereau is the first to break the spell, she shakes herself, draws away, laughing . . . "Really, now, aren't we a pair of old fools, we'd do better to go and do our work. My pudding must be burning."

I experience all at once a sense of lassitude, of boredom, such as we feel at a play that is not very well acted and in which we do not succeed in becoming interested; I would like to leave, but I can't: it's the same sensation of being bogged down, the same attitude of dreary passivity that I have felt so often when we are by ourselves, without Martereau. This time is no longer Martereau's time: a nice, firm, dense matter upon which one can stand up straight, the different stages of which are quickly passed through: we've walked resolutely through one, we take the next one with a standing jump. We admired the new stove, then we relaxed and grew a little sentimental; now we're going to finish nailing up the packing cases, look to the pudding. No, this time is like it is at home, formless, mushy matter, a muddy stream that drags me slowly along . . . a frightening void is going to catch hold of me . . . the Martereaus are holding me back . . . "Do stay, don't leave, we'll have tea, we'll celebrate our silver wedding anniversary, my wife has made a pudding, come on, do stay . . ." I hang on weakly, I catch hold of just anything, tufts of grass, bits of wood floating within reach, drifting along with the current, like myself . . . I follow them into the dining room, we drink tea, we listen to the radio, I feel myself still slipping, I'm becoming bogged down, it's like nausea, a sort of blind stagger, giddiness . . . I must make an effort . . . I stand up too abruptly, all of a sudden, and they look at me, astonished . . . "I must really go home. It's late, they're expecting me for dinner, I'm going to be late. I haven't been so well recently, they'll be anxious."

As soon as their door has closed behind me, I feel better. My strength returns. I feel a bit excited, as though lifted up and pulled along from a distance, I would like to run, the way I used to do when I ran as fast as I could through the dark hall towards the refuge of the lighted room where my parents were . . .

My uncle is there, seated as usual in his armchair, reading his newspaper. He looks at me over his spectacles with that kindly look of a man getting on in years, that he has sometimes, and which always touches me: "Well, what have you been up to?—I've just been to see Martereau.—Again? Why, you pass your time there . . . —No, don't laugh at me, in spite of everything, my mind wasn't at rest, I wanted to see him.—Well, then? What did you see?"

I recognize this faint excitement, this voluptuous, sickening flavor . . . it's the flavor of baseness, of treachery . . . the same I had tasted for the first time, long ago, when, urged on by some sort of inner necessity, I went and told my mother, who had just returned from a trip, that the maid who had taken devoted care of me during her absence, had been stealing . . . "Well, I must say, there's something disturbing about all that, just the same . . . you know the Martereaus are moving." He lowers his spectacles still more, the better to see me. "They're moving? Where to?—Why, into the house . . . Martereau told me that you had asked him to have some work done on it. So it's more convenient for him to be on the spot. But there's one thing that's curious . . . I thought about it on my way home—at the moment it didn't strike me—they've bought a new kitchen stove, and that was before he called you, even: it's just come; they're going to move the old one into the house . . . They seem to be planning to settle there as though it belonged to them . . . They've packed a lot of things . . . They're nailing up packing cases . . ." My uncle straightens up, takes off his glasses, looks sharply into space, then rises, his eyes directly on me, with his hand he makes a tranquilizing gesture: "Come, come now, be calm, let's not get worked up . . . All of that is very strange, what you tell me . . . He didn't breathe a word, to me, about this move . . ."

He is thinking. I watch him in silence. We experience, he and I, a moment of happiness. To obtain this, we would give, each one of us, all the houses and all the chateaux in the world. Indeed, it is towards the achievement of such moments as these between us that my clumsy efforts, which are nearly always unsuccessful, are directed. This time I've fully succeeded. A common enemy to be combated, a threat to be averted, an immediate obstacle confronting us, which we must overcome, have an effect upon us that I might compare to that produced by electroplating: it is as though a strong current, originating outside us, caused a protective coating of metal to settle upon us: the soft, crumbly, inconsistent matter subject to continual frittering and collapse, becomes covered with a hard, smooth deposit. We are handsome, well polished objects, clean-cut and harmonious in form. He feels at this moment the way my respectful eye sees him: a level-headed, just old man, with vast experience, who has always been able to rise above all circumstances, size up clearly the most complicated situations, decide promptly what should be done. And I, standing there before him, I am the fiery young lieutenant sent ahead as a scout, who has come back proudly to report on his mission, and who awaits the general's orders in deferent silence. After a while, he raises towards me a calm, energetic, direct gaze. "Listen, there's no point in making idle suppositions, in wracking our brains for nothing. It's very simple: I'm going to write him. A very courteous but firm note asking him, as a matter of form— you never know what might happen, he should take that as being perfectly natural—to send me a receipt . . . Then we'll see. Be nice and bring me a sheet of paper and an envelope, and also, if you don't mind, my fountain-pen: it's on my desk."

*O*nce more, nothing can resist their actual presence. They have only to make a flesh-and-blood appearance for everything to be swept away: all my anguished apprehensions, my suspicions, my dissectings, all my resolutions and my clever manoeuvring. Madame Martereau's gesture as she wipes her wet hands on her apron, her accent—the Berry? Burgundy?—which I like so much . . . "Well, well, so it's you . . . What a surprise . . . Come in . . . My husband's not home, he won't be long . . . Don't look at my apron, I was cleaning house, I never get through here, it's so big, you've hardly finished before you have to start over again . . ." and right away, here I am, changed from the smart sleuth I had hoped to become, from the justiciary who has come to demand an accounting, into a good little boy whose uncle has sent him to a friend's house on an errand. I re-experience an emotion that I know well, one I have felt so often on entering their house—that of a traveler returning to the scene of his birth—and which the restful coolness of the parlor, with its half-closed shutters, the smell of furniture wax, the friendly unpretentiousness, the nice, soothing ugliness of the mass-made furniture, always give me . . . "Come in, come in here, it's the only room, for the moment, that we have finished arranging . . . if you don't object to that odor . . . some folks don't like it . . . I've just been rubbing the floors . . . Do sit down, I'll be back, I'm going to put the kettle on . . . oh, yes, you will have a cup of tea with me, it will only take a second, there, I'm back again, I'll take off my apron . . ." She sits down beside me on the sofa . . . "It does a body good to sit down for a while, I don't often sit down during the day . . . first one thing and then another, you know how it is . . . Well? What's new? It's been so long since we saw you . . . As for us, we have hardly been off the place. My husband goes to Paris from time to time on business. He just happens to be there today. It's a bit tiring, but on the other hand, it does him good, it diverts him and gives him a change of air . . . He's very nervous just now, he's quite worried . . ." There's something new in her face, that I can't very well define, a sort of frailness, a sort of sad resignation that brings out and delicately accentuates her usual dignity. Her dignity . . . that's it . . . no need to hunt for it, that's what straightens me out, cleanses me, what compels me to remain before her in exactly the same attitude she has chosen to force upon me; an inexorable, gentle pressure; I am all sympathy, all respectful and discreet compassion, my attentive eyes caress her weary face, her white hair . . .

It will be better to do it right away, a second more and it will be too late, I shan't be able to do it . . . "I am extremely sorry to bother you like this, I didn't want to add to your worries, but my uncle insisted . . . He always gets so upset about nothing . . . so he asked me . . . I don't know whether you know about it or not . . . he wrote to your husband nearly two months ago . . ." She looks me straight in the eyes and nods gravely: "Yes. I know. My husband tells me everything. He got your uncle's letter. He's not going to answer it." I feel myself blushing, but she holds me in position, I make a faint sigh of assent, I look her in the eye . . . "Yes, my husband was very hurt. When he agreed to do that favor for your uncle, he never dreamed for a moment that one day it would bring him such a letter as that. He was dumbfounded. If he had known, you can imagine that never . . . I said to him when your uncle came to dinner with us . . . I told him that very evening, as soon as your uncle had left, that he should never have accepted . . . —My uncle realized perfectly . . . Please believe that he was very appreciative . . ." She raises her hand: "No, don't say that. You know quite well that it's not so. Your uncle thought that my husband wanted to profit by

166

the affair. Whereas if you knew . . . what it has all cost us . . . Just think, at that time, we were considering buying a place of our own; yes, indeed, and we had to give it up: the income tax authorities would never have conceded that my husband could have bought two places at the same time, with our limited means. Now prices have gone up, you know that, since last year prices have nearly doubled, and we're spending a lot here on repairs. First one thing and then another . . . you know how it is, you never finish. And at that, my husband does a lot of things himself . . . he's taken any amount of trouble . . . a bit of masonry, carpentry . . . actually, he doesn't complain about it, there's nothing he likes better than doing little odd jobs. And it would never have occurred to us to ask for a promise or a guarantee of any sort . . . Only, after all that, for your uncle to ask for one, you'll admit that was rather unexpected . . . For your uncle to ask my husband to prove his good intentions, to give him a pledge of his honesty, proof . . . That he'll never do. You don't know him. When you approach him like that, it's finished. If you hurt his feelings, he grows obstinate, and then, there's nothing you can do, he will never go back on what he has said . . . Oh! if he had listened to me . . . I had a presentiment that all that would bring nothing but trouble. I said it to him that very day. But he wouldn't listen, he lost his temper; you don't understand, I couldn't refuse him that, those are things friends do for each other . . . he's a charming man . . . He held your uncle in very high esteem; that I can tell you: he was proud to have him as a friend: he felt that

167

he deserved great credit, he considered him an unusually intelligent man, and a perfect gentleman . . . Ah! I can assure you, he can't get over it, that your uncle should have acted like that; for him, friendship is something sacred . . . nothing is too nice, too good for his friends . . . Your relatives are spoiled, your uncle has the reputation of being open-handed, very generous, therefore my husband didn't want to mention his own problems, didn't want to seem petty . . . And so, to make a long story short, he accepted like that, without a word. As for me, I didn't agree. Now my husband is all the more resentful towards him, naturally. He feels that he's been wronged. I say nothing. If I were to say now: 'You remember, I warned you . . .' he would go into a rage . . . My husband's a good man, only, he's like that: you can't risk a direct attack on him; your uncle made a mistake to handle him so roughly, he felt affronted, and he'll never go back on what he has said. He said to me: 'I'll never answer such a letter as that. Never.' And you can believe me, I know him. It's no use, even, for you to speak to him about it, it wouldn't do any good." She folds her hands on her knees and looks away . . . "Ah! really, sometimes . . . Life is too ugly, too stupid . . . And yet I do all I can; as for me, I want more than anything to live in peace, I have a horror of bickering, quarreling . . . And I realize that for you too it's very painful, all that; your uncle must not always be easy to get along with, either . . . But that's that; we can't do anything about it, neither you nor I . . ."

We hear the tinkle of the little bell on the garden gate,

168

the creak of gravel . . . "There he is. Above all, don't say anything; not now, I beg of you, not a word about that; you may believe me, it's no use." An act of treason, embryonic treason, in the suddenly frivolous, carefree, natural tone with which she tells him: "Look who's come to see us . . ." He raises his eyebrows, holds out his hand: "Well, well—it's so slight, so quickly vanished, that it seems to me I must have imagined it, that ghost of a sneer, like a suppressed hiss, in the inflexion of his "Well, well"—We had begun to think you had forgotten us . . . What fair wind brings you here? How are you?" He shakes my hand hurriedly and turns towards his wife without listening to me . . . "You forgot the fire under the tea-kettle, I turned it out, the water was boiling over. Well, then? How was it here without me? I hurried as much as I could: that idiot almost made me miss my train . . ." Madame Martereau raises her head in his direction, he searches her face with an anxious look . . . Together, they two alone, a single block before the rest of the world, before me. The entire world is thrust aside, held at a respectful distance, and I pushed into a corner, negligible, insignificant . . . "I was anxious: I'm sure you took advantage of the fact that I wasn't here not to take care of yourself . . . I bet you didn't stop once, again this time . . ." From the corner to which I am relegated, I make a faint movement in their direction . . . "Madame Martereau isn't well? . . . I didn't know that . . . I am so sorry, she didn't say anything . . . If I had known . . ." She looks at me, smiles at me: "Oh, it's nothing . . . Don't listen to him, it's nonsense. If I listened to him, I'd spend my time in bed." But he brushes me aside: "I mean it, if you would take a little more care of yourself instead of working here all day long, killing yourself working here" . . . Without even looking at me, he jostles me, pushes me away with his foot, I feel the pointed toe of his shoe . . . "You'll end up by killing yourself, that's how it will end, all that, all this nonsense . . . You know very well what the doctor told you . . ." She lends me a friendly hand, she tries to help me up . . . "Do tell him, you have seen so many of them, tell him they know nothing about it, doctors don't; if you had listened to them, you would be dead and buried, isn't that so?" I seize her outstretched hand gratefully . . . "That is certainly true. I know something about it, sometimes they scare you to death about nothing. You can either take it or leave it, what doctors tell you . . . they gave me six months to live. Only, your husband is right" . . . One look from Martereau . . . just one reassuring, kindly look, as before, that's all I ask for . . . "only, your husband is right, you really should be very careful, I rested for months on end and I believe that if I have the upper hand now, it's thanks to that, just the same; I still take a rest after lunch every day, but of course what I had . . ." He turns towards me finally: "Do you know, young man, what you had, do you know what they call that?" I shrivel up a bit, withdraw . . . "Do you know what it's called, your illness? It's the rich man's illness . . . Not because only rich people catch it, the contrary is true, but because it's only good for the rich, they're the only ones who can get well of it . . . You may consider yourself fortunate, not everybody has your luck . . . a family that waits on you hand and foot, an aunt who coddles you . . . she'll miss that, eh, your aunt will, when she won't have you to take care of any more . . . As for my wife, what she has is that she wears herself out, she shouldn't do that at her age, she should be careful, rest . . . Excuse me, I don't want to seem to be putting you out, but she must go and rest, she looks badly . . . and I myself, I must admit that I too am dead on my feet today, I'm very tired . . ."

In the entrance hall, as he turns to open the door for me, I'm struck by how thin he looks. His lean neck, like that of an adolescent, floats about in his collar, which is too big for him. There's something vulnerable about him that moves me to pity. I would like to show him my confidence, my friendliness, I shake his outstretched hand hard. He gives me a light pat on the shoulder . . . "There now, please excuse us . . . come and see us again another time . . . we'll always be glad to see you, but today you must excuse us . . . You do well to dress warmly. The weather's changing . . . I say, that's a handsome scarf you've got there . . . whew! . . . is it your aunt who knits you nice things like that? So then, good-bye, and do excuse us. We'll see you soon. Good-bye."

"Well, I must say, that's a good one. That really is a good one . . . so that little show was all that was needed for you to make a complete about face . . . for you to come and say to me now, to me, that I'm the crook, I'm the exploiter, and they are the poor honest folk that I've wronged, ruined. Really, that's the best yet . . . Poor Martereau, he's affronted, I've wounded his self-esteem, he's so sensitive, I've attacked his honor. His honor, just imagine. Ah! they're all alike: as soon as they start to cheat, they can talk of nothing else: their honor with a capital H. I've seen that before. It's a very bad sign, my boy, experience will teach you, when people begin to talk about their Honor, when they become too touchy on that subject. Now listen, I beg of you, don't try to make a fool of me. And so you didn't ask a single question, you didn't say a thing, you listened without making a move to that cock-and-bull story? Martereau made you feel sorry for him? They're really appalling, all these sensitive souls . . . Fortunately, however, for me, I've got a hard heart, and a brain that's still sound enough, for the moment, not yet gone entirely soft, I can't see in what way I have so seriously offended this gentleman who pocketed two million eight hundred thousand francs without batting an eyelash—he wasn't affronted by that—who didn't even consider it necessary to let me have a paper of any kind, who is occupying my house bought with my money as though it belonged to him, and who refuses to write me a letter because it might be used as proof against him. Really, listen, excuse me while I laugh. And they are laughing out there, that I'll guarantee you. They're laughing at how they 'took you in'; at your age, that's not allowed, you're not a milksop, you're not four years old. But the whole story is so easy to see through . . . 'Above all, don't say anything to him about it, he's so offended, that would hurt him so, it has all but ruined him . . .' His wife is in cahoots with him, of course, that's obvious, they cooked all that up between them, and it succeeded, and for the moment, they've got rid of you: that's all they want, that will allow them to let matters drag, and wait and see what happens. Meanwhile, they're keeping everything. And they're taking no chances, they're not giving the slightest guarantee, they're not so dumb, not the slightest word in writing that I could use against them. As for me, my boy, I'm not one of your dreamers. You know perfectly, what count for me, are facts. I don't give a rap about all the rest. I'm not at all touched by points of honor and offended looks. What's important is that they have kept both the money and the house. And if you were a little less scatter-brained—I can tell you, at your age, I wasn't like that, life has taught me a lot but, just the same, I was not like you—you would never have allowed yourself to be led about by the nose like that."

That's his force, his surest element of charm, and he uses it quite consciously. When he succeeds in extracting the fact from the treacle I'm floundering in, the way we extract a diamond from its matrix, and starts brandishing it before me, I'm won over. He has a marvelous scent for discovering it. His sharp, experienced eye unearths it right away, however well it's hidden. He takes it out and holds it up at arm's length. How often I've seen him use it, give one single well-aimed blow, in order to strike and anni-

173

hilate his opponent. How often, when I've come to tell him
—and nothing exasperates him so much as this sort of
supplicant bragging—that they were going well, those little
inventions of ours, that people liked our chromium chairs
and wicker sofas: I approached him groveling, my eyes
lowered, I was so ill at ease, I told him that Mme. X . . .
had spoken of them . . . she had asked the price, she had
come twice to the shop . . . there had been a little note in
the smartest art magazine . . . he would listen in silence,
annoyed, his eyes puckered—he hates to give when people
try to force him like that—he would remain turned away
from me in profile, he never looks at me in such cases,
he would look for and find right away the contusing implement, deal me a telling blow: "How many?" I was reeling.
Trying to catch hold of something . . . "What do you
mean, how many? . . ." He struck another blow: "Yes,
how many? How many of your chairs and sofas have you
sold? How many? What are your sales? You know, what
people say, compliments, all that means nothing to me.
I like sound realities. Facts."

I too, I must admit, under his influence, I've almost come
to like them. Only, I haven't his flair, his hunter's ferreting
glance, his relentless eye, for unearthing them. Once he has
hold of them, nothing can make him give them up. He
hangs on in the face of everything. I myself don't distin-
guish them very well. When, more often than not with his
help, I think I've got them, the slightest thing makes me
let go. Then I make excuses to myself. I tax my uncle with
his ferociousness which ends by giving him a false view of

things, his crude mind which simplifies things out of a secret penchant for a certain brutality: he hasn't, as I have, a liking for the fine shadings in which truth is sometimes to be found, he lacks forbearance, kindliness . . . I myself prefer, at times, I'm always so afraid of not seeing clearly enough, of being too easily satisfied, even though the fact may be obvious and destroy everything, to deny the evidence, question my own senses . . .

This time the situation presents itself favourably for him. He can keep repeating in that obstinate tone of his: "Yes or no? Yes or no? Did he keep the money? Yes or no, has he given back the house? Has he answered my letter, yes or no?" But I'm not so sure . . . It's not "so simple" after all: an expression that has the knack of driving him wild, because of which he starts to hate me—and rightly so. He senses perfectly that I'm paying him back in his own coin: I do with him what he wants to do with me when he tries to give me those staggering blows with his "facts." I'm trying to weaken him, to overwhelm him, to make him aware of his brutality, of his childish simple-mindedness, to lure him onto the miry ground he has a horror of—he knows that he would end by being bogged down—into what he sneeringly calls my "psychology" . . . The rage, the contempt in his tone when he fairly jumps down my throat: "Ah! no, I beg of you, no psychology . . ."

Everything must have gone for the very best. They shook hands one last time on the landing. My uncle, as he does when he has one of his outbursts of affection, held Martereau's hand in his two hands, apparently quite moved . . . "We'll see you soon, very soon, and thanks again, thanks. No, really, it's very decent what you're doing there . . . It's good to know that there are still friends to be found who can be counted on. It's understood, then, that I'll send you the money and we'll telephone each other to settle on an evening. My wife will be so glad. She was very sorry not to have been able to come . . ." Even the little click of the street door down below, is heartening—a last friendly sign, a last caress. What Martereau had vaguely foreseen (it had been like a draft of icy air that had blown against him all of a sudden at the very heart of their warm, friendly intimacy) had not come about; the thing he had dreaded, that sensation, when they were about to leave each other, of uprooting, of falling into space, had not taken place. At present, the only feeling he has is one of joyful confidence. And he still has an overflow of energy and good humor to be expended. He walks up and down, whistling to himself . . . "I can't think of going to sleep. That coffee has got me excited. If I did what I feel like doing, I would go out for a walk . . ."

His wife doesn't mistake it, they've known, both of them, for a long time now, how to decipher without an error each sign of this code language: that little whistle, that delighted, off-handed, airy manner, she knows what they mean! They mean treason. They mean revolt, defiance. And he, he knows that she knows. He had noticed all evening, without even having to look at her—they don't need that—her reproofs, her entreaties. It never fails, she's there for that. As soon as he lets himself go a bit, sticks his nose out of doors, takes a bit of air, care-free and happy—for instance, already in the past, in the casinos, in the gambling rooms, amidst the brilliance of the chandeliers, the sheen of silks, of jewels, the inviting looks, the smiles of pretty women, when, beaming, intoxicated, suddenly released, he threw a packet of bank-notes on the table . . . "Come on, gentlemen, put up your stakes, all bets are off . . ." right away he felt her behind him, pulling him away: "Listen, what are you thinking of, you must be crazy. That's complete madness, look here, we can't afford . . . that's really all we needed . . ."

She's always there busily engaged in her ant-like work, with never a moment's respite, continually patching up, repairing the damaged hill. The door is hardly closed before she has set to work, putting everything back in order, doing away with all traces of the intruder. She clears away the table, empties the ashtrays, pushes the chairs back into place . . . That mania of hers, just as soon as guests have gone, to quickly put each object back in the place that has been assigned to it once and for all . . . He does it too, in fact,—they have shared the same manias for years now —usually it's his way of keeping from slipping into space when the door closes and they remain alone, of regaining his foothold.

But this time he feels perfectly steady, he has no desire to help her, the way he usually does, to do away with the traces. On the contrary, even. He walks up and down without looking at her, his hands in his pockets, he whistles softly, smiles at his thoughts . . . He feels that she's watching him . . . She knows what he's thinking . . . Well, so much the better, this time he won't let himself be bullied. He's always been too weak, too sensitive, too busy, too fascinated trying to decipher the signs she was making to him. Even now, no matter how he tries, he can't help noticing them, he records them in spite of himself, like a sensitive plate. But he's not going to let anything interrupt his momentum, spoil his pleasure . . . He must pretend not to notice that obstinate, resigned manner she assumes, her disapproving silence, her look of not wanting to take part in things, of sticking to her own point of view . . . he must shut himself in, be hard, surround himself with a shell against which all those corpuscles she bombards him with will bounce off, without penetrating. He comes to a halt in front of her, stretches himself: "Ah! I certainly did enjoy this evening . . . he's really an extraordinary fellow, don't you think so? . . . What vitality he has! . . . and he's damned intelligent . . . It's a pleasure to talk to people like that . . ."

Mixed with his defiance, they both feel it, there's about him a sort of timorous pleading, an entreaty . . . a need— it comes, doubtless, from his overflow of good humour— to attract her to him, to force her to share with him, to take part . . . why can't we all be happy together? . . . she should agree, she should consent to understand . . . If she could share his tastes a bit, his ideas . . . why does she always have to snub him, put a spoke in his wheel . . . it would be so easy to be happy . . .

Occasionally, in the past, when they were young, when he happened to come a little late, when he had been, as she called it, "hanging round the cafés," he used to bring friends home for dinner . . . "Why, of course, come on, my wife will be delighted . . . there's always plenty to eat in the house . . . come along . . . you must come . . ." he would run up the stairs two at a time, joking, excited as a kid . . . "You wait, I'll go get her . . ." he went softly into her room . . . "hoo-hoo, here I am, it's me . . . I've got a surprise for you . . . guess, darling, who's with me . . . And above all, don't bother, we're not hungry, a sandwich and a good cup of coffee will do . . ." Something in him, just seeing the resigned way she laid down her work, suddenly collapsed. All his light-heartedness, all his high spirits vanished in a second. His voice grew husky. His friends noticed it when he came back wearing an expression that was a poor imitation of the care-free one he had had a few moments before. Little by little, she has got the better of him, he has ended by giving in . . . it's because of her that, for twenty-five years, they have led this cramped, shut-in life of theirs . . .

This time too, it won't take long, she'll get him: the flickering light, the timorous entreaty, the trembling hope she perceives in him, provoke her, excite her . . . few people can resist that. And then she takes a sort of pleasure, when she sees him preening himself, disporting himself with the heedlessness, the high spirits of a young dog turned loose in a field, in taking him up by the scruff of his neck and setting him down face to face with reality. Implacable.

Hard on herself and hard on him. Death, illness, old age: she has always taken a bitter satisfaction in pretending to be older than her age, in adding on one or two years, for the sake of a round figure, and in making him older too . . . he has a horror of that, something retracts, bristles inside him when she says: "Oh! you know, for old people like us . . ." Or, if he complains that he's tired, that he has pains in his joints: "Well, what do you expect, you're not twenty years old, it's a little gout probably, rheumatism . . . After all, the ailments that go with our age are beginning . . ."

Jealous . . . in reality it's that, wanting him entirely to herself . . . that impatient, irritated tone of hers in those moments, like a little while ago, when he was leaning across the table, discussing, flashing his wit about, laughing, making, as she says, long speeches . . . the tone in which she said to him: "Do help yourself, go ahead" . . . or: "Won't you please pass the gravy, everything's getting cold" . . . nose to the ground right away like her, in something real, firm, instead of standing there baying at the moon, losing time with a lot of idle talk . . . discussions that are of no earthly use . . . high-flown notions . . . so much bluster . . . come on there, nose to the ground at her side, head down, close to each other, inconspicuous, attentive and very discreet . . . she hates the intruder who leads him away from her into an unknown world to which she has no access . . . Now she's going to sever the slender thread, the frail tie, that stretches between his friend and him . . . what she's about to say is so inevitably certain, he feels it so clearly, suspended there already in her silence, that it's perhaps, too, out of impatience, in order to hasten matters that he says this to her: "He's damned intelligent. Really, very much alive, don't you think so? . . ." and it doesn't fail: "Intelligent . . . Oh! as for that, yes, you can't deny him that. Too much so, even, for my taste, far too much. Ah! he knows what he's doing. In fact, I think he's by way of getting the best of you, in a marvelous way, he's trying to take advantage of you, to make a fool of you. You made a great mistake to accept. We're in a pretty mess."

Debase him, belittle him, humiliate him—she alone in the world can do that. For a long time now there's been no reserve, no sense of loathing between them: they spread out their wounds, their weaknesses, their baseness before each other, they tell each other the "plain unvarnished truth," after all, they're joined together like Siamese twins aren't they? . . . of course they are . . . he's deceiving himself, he's let himself be carried away somewhat . . . he thought—old idiot, old fool that he is—that he had inspired real confidence, real friendship: she'll set all that straight: "Those things don't happen to us, you know that, you are crazy. What need has a man like that who, in his position, must have so many connections, lots of brilliant friends, to come and let himself be bored all evening with us? Really, you've lost all sense of perspective, you don't see us as we are . . . What interest do we offer, if not the obvious one, that he can make you do what he wants like a good old horse, just as everybody has always done,—it has cost us dearly enough—that he can make use of you."

He knows all that by heart. Before she speaks, he knows everything she's going to say. Ah! no, this time, he won't have it, he doesn't want to play that particular game. He feels the rage we experience when things, table corners, or chairs, set in our way—it makes no difference that we knew they were there, stretched out our hand to recognize and feel them—knock against us stupidly in the dark, on our sensitive spots, on our knee, our elbow, we feel like cursing them, knocking them back, hurting them . . . But he is still controlling himself too well, he's still too happy, he feels too strong, and his friend is still there right nearby, affable, generous, maintaining him within the limits of decency, of politeness, of propriety . . . "We'll see you soon, see you very soon, my wife will be so glad, she was extremely sorry . . ." He is holding on to himself to avoid an outburst, he cuts her short: "Oh, listen, I beg of you, you understand nothing about it, so don't mix into it. I know what I'm doing. You always think you're surrounded by enemies. In fact, that's why we've always led the life we do . . . Oh! well, I'm going out . . ." He feels a joy which he well recognizes, that he should have made use of his most trusted weapon. He relishes the distress that rises up in her immediately, her bewilderment . . . he opens the door . . . "Well, I've had enough, I'm going out, I'm going to take a walk . . . No use to wait for me. I'll probably be home late, don't wait up."

The click of the street door being cautiously closed is a disquieting sound: it's the telltale noise of sly vanishings, desertions . . . The crevice, a gaping hole, that Martereau had felt open up in him at moments during that evening, then close right away, re-opened wide this time, an icy draft blew into it, the moment my uncle stood up suddenly, looked at his watch: "Good heavens, this is madness . . . What am I thinking of? You know what time it is? You must be dead tired . . ." Nothing, neither affectionate hand-shakes, nor assurances . . . "We'll see you soon, very soon, we'll telephone to settle on an evening . . . my wife will be delighted . . ." has succeeded in filling up that hollow: by now it's become an enormous hole, an immense emptiness. And she, with her detached indifferent manner, her distant calm (the door's no sooner closed than she's there already, busying about as though nothing had happened, putting things away, clearing off the table, pushing the furniture into place), like the flat lands we see spread out quietly down in the valley, while we're leaning over the edge of a sheer cliff, she increases his sensation of dizziness, his heart stands still.

He walks up and down, hands in his pockets, whistling to keep in countenance, he can't help looking at her: she trots about, brings in a tray, shakes the tablecloth. She feels perfectly steady on her feet. She has the faculty that cats have of being able to walk along the edge of a roof without growing dizzy, or to jump from high up and always land on her feet. She doesn't look at him. She's a bit ashamed for him. Even between them, after so many years, they have such moments of reserve. The contrast is too embarrassing between the excitement that she saw in him a few moments ago, his high spirits, his outspokenness, his good humor, his jokes, and this sudden collapse, this sagging, played-out look—what's the use? it's all over, the shadow he had tried to embrace has vanished, the ghost has fled, all his efforts were in vain . . . There's nothing left but that strain in the cheek muscles that comes from smiling too much, laughing too much, and which she calls politeness cramp. She doesn't look at him, she knows quite well and he knows that she knows, what it comes from in him, that cramp, and that sudden distress, that self-loathing that he feels now . . . She is familiar with his vanity, his coquetry, like that of a pretty woman, the necessity he feels for people to like him, to make a fuss over him, flatter him . . . as though you could believe a word people say, but he's like all men, a big baby . . . And today, think of it, it wasn't just anything . . . an important man . . . really somebody . . . What would he not do? Why he'd go into debt, he'd reduce us all to beggary in order to show him that he's his equal, in order to charm him . . . never would he dare admit to him that he can't do that kind of thing for him, no, never! . . . She sweeps the carpet, piles the plates one on top of the other . . . Well, he's sobered up now, it's made him think a bit, there's plenty to think about. She passes in front of him without looking at him, the tray in her hands, and a look on her face that says: come on, there, the party's over, and that's not all, now we've got to pay the piper . . .

Their great force is never to stop, never to daydream, build castles in Spain . . . things about them, people, "life" itself, don't allow them to be idle, don't allow them to waste a moment, they've always got their noses stuck in things, they never raise their heads, that's no affair of theirs . . . Death, it's not all that . . . Eternity . . . all those ravings, vague aspirations, lofty ideas . . . the corpse is there on the bed, it must be washed, dressed, the candles must be lighted . . . they clean and swaddle the new-born infant without wasting a moment, dress, scrub, cook, mend . . . we weren't put here to amuse ourselves, she often says that . . . Life is made up of chores, when you've finished one, right away you start another . . . that's her strength, her dignity, which, at certain moments, he can't help admiring, to stand steadily on her two feet, perfectly at home on earth, to always have, as she says, "other fish to fry" . . . She never really "needs anybody" . . . not like him . . . he's so malleable, so dependent, tremulous, changeable . . . at each moment he's like the reflection of himself that he sees in people's eyes . . . Forsaking the substance for the shadow . . . tilting at windmills . . . Life makes him pay dearly for it . . . he has always paid very dearly, the highest price, for the slightest pleasure that life has afforded him . . . As soon as he stretches out his hand, it has never failed to happen: a sharp little rap on the knuckles to call him to order; as for her, she doesn't even try to stretch out her hand, she doesn't feel like it, she needs nothing, is satisfied with little, moderate in her tastes, active, an ant . . . She's already examining closely, without wasting time the way he does, the wine spots on the table cloth, she shakes her head . . .

Now, as he walks up and down whistling to himself, he feels something inside him weighing painfully upon him, sharp twinges: all his unemployed force, all the over-flow of force accumulated in him a while ago in order to capture, to clasp to him, to possess . . . he didn't know what . . . a little human warmth, a little friendship? . . . or rather, no, not that . . . what he wanted was an assurance, a certainty, the certainty that he too—and why not? a little luck might have changed everything—could enter into that forbidden zone, that brilliant, exclusive circle, among the men who have the power, who have "arrived," in their company one must feel an added vitality, feel oneself being borne along, intoxicated by bracing air, sprinkled with salt spray, on the crest of the wave, in the very vanguard of ones time . . . "Do you know what I was told? . . ." my uncle had leaned over to whisper in his ear . . . "And you know, I have this from a very reliable source, someone you can be sure of, a high official, a man right up at the top, the other day, at the British Embassy reception . . ." hearing that, he had felt a satisfaction, an excitement and, at the same time, as he, in turn, leaned in an appreciative, respectful manner to listen, a slight malaise, a vague fear . . . the door of the brilliant ballroom to the threshold of which he had been brought, into which he was about to enter, could suddenly close, he would be on the outside once more, stamping his feet in the cold, in the dismal grayness . . .

There she is back again, carrying the empty tray, about to take on a new load . . . colorless, a bit flabby already, a bit stooped, no desire to please, no make-up, dowdy . . . it was about women of this type that that character had spoken, in a popular play (he had seen it a long time ago, but had never forgotten the remark) when he said: "For us lower middle-class men, it's our lot to marry women like that . . ." She passes in front of him with the heavy tray in her hands: "Open the door for me, will you." Her dry little tone is like a slap meant to wake him up; set him on his feet again . . . come on, now, sober up a bit, come down from out of the moon, quit acting like a child . . . help me, why don't you, you'd do better. He opens the door for her. She's right: he should bestir himself a bit, pull himself together, it's beneath him, absurd, these nostalgic dreams worthy of a retarded adolescent, he must make an effort, take off those distorting glasses, see things the way she sees them, reasonably, reduce them to their proportions and learn to be contented with them: they've just spent a pleasant evening with an intelligent man . . . say it out loud, say it to her, and let her agree quietly, that would be the best of exorcisms . . . he lays his hand on her shoulder . . . "It was a nice evening, wasn't it? didn't you think so? He's very amusing, that fellow, very intelligent . . . It's a pleasure to talk to him." She looks up at him with amazement: "Ah! that he is . . . When it comes to being intelligent, he's that all right, too much so even, far too much. He certainly took you in with regard to the house . . . Now we're in a pretty mess . . ."

He had wanted to reassure himself, he had tried to persuade himself that what he had paid for so dearly was not, after all, to be despised: it was something that was agreeable to use and of excellent quality . . . but she knows all about it, you can't fool her . . . can't he see that what he has brought back there is a real fake, a sham, so much trash that nobody wants. And as for the price he paid, let's not talk about that, it's a shame to admit it, he had been gulled like a child . . . fleeced . . . Now she's going to show him pitilessly to what extent the goods had been falsified, examine the object from every side, make it resonate to show what a hollow sound it gives . . . Ah! no, that will do, not now, that's enough . . . "Oh! I beg of you, let me alone, don't you mix into it . . ." escape right away, flee from her . . . He opens the door.

It was nothing, what we call nothing . . . just a little something perhaps, at the moment when my uncle got up to leave, in the way in which, when they begged him . . . "why no, certainly not, it's not late, stay a little while longer, we're not at all tired, do stay . . ." he sat down immediately, complied without a moment's hesitation . . . a rather too prompt acquiescence in which could be glimpsed cold-blooded determination, resignation (badly acted, it can't be helped, there's nothing to be done about it: they haven't yet got what was coming to them, they're asking for more, it's perfectly fair, I'll have to pay up without a murmur) . . . a vibration inside him, hardly perceptible, but which,

188

like the ripple, the slight cracks on a canvas, suddenly revealed the illusion . . . And right away, everything that had surged up for a moment in Martereau, then disappeared—all the doubts, ghosts of suspicion, vague uneasiness and anxiety that had stirred in him in the course of the evening—reappears and gathers in one spot, a tumor that swells and weighs upon him. He would have to feel it to see what it is exactly, look at it closely in order to examine it, but it can't be done, this is not the moment, the other fellow is there in charge, directing all his movements . . . he must maintain, at all costs, without letting it lower so much as a tenth of a degree, their excitement, their urbanity, gayety and high spirits . . . at the slightest hesitation, the entire edifice so painstakingly constructed, at the cost of such effort, would suddenly collapse . . . the politeness cramp makes their cheeks hurt, they smile, laugh, pat each other's hands, look affectionately at each other . . . "Well, we'll see you soon, I hope, it's a promise, we'll telephone" . . . not a single gesture of retreat as long as he is there: even after the door is closed, it's wiser to keep smiling, to maintain a lively, gay expression . . . perhaps he has forgotten something, suppose he comes back . . . Only the quiet click of the street-door down below, gives the signal of deliverance. The aching lasts a few moments longer, the cramp . . . they stretch themselves, relax gently . . . their smiles wear off, their eyes cease to shine, their features sag . . . Martereau begins to walk up and down . . . Come on now, let's have it out between us, what is it exactly, where is it? He doesn't have to look long. Already,

189

before he distinguishes it clearly, he is suffused by a sensation of warmth, of scalding steam, he feels himself blushing. This blushing and this warmth are premonitory signs, the flash that precedes the clap of thunder, almost at once, with a deafening crash, the lightning strikes: a cat's-paw: that's what he is. He remains glued to one spot, petrified, burned to a cinder: a cat's-paw. It's all quite clear: there's no use hunting any longer, it's useless to cheat now, to try to hide that, to cover it over: mutual favors . . . what wouldn't we do for a friend . . . why, of course, it's nothing at all . . . a friend who is in a slightly awkward situation, momentarily a bit embarrassed . . . he can't make the investment himself, so he asked me . . . for me, it was no problem . . . from his standpoint the sum involved was so insignificant . . . Useless, there's nothing you can do . . . it's there, like gold nuggets in sand, like a diamond surrounded by its matrix, hard and pure, impossible to scratch it: a cat's-paw.

They're smart. They're very smart. They do everything deliberately. You can count on them . . . A cat's-paw . . . They made that discovery a long time ago, they succeeded in extracting that from the greatest variety of mixtures and combinations, a simple element that combines with other simple elements in a hundred different ways and forms a hundred compounds, but they have succeeded in isolating it, and they have given it a name, they have studied all its properties; they know them so well, everybody knows them so perfectly, that the name alone now, as soon as it is pronounced, suffices to disclose them all at one time: you can't go wrong, there's nothing more to be discovered, nothing more to be invented, it's all known, well known, acknowledged, classified: a cat's-paw—that's it. And that's what I am, me, me! His cat's-paw. Another flash, a clap of thunder, the lightning strikes, it burns: his cat's-paw . . . for him too . . . that's what I am for him . . . He looked about, passed in review everybody he knew . . . who might accept that . . . why, of course, good old Martereau, that would suit him to a T . . . small savings . . . honest income-tax declarations . . . would never dare cheat the Treasury . . . much too timorous, too prudent . . . doesn't cut much of a figure . . . only too flattered to do a favour for an influential man, to be in his confidence . . . that will increase his stature, give him importance, he wouldn't even dream of refusing . . . he isn't intelligent enough, hasn't enough cynicism or pride to think of calling it by its name, even to pronounce the word, to take offence . . . it will suffice to gild the pill! Another flash. A terrible burn . . . Naturally . . . he was right . . . he was playing on velvet . . . All attention, both of them, she too, on the alert . . . trembling, quaking, dashing about loaded down with parcels . . . nothing's too good, too dear . . . hurry, he's going to arrive, go dress quickly, imagine, what an honor . . . all smiles and bowing . . . give Monsieur a glass of wine, pass the cakes, the liqueurs . . . their flattered, delighted laughter when he deigned to express a word of appreciation . . . Martereau hears his own obsequious, rapturous, mushy laughter, when the other fellow touches him on the shoulder . . . "At our age, eh? isn't that so? . . ." It's men like that who are chosen to play those roles . . . he was just the right one . . . and the other fellow was there watching him, turning the handles, the levers of control: he knew all about these machines and this one worked so well, it was a pleasure.

Martereau is walking up and down, his hands in his pockets, he's whistling to keep himself in countenance, because she doesn't lose sight of him, she sees him without looking at him, while she trots about, pushes the furniture, puts the plates away . . . She sees everything, she's there continually watching him, she has seen everything, his eagerness, his jokes, his high spirits—export products for the use of foreigners: at home he is on the whole uncommunicative, always absorbed in thought, annoyed by the slightest thing . . . But that: a cat's-paw . . . she hasn't thought of that, she doesn't even know what it is . . . that means nothing to her, and even if she knew, she wouldn't blush at such nonsense as that, what-people-say . . . My husband let himself be impressed, which was understandable, he's an important man, influential . . . who are we, after all, an obscure couple . . . we have to look at things the way they are, life is not a novel, you have to make the best of it, no, she really hasn't got time to amuse herself with such over-refined sensibility and suffering. What she's worried about is something real, something substantial: what's to be done now? He went a little far this time; it was hard to refuse, but just the same, he shouldn't have accepted . . . She says nothing . . . He knows that she chooses her moment . . .

192

When we swallow something like that, without retaliating immediately, we retain it all our life, it ripens inside us, grows, rots . . . We should retort right away, give tit for tat, return the ball at once . . . but that he never could do, timid really, timorous . . . he would have had to fall out of step, tear himself away from the embrace, break the charm, take a big leap backwards and, from there, at a safe distance, with perfect composure: "My dear fellow, I understand quite well, I should have been glad to do it, believe me, only it happens to be a difficult moment for me, I'm sorry, I really can't," and the other man would have backed out, a bit uncomfortable, but filled with respect, hat in hand . . . and that's just what he lacks, the strength required to stand seeing the other person back out crestfallen like that before him, and not feel right away like doing all he can to prevent him, to detain him, to make amends . . .

Now he would be receiving his reward, he would walk towards her, head high, wearing a wreath of laurel, and bowing gracefully, pick up the gauntlet she has thrown him. She would drop her tidying then and there, they would sit close to each other on the divan, the way they used to do, they would exchange their impressions, starting from the very beginning . . . As for myself, already, at the soup course, I felt something . . . He was paving the way . . .— No, I didn't suspect a thing, I was even surprised when he began to talk about his tax declarations, when you told him . . .—That was because I saw what he was driving at, the old fox. Only, I wasn't born yesterday, either, I know

how to defend myself . . .—Oh! that you certainly do . . .
you never let people walk over you . . ." She takes his
hand, looks at him, smiles her youthful, affectionate smile,
slightly teasing . . . That would be so nice: he so needs a
little tenderness, a little support . . . Things aren't perhaps
as black as they look, he always has a tendency to take too
dim a view, to exaggerate . . . that's his weakness, his mania,
to magnify, simplify, to give clear-cut outlines to things
and then to stand there at a loss, before them: A cat's-paw
. . . Why, who ever said that? What an idea . . . What could
he have been thinking of . . . But people are shrewder than
we think, they understand us quite well, in reality; that
old fox has rubbed up against too many people to be
wrong; he recognizes disinterestedness and generosity when
he sees them; he didn't even dare to suggest that there
would be anything to be gained, any sort of remuneration,
no, a simple favor between friends . . . that grateful look
of his, when they shook hands in the hall . . . it was sincere . . . there's no mistaking things like that . . . and
she . . . whom does she lean on proudly, at times, on whom
has she ever counted when times were hard, if not on him
. . . naturally, she's like everybody else, she has her little
weaknesses, but you have to be lenient, not even think
about them, you must have confidence in people, give
them credit, approach them through their good side, never
lose sight of the only thing that counts, really deep feeling
. . . she loves him, he knows it perfectly, she knows him,
she loves the manly way he occasionally likes to take risks,
his impulsive generosity . . . he goes up to her and lays

his hand on her shoulder . . . "Well, have you nothing to say . . . what did you think of him? It was a nice evening . . . He's damned intelligent, don't you think so?"

Just here, in Madame Martereau's place, certain people, whom I know well, would have been unable to resist: "Intelligent, ah! that I should say he is . . . it finally got to be amusing . . . I began to wonder how far his cynicism and your weakness would go . . . When I think that you wouldn't have hesitated a moment to refuse that to friends, real ones . . . especially if they were friends of mine . . . or my family . . . with us you don't care . . ." Hearts beating, panting, they would have pressed their vampire mouths there where the warm blood gathers, where the pulse beats, they would have sucked, bitten. "At times I felt like laughing . . . If you imagine that's the way to inspire friendship and gratitude in a man like him . . . he thinks he has done you a great honor . . . he must have seen that it flattered you . . . You saw it yourself . . . when he condescended to sit down again in order to grant us a quarter of an hour longer . . . a little extra . . ." But Madame Martereau has little of the vampire about her. She has no liking whatsoever for revelry, for magnificent festivities, for orgies that end by the participants rolling under the table in vomit and wine, clasped in each other's arms. No liking for unwholesome play. If she could, she would say nothing, what's the use? What's the point? People are what they are. We shouldn't be too uncompromising in life, ask too much. Just the same, she can't complain, really, she could have had worse luck, you have only to look about you. She's fortunate enough, after all, to have what people call a good husband . . . If she could, she would brush him aside with just a touch of annoyance . . . (really! men are big babies) . . . "Yes, yes, but let me pass, will you . . . I haven't finished . . . I haven't time to talk now . . . it's after midnight . . ." Only, this time it's a serious matter, there's something important at stake, something you can't joke about, the purchase of their own house is jeopardized, she hasn't the right . . . She hates to be obliged to take him to task, poor chap, he looks upset, she would prefer to be able to reassure him, but she must do her duty, it's a question of their security and their future, ah! if she were not there to warn him, to protect him . . . "Yes, you can say he is. I should say he is intelligent, too intelligent even, too much so, he certainly wound you round his finger, the old fox, he certainly knew how to make use of you . . . At present, what are you going to do? We're in a pretty mess."

Now he realizes: he can no longer choose. This is the price of all his weakness, all his compromising, of this latest act of cowardice, the worst of all: to have tried to cheat, to lie to himself, to have pretended to hope to obtain her collusion and stupidly exposed himself to her as well. The only thing he can do now is to beat an orderly retreat, cut his losses and, if there is still time, save his face, at least before her . . . she can't really think that she is the one who's going to manoeuvre him now—that would be the limit, the last straw—that he's going to let her take her turn at pulling the strings . . . Put her back in her place as quickly as possible, force her to withdraw, with her that's easy . . . "Ah! no, I beg of you, keep out of it, will you, don't you mix in, I think I'm old enough to know what I'm doing . . ." Down dog . . . He should be left in peace. Alone, far from them all, to walk alone under a starry sky, in the great out-of-doors, breathe in a little fresh air . . . He moves towards the door . . . "Well, I feel like going out. I'm going for a little walk. You must be tired. Go to bed. Don't wait up for me."

Years ago, at the very beginning, as soon as she looked at him that way before people, to make him a sign, restrain him, put him on his guard, at once all his pleasure collapsed: for him the party was over, he now had only one desire, which was that everybody should leave, that they should be left alone . . . he must know immediately . . . she must tell him . . . perhaps he had been wrong, it was perhaps not that at all she had been thinking about, perhaps she hadn't even looked at him . . . he knows well that he is so suspicious, that he always, as she says, imagines things . . . The door was hardly closed when he would look at her with a supplicating expression . . . "Listen, darling, tell me, promise me you'll answer me frankly . . . we agreed we would tell each other everything . . . Tell me, a while ago, when I agreed to make him a loan, it seemed to me that you looked at me . . . ." At first, she didn't suspect anything, she replied quite simply: "I should say I did. I hoped you would understand. Why, really, you must be crazy. He'll never pay it back . . ." Inside him something tore, fell: so that was it. The worst. What he had feared. The magnificent fruit he had picked was worm-eaten, rotten . . . Sly, cold, petty, suspicious, never a generous impulse, never a kindly reaction . . . Why no, he's too afraid . . . he can't stand it, he doesn't want to, there's still perhaps something that can be done about it, she's still so young, he can teach her, she can change, all he'll have to do will be to explain to her, she'll understand . . . "Listen, darling, you mustn't . . . I've already told you, I hate all those signs in front of other people, those looks . . . they see them, I assure you they do, it's very offensive . . . If we act like that, we won't have any friends . . . you know that's not friendship, that's not being a good pal. Naturally . . . you've lived a kind of sheltered existence . . . But if you knew what a joy it can be sometimes, to give . . . I never was so happy, in fact, as in the old days when sometimes I would spend my last hundred francs on a round of drinks for the boys . . ." She gave a sort of bored, old wives' laugh . . . "Ah! you're a fine one, you are . . . That's all very well, all that, but afterwards, it falls on me, I'm the one who has to drudge to make up for the crazy things you do . . . I work myself to death . . . Look at my hands . . . I deprive myself of everything . . . It's always like that: you make the fine gestures, while I take care of the sous . . ."

But little by little she had noticed that it had become a sort of mania with him, like the one he had of getting up several times at night to see if the gas was turned off; he ended by imagining on all occasions that he had caught her making a sign, looking at him . . . when he opened a fresh bottle of wine, filled the glasses a bit too full, passed the cigarettes . . . She had got into the habit of avoiding his mealy-mouthed cross-examinings which always ended in interminable moralizing, reproaches, scenes . . . When he asked her: "Why did you look at me like that?" she immediately assumed that weary, exasperated manner of hers . . . "Oh! I couldn't say, I don't remember. I don't know what you're always driving at . . ." And he was tortured by doubt, by frightful pangs which he succeeded in calming for a few seconds by persuading himself that he had been mistaken, that she was telling him the truth, then the pangs started up again.

But for a long time now, he has asked nothing more of her and put no questions to himself: he knew, as soon as he saw her look, that the trap-door had just shut on them. He was alone with her at the bottom of the hole. Nobody could do anything for him now. Neither the innocent warm looks of his friend, nor his thanks, his assurances . . . which he perceived as though they came from far off, separated from him by a great distance . . . could get him out of it. He'd do better to go away entirely, the sooner the better, abandon him to his fate. A fate that he had chosen for himself . . . a fate he had deserved because of his childish confidence, his cowardice . . . He had fore-seen, sensed all that, from the very first time he had met her, but he still tries to lie to himself, to cheat. Now he must pay. As we make our bed, so must we lie in it. The cup is there: he must drink it.

He walks up and down, his hands in his pockets, whistling softly, he casts a glance of hate at her . . . it never fails . . . she's already put on her martyred expression: Ah! that's the kind of thing he always does, she ought to be accustomed to it, but just now, she's at the end of her tether, she's growing old, she's weary, will it never end, this dog's life, there are moments, really, when you feel like . . . But what can you do, you have to carry on . . . She has a falsely resigned, too sweet look about her: a poor, defenseless woman in the hands of a brute . . . he knows that that's how she sees herself. Just now she's enjoying it, sad, weak . . . The entire female sex with its enduring patience, its sufferings,—what women have to put up with —each of her gestures expresses it as she empties the butts left on plates into the ashtrays, examines the table cloth with a shake of her head, lugs the heavy tray, her arms spread wide, her lips tight: "Let me pass, will you. Open the door for me, please."

She could incite him to commit a crime when she assumes that tone, that manner, she could drive him to heaven knows what extremes. A brute: she's right: a torturer. Alone, here, the two of them. She should pull off his boots when he comes reeling home from the corner saloon. A wine-sodden brute who hiccoughs, takes his stand there in front of her, keeps her from passing and bursts out laughing as he looks at her blue eyes wide with horror: Well there, my girl, she's not laughing, is she, doesn't feel like smiling, showing her pretty little teeth? He would take great pleasure in pinching her to make her cry out, to give a good punch with his fist and knock the whole thing down on the floor, tray, glasses and all. He seizes her wrists: I've had enough of your play-acting, let's talk a bit, old girl, all alone, now, just between ourselves, it was, don't you think so—he takes her by the chin—a very nice successful evening, wasn't it, my little kitten . . . "He's charming, damned intelligent, eh? Don't you think so? We had a nice evening . . . It's a pleasure to talk to men like him . . ."

She appears to retract, to shrink, on her face there is a secret look of fear and defiance . . . "I'll say he is . . . Ah! as far as that goes, yes, he's intelligent . . . too much so, even . . . he certainly wound you round his finger . . ."

He pressed hard, just in the right spot, and it spurted out, he got it right in the eye . . . The sudden tightening of his heart-strings, his instantly dominated sense of confusion, make him realize that, in spite of everything, old idiot, old fool that he is, he had retained a tiny ray of hope . . .

Now that the pocket in her has burst, she's going to want to empty it entirely. But he won't have it. Let her swallow her bile, her venom. It can swell up again in her, poison her, till it hurts . . . "Ah! no, I beg of you, my dear, let's not get started. I've got my own ideas about it. But you'd better go get some sleep. Go on to bed, I'm going out. Don't wait up for me."

"It's like the last scene in Kafka's *Trial*" . . . this had crossed my mind all of a sudden, that day, while we were visiting the suburban villa, while we were walking, the three of us, my uncle and Martereau flanking me on either side, on the path leading to the house . . . "The Gentlemen" . . . they reminded me of them because of their quiet, rather rhythmic gait, their long dress overcoats slightly fitted at the waist, their dark, broad-brimmed felt hats, and the stubborn, relentless, slightly saccharine gentleness with which they escorted me. And I, like the hero of the *Trial,* let them do it, willingly, almost abetting them, a bit disgusted . . .

Ridiculous, obviously. I had thought that was ridiculous. I had thrust it aside right away, it had disappeared immediately, it must have become embedded somewhere in me and remained there, buried. Now, all at once, it crops out again, it tears to pieces the thing I was busy manufacturing, the intangible, trembling web made by weaving the arachnoid threads I was secreting and in which I was trying to catch Martereau. I wanted to crush him slowly, to agglutinate him, to make of him the formless, mushy, ever so insipid substance that we are made of here, the same that I feed upon. But the tenuous ties are severed. Martereau frees himself. "The Gentlemen" . . . of the two, Martereau was the one who directed the operation. Martereau knew where he was leading me: no fuss, no make-believe, useless to balk. You'll be forced to walk straight. That little smile of his as he watched me struggling weakly, seated on the little folding seat in front of him, when I asked him timidly: "What's it made of, the house?" and when my uncle, unwittingly playing into his hand, tightened his grip: "You don't know them, my dear Martereau, mill-stone is their pet aversion, the very height of abomination. What they want is an old thatched cottage . . ." A god-send for him, this game . . . And afterwards, when I saw him waiting for us beside the car with the owner . . . His back was turned . . . he was swinging gently back and forth. His long, dark overcoat, pulled forward by his hands thrust deep into his pockets, outlined the shape of his back. He suddenly grew silent when he heard us coming, then started to talk about just anything, the way people do in such cases, as though nothing had happened . . . It was in order to speak to the owner that he had gone ahead, leaving us in the basement, busy admiring our nice new toy, studying the instructions on the various levers of the furnace . . .

And the day when we gave him the money . . . What a treat I could offer my cousin if I went and said to her now: "Listen, have you a second? I'd like to speak to you . . . It's about Martereau . . . you know, that whole affair worries me, I wish you would tell me if I'm going crazy . . . but that day when we went to see him . . . tell me . . . sometimes you have remarkable intuition . . . didn't you feel . . . sometimes you feel those things so clearly . . ." (in this way I would immediately forestall her irritating demonstrations of naïveté, or childish enthusiasm: "Oh! what are all of you driving at about Monsieur Martereau, I like him, so there! he's adorable . . .") ". . . try a bit— you do it so well, when you want to—to play the extra-clairvoyant crystal-gazer . . . Remember . . . didn't it seem to you at the moment when you handed him the money . . . didn't you have some presentiment, some feeling of certainty, that you would never see that money again, that it would cause all kinds of trouble . . . As for me, I'm certain that I must have felt it . . . it comes back to me now . . . it came over me like a flash . . . at the moment, it seemed to me that I gave him the money without proof, without a receipt, as a mark of our friendship, our confidence—I always have the impression that your father . . . you know how he is . . . that he must annoy him at times, humiliate him—I thought that Martereau had appreciated that, that he was moved by it, but that wasn't it. There was something else in his look of satisfaction as he took the money, when he tied up the parcel . . . do you remember how he looked at us? . . . that satisfaction known only to him, hidden . . . As though he were saying to himself: 'Phew, so that's that . . . the trap worked. The spring snapped. They're caught. In the clink.' " She listens, her eyes shining, her mouth half open. I feel her clinging to me, vibrating in unison . . . "Listen, you're right . . . it hadn't struck me . . . but now that you speak of it, I'm going to tell you . . . it's even much more extraordinary: I felt I wanted to get rid of that money, I would have liked to throw it out of the window . . . I always feel like throwing everything they give me out of the window . . . everything they own . . ." I nod approval . . . "Yes, yes, I know . . ." We're walking slowly along, hand in hand, Tom Thumb and his little sister seeking their way in the forest, one by one, we find the pebbles . . . "You know how I infuriate Maman with my disorder and my heedlessness . . . I lose everything . . . Not long ago I discovered what it was . . . a form of refusal . . . of revolt . . . I don't want their money . . . that hold they have over me . . . My mother certainly realizes it, otherwise, she wouldn't dramatize things so . . . I said it to them, you remember, when there was that awful scene because I had lost my purse . . . They thought I was crazy. Well, what I said to them was true . . . When I gave the money to Martereau I knew that he would keep it. I wanted him to keep it . . . It was on purpose that I said nothing about a receipt . . ." I interrupt her: "That's probably true . . . Only, I'm going to tell you something else . . ." we both feel the exquisite titillation, the voluptuousness that you feel when you're sinking down, when you let yourself fall farther and farther down, to the very depths . . . "I'm going to tell you . . . Even if you had wanted to speak of it, you couldn't have . . . Martereau kept you from doing it . . . Martereau was pressing down upon us with all his might . . . A very strong current emanating from him held us . . . we couldn't ask him, remember that . . ."

Yes, we could have a good time, she and I. But it would be just so much time lost, useless squandering, a real waste. I can realize much greater profit from that little treasure I discovered. I've got a better customer for it.

This time, I believe that all the luck is on my side, the risk of failure just about nonexistent. My satisfaction, the fact that I am so conscious of my strength, lends skill to all my movements. My uncle seems glad to see me . . . he is wearing his friendly expression, pleasantly mocking and affectionate: "Well, well, so it's you . . . Tell me, . . . what's the latest? What have you been up to now? What's new about Martereau?" My joy makes me modest, generous: "Listen, uncle, it's incredible: how right you were . . . I've come to apologize." He raises his eyebrows very high, opens his eyes comically wide to underline his surprise, his interest: "Ah? Ah? There's something new?—No, nothing special. Only you were right; you've only got to think about it a moment and it stands to reason." Without hesitating, I now choose the suitable method of convincing him . . . There are two for me to choose from, as, for certain problems, there are two ways of proceeding: one by the use of algebra, the other by the use of arithmetic. As a rule, I prefer arithmetic for my own personal needs. For him, it's no good: all these concrete data, sensations, vague impressions, reminiscences, presentiments, fluids and currents would arouse his distrust, or his rage. Only a currently accepted, indisputable sign, of a general nature, convinces him. Nothing easier than to use it. The demonstration takes care of itself when you know the final result: "Listen, it stands to reason . . . You have only got to think about it a moment . . . I don't know what I could have been thinking of: the facts are there; there's no point in twisting things. It was as clear as crystal from the beginning. First of all, he takes the money without offering to furnish a receipt, but that, we'll let that pass. Yes, I'll grant you, that was not the proper thing to do, but we didn't ask for one either. Then afterwards: he moves into the house; he settles there as if it were his own, spends money on it, supposedly rather expensive repairs, without asking you . . . just like that . . . of his own accord . . . And the story of the letter: he gets mad, supposedly because you dare to ask for a receipt, but in reality it's always the same thing: he doesn't want to let you have a paper of any kind. Above all, no proof. Nobody's the wiser. Why, that would be more than enough to have a man sentenced in any court. And the court would be right. The facts: they're all that counts. And the facts are eloquent."

I feel again the delightful sense of security that Martereau has always given me. From one fact to the other, my thought stretches clear, direct, the shortest road. Joining one of the exactly situated points to the other, it outlines a drawing that has all the precision of a geometrical figure. One look suffices: the definition is evident. No doubt is possible. Martereau is a crook. My uncle enjoys this moment as much as I do. This is the delightful moment when the demonstration comes out right, when the result proves to be accurate within a thousandth of a point. And

I'm the one who has found the solution: a hard-working little boy who has known how to apply what his teacher taught him. He laughs happily, gives me one of his nice big friendly slaps on the shoulder: "Hey, there . . . not so fast, young man . . ." He's so pleased that he would like to amuse himself a bit, make the pleasure last, tease me, perhaps, before giving me a good mark, ask me one last poser . . . "not so fast . . . How you do exaggerate . . . A crook: that's a great big word. You certainly do go at it with hammer and tongs, I must say, once you've started. No, let's not magnify matters . . ." He must feel that I'm spoiling him too much, that I'm really too generous . . . that's madness, see here . . . he hadn't asked for all that . . . But I present it to him with joy, I'm so happy to give it to him, I beg him to accept: "Yes, yes. I assure you, that's the word. Martereau fixed all that up from the start. I'm sure that he was already in cahoots with the owner. Afterwards, the opportunity was unhoped for, he jumped at it. I let myself be led round by the nose." He's delighted, moved, his eyes caress my face, his fingers feel my arm, he pinches me affectionately the way he does in his rare moments of emotion . . . "No, listen, things aren't as simple as all that . . ." he wants to compete with me in generosity, pay me back in my own coin, he's ready to make all kinds of concessions. The roles are reversed, he has assumed the one I usually play. Now that we are so close to each other, and he is certain of my submission, my respect, he can relax a bit, let himself go, show me that he too is capable, like me, of distinguishing half-tints, shadings . . . "Things aren't so simple . . . Ah! these young people, they always imagine that an abyss separates them from the preceding generation, but we too, whatever they might think, we understand all that, all their subtleties, their 'psychology' . . . today they have other names for it, that's all, but people haven't changed in spite of their fashionable psychiatrists . . . I too, have a certain flair, I've rubbed up against quite a lot of people in my time . . . you are certainly right, roughly speaking, but it's not so simple as that . . . People are not all of one piece. He's a decent enough fellow, Martereau. Not very capable. Not very intelligent. He's never done very well. They scraped together a few savings by cutting down here, then there, all their lives, in order to put a little money aside . . . they're honest, cheat a bit from time to time, like everybody else, but in the long run, they'll die without ever having done anything that was flagrantly shady . . . a decent sort, a good father and a good husband . . . and then all of a sudden, the opportunity arises . . . imagine . . . two million eight hundred thousand francs . . . given to you like that, in your hand, without a scrap of paper required . . . well, what can you expect, it's hard to let go of it, the temptation is too great . . . You see, my boy, now that we're talking heart to heart . . . you'll remember that, before, nobody was allowed to say a word against him, you swore by him alone . . ." It seems to me that the temptation is too great for him too, he can't resist, the tender flesh is there, his for the taking, he has only to stretch out his hand . . . I feel his hot breath upon me . . . "Nobody could say a word

. . . it was Martereau this, Martereau that . . . But I myself had sized him up long ago, I've known him for a long time, your friend Martereau, I had sort of lost sight of him, but I know, people don't change: he's a jack-of-all-trades, he's tried everything . . . and it always cracked up, there was always something that went wrong . . . he's lazy, really, weak . . ." As I listen to him I experience a sort of amazement mingled with fright . . . "Yes, indeed, my dear Martereau, believe me, that's the only way to succeed: hammer on the same nail, have one passion only . . ." His indignation, his rage, in those cases, when we try to unmask him: "Now what kind of a story is that? What will you invent next? . . . How should I know whether he changed jobs or not, your friend Martereau . . . What a lot of sensitive plants, thin-skins . . ." He succeeds in putting us off the scent, in making us ashamed of ourselves. We feel like low swine even to have dared harbor suspicion . . . But this time, he's given himself away. He's unmasked. Doubt is no longer possible. So that was it! And all of a sudden I feel cleansed, scoured: a sensation of salutary burning like that we feel when a wound is disinfected. He's off now, he's got a free rein . . . "Yes. He's lazy, really, your friend Martereau, he's a failure . . . However, I thought he was just the person to do me that little favour . . . I thought he would be flattered. I expected to pay him later for his services . . . He must have guessed that I would compensate him in one way or another . . . But he was playing for high stakes . . . apparently he has a real passion for gambling . . . Did you know that, by the way, that Martereau likes to gamble? When he used to go to the Casino, they couldn't hold him back: a sheep gone crazy. His wife said it again recently, that evening I dined there: at one time they went to Enghien every Sunday. He used to play roulette . . ." My uncle is in seventh heaven, he's laughing with the thin, shrill laughter of an old man . . . "Oh, yes, indeed, he's a real dare-devil, your friend Martereau, an enthusiast . . ."

We suddenly stop talking . . . there's my aunt. All dressed to go out, gloves on, made up, she's standing in the doorway looking at us with an icy glare, while we sit there sheepish and abashed, congealed, like children who feel they've been caught red-handed. She hates these moments of intimacy between us, our suspicious gayety, our collusive laughter . . . She feels him shrivel up already, hunch his shoulders, waiting for the blow. She knows that she can strike: the moment is propitious. She doesn't miss him: "Again? Not finished yet? You're still at it? It's still Martereau? Really, my poor dear, once you get started, you don't know how to stop. It's become a veritable mania . . . an obsession . . . watch out, at your age that can be dangerous, you're beginning to talk drivel . . . that's senile decay . . ." The same sensation of warmth suffuses us both. His cheeks can still, at his age, grow as red as those of an adolescent . . .

Tender, weak, numb with cold, stretching out a misshapen hand in front of restaurant doors . . . the street urchins throw stones at him . . . she has ridiculed, dishonored, ruined him . . . With his face painted, rigged out in an absurd get-up, she forces him each evening to play the clown, to crow "cockle-doodle-do" on the stage of a cheap cabaret, while the audience howls and hoots . . . The bitch . . . she pulls her skirt up very high and makes him kneel down before her to put on her stockings . . . the schoolboys split their sides laughing . . . Professor Unrat . . . that's he . . . my heart bleeds, I would like to comfort him, protect him . . . Don't be afraid, uncle . . . I'll take you home. Let's get out of here. Take my arm.

The dully harrowing throb of the apparatus in the next room hums in my ears. The stuffy heat peculiar to operating rooms and nursing homes makes me sluggish. Here I am, forgotten, I can't remember for how long, sunk deep in an easychair, my head reverberating and empty, as though half way under an anaesthetic. I should make an effort, get up, go out into the hall, call someone, but I don't move, I prefer to wait . . . my aunt is going to come, she insisted on calling for me, she will arrive soon. Like the young girls of other days who, in order to learn their future, used to sit in front of their mirror, between two rows of candles, and stare into it until, in their half-sleep, in their dream, they saw the eagerly awaited image of their future husband appear in it, coming towards them, I keep staring through the window at the garden gate, in the hope of seeing her appear . . . Spick and span, with her smooth, compact face, her afternoon face, she will walk quickly up the path, I shall hear the sound of her hurried little steps in the hall . . . "What! you haven't been examined yet? Why, that's outrageous, we must complain; wait a second, I'll go and shake them up a bit." And she'll go, erect and a bit stiff on her high heels, to "shake up" the nurses gossiping in the little glass-enclosed office at the end of the hall: "Really, Mademoiselle, this is incredible, this young man has been waiting for an hour and a half to be X-rayed . . ."

Finally, the little wooden gate at the end of the walk— am I dreaming—opens partially . . . it's she, I recognize her little fur tippet and her black velvet toque, but how strangely she's behaving, she turns her back, she doesn't come in, keeps her back turned, motionless, in the half-open gate . . . there is someone behind her, a tall, dark figure . . . she takes a step backward, the figure comes forward . . . broad shoulders, pink complexion, wide-brimmed felt hat . . . Martereau . . . so he came too . . . they're going to come in . . . but she still has her back to me, it's as though she were keeping him from coming any farther . . . he leans over, his chin brushes the black velvet toque, he straightens up as if he had been pulled from behind, and she closes the gate between them.

She's coming up the path alone, spick and span, her face smooth, compact . . . I hear the noise of her hurried steps in the hall, she's almost running, she opens the door of the waiting-room . . . "It's terrible, I'm very late . . . What! you haven't been examined yet? But you'll be here till tomorrow if you don't say anything . . . Wait a moment, I'll go and shake them up . . ."

These words that I had been expecting have a funny sound. They are unreal, distant, like people's voices we hear when we're on the point of going to sleep.

They float between her and me, as different from the words she usually speaks, whose genesis I can trace without too much difficulty, as branches broken off for military camouflage from well planted trees rooted deep in the earth.

Camouflage—that's all they are, those words, that voice —which she sets between herself and me in order for me not to see her, behind which she watches me, invisible, formidable, from where, by means of powerful waves, she directs all my movements. I obey. Like hers, my voice has a strange sonorousness: "Oh, do, I beg of you, I'm so tired, I dozed off a bit, I haven't the energy to move. Tell them that I was down for three o'clock. They must have forgotten . . ."

The regular sound of her short steps on the linoleum in the hall has a relentless note that says: no fuss, I beg of

you; no long-drawn-out musings: come down to earth; behave yourself—they say that to me. She's back: "Come on,
they're going to take you right away. Hurry up."

So Martereau has accomplished that extraordinary feat:
he has seized us in his firm grip and dragged us out into
the open air, out of our stagnant pond. So they can take
place among us too—genuine, expansive reactions. Not our
usual unnameable, barely discernible quakings, our pale
mirrorings, but something strong, clear-cut, perfectly
visible: a real act. Something that everybody recognizes
right away and calls by name: adultery . . .

But for me, unaccustomed as I am to the open air and
to light, it still seems to me all the time that it hasn't really
happened to us: I'm like those sophisticated travelers in
distant lands who, when they see for the first time Esquimos
in their igloos, or Arab street crowds, almost too pictur-
esque for their taste, the veiled women, the men with their
turbans and burnooses, the public story-tellers, the water-
carriers, the snake-charmers, have the impression of watching a performance at the Opera, or at the Chatelet. It had
seemed to me that day, at the nursing home, that it wasn't
quite real, that appearance of my aunt and Martereau in
the gate-way: a bit too stagey.

And since then, it's still the same. It's really as though
we were at the theatre. We are actors playing in a play.

All about us, in the darkness, a silent audience is watching us and waiting to know what's going to happen.

The setting: an upper middle class parlor. Evening, after dinner. At the left of the fireplace, seated in a big easychair reading his newspaper—the husband (my uncle). At a table, in the light of a lamp, wrapped in a shawl, her head leaning on one hand, holding up a playing card in the other—his wife (my aunt). Beside her: their young nephew (that's me) is watching her play solitaire and, in his impatience, picks up a card from time to time and lays it elsewhere. Silence. Stifled exclamations round the card table. Irritated rustling of the newspaper. Suddenly the husband throws his newspaper down, rises. He crosses the room and takes his stand in front of the card-players.

The husband: "Drop that for five minutes, will you? I've something important to say to you."

(The wife, eyes still lowered on her game, says nothing, plays a card).

The husband (in a hissing voice): "Now listen, will you, I can assure you that this is a bit more interesting . . ." She, sweetly: "But I am listening.—Well, I had a telephone call from Martereau. In reply to my letter. About time. Really, it's worth its weight in gold: the house, he doesn't know yet if he can give it back just now. His wife and he both need fresh air, it will depend on what the doctor advises. As for the expenses incurred, he doesn't know. I asked him to let me have an idea, approximately . . . he must have bills, estimates . . . Bills! He saw red. I dare to mention bills to him! Who do I think he is, anyway? My contractor, my overseer? This time, I also saw red. I shouted at him: And you, who do you think I am? A damned fool? You think I don't know why you haven't written? You're afraid to let me have some proof: nothing on paper, eh, between us . . . At this point, he came out with something . . ." He seizes the nephew's arm: "Do you know, my boy, what he said? Would you both like to know what he answered?" Just here, his wife looks at him: "Well, he said: Ah! now we have it. You've finally come out with it. I'm no damned fool, either. I understood what it was all about a long time ago. I know. I know what you say to people—the wife and nephew make a slight movement— I know what you say about me . . . that I schemed it all up from the beginning, that I didn't give a receipt on purpose . . . I know, don't deny it, there's no use. You accuse me of God knows what dirty dealings, you drag me in the mud . . ." Silence. The wife and nephew remain motionless, as though petrified. The husband, his hands behind his back, begins to walk up and down the stage. His voice has come down a tone: "The house, the money, I don't give a rap about them, you know that perfectly well. But there's one thing I want to know . . ." He comes to a halt in front of them, casts a quick glance at his wife, then looks his nephew directly in the eye: "I want to know who's the traitor round here." He raises his voice: "Who is it that tells on the outside what's said at home, what goes on here, in my house? Huh? Who is it that does that?" Silence. The audience, in the shadow, is waiting. I blanch. I straighten up. I realize that my role requires me to look at my aunt, but it's beyond me; even here, in these great open spaces, in the midst of these vast currents, I cannot . . . My voice trembles: "There's one thing I can swear to you, uncle, I can give you my word of honor: I haven't said a word about all that to Martereau." My uncle looks at me, then goes and sits down again in his chair. All his excitement has subsided. His voice sounds weary: "Then, how did he know about it?" Silence. All eyes are turned on my aunt and me, seated in the light of the lamp. My aunt is looking down at her game of solitaire. Thoughtfully, she picks up a card. She holds it suspended in the air then says, in a very soft voice: "Now that you've calmed down a bit, I may perhaps say a word. When you get excited, it's useless to explain anything to you, you don't even listen. You, yourself, asked him for a receipt, you wrote him, you sent this boy to see him . . . How do you expect him not to understand what you think? You always think people are stupider than they are. He wanted to impress you, so he told you he knew about it. And you were taken in right away. Then you come and accuse this boy . . . Really, once you get started . . ." My uncle seems weary, as though deflated, and also a bit ashamed of himself. He makes an irritated gesture with his hand to silence her, the way we drive off a fly. He picks up his newspaper. Just here, I rise and, in a dignified manner: "If you have nothing more to say to me, I believe I'll go to bed." With a little bow of the head, I leave the room. After my exit, they remain seated for a few moments, each in the same spot, in silence, she going on with her solitaire, he absorbed by his newspaper. And then the curtain falls.

But I can't last for long outside my own element; light blinds me, air hurts me, strong currents make me dizzy. As soon as I am out of the wings, alone in my room, I long to sink down again into the mushy, putrid ooze that quivers on the bottom of stagnant waters. Very soon I'm at it again . . .

"Hammer on the same nail . . . believe me, my dear Martereau, that's the only way . . ." and I, wavering between them, a liana, a trembling bit of seaweed, borne from one to the other, clinging to each of them, first to one then to the other, wanting to stand up for my uncle and protect Martereau . . . How amused Martereau must have been by my awkward, panic-stricken efforts . . .

The lady with the unicorn, the Tanagra statuette, the little fairy . . . Married so young, almost a child . . . Looking wistfully into the distance, while seated beside her on the banquette in some café, or at a tea-room table, he gazes at her. He presses her slender fingers. Sighs. Secrets. Tears dried unobtrusively with the corner of a tiny handkerchief . . . "Ah! if you knew . . . I've spent many a night in tears . . . He can be so hard . . . you could be dying right beside him and he wouldn't notice it . . . he's the only one that counts. Full of himself. Puffed up with vanity: I. I . . ." Martereau listens, all sympathy, moved, a little embarrassed at times to be intruding like this, to be listening at key-holes: but women don't feel the same way about those things . . . It's delightful, nevertheless, the role she makes him play, that she has chosen for him: the knight, the protector of the weak, the just. Comprehensive, sensitive and strong. Generous towards a vanquished rival whom she drags before him barefooted, in chains.

At times it was a bit embarrassing, too ridiculous, but the show was worth the price, it was really out-of-the-ordinary, a magnificent exhibition, a first-class performance. Martereau amused himself a lot. It was really astonishing, too good, here again, to be true, to see how my uncle surpassed himself that day: it was as though he were trying to do his best to resemble perfectly the portrait she had painted; fascinated as he probably was, this happens to nervous people, by the image of himself that he saw in Martereau, carrying out obediently the movements that an invisible baton in Martereau was directing. Martereau felt like shouting bravo! the portrait was such a good resemblance (women often have that gift, that clear-seeing, pitiless eye), he felt like applauding. Comfortably seated on his cushioned balcony seat, wearing an indulgent, amused expression (I admired so much that expression of his), he looked at the figure lying at his feet in the dust of the ring, in the glare of the spotlights, playing the clown, beating his breast, railing at him: "Look at me, me, I know what it means to drudge, that I can guarantee you, I know what it means to work, I've worked a twelve-hour day, yes, sir, I

used to get there at the same time as the workmen . . .
I've worked all my life . . . Hammer on the same nail . . .
That's the secret . . ." Hands folded, leaning slightly backward, Martereau observes him: crude, coarse, no time to
waste on subtleties: as soon as a man sets foot in his office,
in a wink he has sized him up, he knows who he is, what
he wants . . . Now he thinks that this is what he should
serve to him, Martereau, in order to subjugate him, crush
him . . . A little woman like her, a frail little exotic bird
like that, pines away with a man like him . . . delicate hot-
house plants, for them to flourish they need a bit of tenderness and warmth, little attentions, petting . . . How
touching she is just now, it's moving to see her here, in
the dragon's lair . . . a gentle prey . . . a frightened little
bird . . . it's for him that she's trembling, he senses it,
while the other comes nearer, looking for his vulnerable
spot . . . he would like to reassure her, she should have no
fear, he's strong, very sure of himself. All those words that
the other is sprinkling him with are nothing but dud shells,
disconnected bombs. Seated side by side in cafés, over tea-
tables, they have emptied them of their contents: a substance which has now become inoffensive, which they have
taken between their fingers, held up to the light, ap-
praised . . .

Martereau smiles like a psychiatrist who listens with
satisfaction to the insults being hurled at him by a patient,
insults that manifest the latter's condition, characterize his
case. He feels like turning to her, his assistant, and saying: "Well, my dear, I congratulate you, your observations

were very good. Your diagnosis was excellent. It's really perfect."

Her laugh when she speaks to the chauffeur, to the hair-dresser, a little laugh she has, like a sort of sneer, abrupt, shrill, icy, and her questions, like tickling, caresses given the wrong way, little pinches, tantalizing and provoking . . . "Do you like to dance, Julien? hm, hm, are you a good dancer? Do you often go to dances? In Montmartre? What do you dance? the tango? my favorite dance . . . Why certainly, certainly, you're too modest, you must dance very well . . . hm, hm, . . . your partners must surely agree with me . . ." and that will-o'-the-wisp in the depths of her eyes which suddenly dilate, pale . . . No, they're not going to a café, what an idea, she wants to go to a tea-room, to Poiré's, or to Colombin . . . "Have you never been to Colombin? Well, my dear, you really have a lot to learn . . . hm, hm . . . And you have never in your life invited a pretty lady to take tea at Colombin? I'm going to lead you astray, hm, hm, . . . You'll see, it's the best place in Paris for a good cup of tea, and where they have the best cakes. You must learn to be greedy, hm, hm . . ." Ex-quisitely fresh odor of her perfume, of her fur, softness of her fur, of her skin . . . Martereau kisses her slender wrist, her tiny hand in its fine suède glove . . . Wherever she wants, of course . . . he'll follow her to the end of the world . . . She adores that, when she's with him, to feel herself like that, the spoilt great lady, capricious, whimsical, and he, admiring, submissive . . . Madame Récamier in the presence of the little chimney sweep, a good fairy distributing exceptional moments, transforming with a gracious gesture of her magic wand, a dreary life. All of that he senses quite well, he perceives it perfectly: it is deposited somewhere in his very depths, a fine, impalpable dust, a thin sediment . . . nothing that meets the eye, he doesn't let it . . . he's going to seize the passing moment, she is in love with him, he is well aware of it, he's amused, delighted, he offers no resistance, lowers his head obediently when, before entering, she runs her hand through his hair, whispers . . . "Just a minute . . ." she rumples the lock on his forehead . . . there . . . she doesn't like that wave, it would be becoming cut short, so little would be necessary—she knows exactly what he would need—for him to have a real air about him, look a real blood . . . she likes to do that, to trim, model, cut, according to patterns she has in her head . . . "Go quickly and pick out the cakes, you can choose for me, they're all delicious . . ." As he makes his way between the tables amidst whisperings, chirpings and swishings, he feels her piercing, observant eye on his back, an eye that nothing escapes: his right shoulder is higher than the other, his hair is badly trimmed in back, the somewhat questionable cut of his suit . . . she forces him to go ahead, gives him little taps on the back . . . go on, go on . . . absurdly rigged up, crowing "cockle-doodle-do," amidst hoots and howls of laughter . . . Pastry fork in hand, with a resigned, remote expression, the waitress, a minx with a haughty, superior air about her, stands waiting . . . He feels that he is making himself ridiculous by hesitating, he must appear to be counting costs, the waitress, who had sized him up at a glance, probably thinks that he considers the price too high . . . When he returns to their table with his plate loaded with cakes she raises an amused, affectionate glance towards him . . . "But, darling, you're mad, you've got enough there for an entire regiment . . ."

It's nothing, all that, the finest sort of deposit, a thin invisible sediment, but one that remains in him, which nothing alters, and which can become visible all of a sudden. As dangerous as the overdue eruptions that make certain fevers all the more malignant.

All of that, the little games, the tantalizing laughter, the pointed looks, the smiles, Madame Récamier and the little chimney sweep, the good fairy, my uncle knows it all. It has gathered in him little by little—a single compact block, a single compound body, concerning which it has never occurred to him, perhaps he was afraid, to separate and examine all the elements—it's there inside him too, as he comes forward, aggressive, presumptuous, beating his breast: "I, I, I've worked all my life . . . I've never counted on anybody but myself . . . Hammer on the same nail, my dear Martereau, believe me, that's the only way . . ." He knows perfectly well, as he comes to the front, that he is not the piteous, vanquished foe being led before his triumphant rival: he is the knight arrayed in brightest armor, who enters the ring under the eyes of his lady, whose colors he is wearing. They have, he knows it, he and she, the same colors, the same scutcheon. She admires him for his courage, his skill, his proud daring, his power. An indestructible tie binds them together. The others— mere pastimes, playthings, poor jesters. That's what he shouts now and what she hears as he enters the ring, brandishing his arms. Even I, when I try to hold him back, to come between them, I can't help admiring him: because of his too great force, which he doesn't quite know how to control, we are afraid. We're embarrassed to watch Martereau being brutally overwhelmed, humiliated, we beg for mercy . . .

That war-cry, that shout of victory, Martereau also hears it. It's not the absurd clown that he sees making an exhibition of himself in the dust of the ring, the captured foe being dragged into the arena—or perhaps he sees that too, at the same time, as though it were super-imposed, this is a thing that happens quite often, we perceive several very different images of the same object—what he sees is a powerful opponent, armed to the teeth, parading in the arena before an admiring and slightly frightened audience, an opponent who charges at him, and strikes . . . "Hammer on the same nail, my dear Martereau, believe me, if you want to succeed, that's the only way . . ." He's clever, his aim is straight. Exactly in the right spot, there where, little by little, it has gathered, the deposit, the sediment left in Martereau by the games, the little tea-parties, the looks that she pressed against his back while she forced him to make his way amidst the laughter and the whispering . . .

her smiles at the plates over-loaded with cakes, at his over generous tips . . . and so many other things . . . certain of which, and they leave the thickest deposit, are even more infinitesimal, barely discernible . . . Under the blows that are dealt him, all that, which had been buried, emerges, is brought to light. Martereau sees it clearly. He knows that he is alone, in enemy territory, forsaken, betrayed. She is on the side of the foe, she belongs to the same species as he, they are of the same blood. They have the same motto, they use the same weapons. There has always existed between them, despite all the sighs, the secrets and the tears, a hidden collusion, a pact. He, Martereau, is nothing—a source of amusement. Even I, he senses that, at bottom, I am on their side—like uncle, like nephew—all the same breed.

Really, my naïveté is touching, my stupidity, when I recall that at the moment when Martereau, having succeeded in saving his face, withdrew with dignity, I followed him . . . I was so upset, I wanted him to tell me . . . it hadn't hurt too much? . . . to reassure me . . . With what repulsion he must have watched my movements, when I crawled to him with such precaution, tried to get closer to him in order to examine his wounds . . . "Tell me, Monsieur Martereau, frankly, my uncle, what impression does he make on you?" . . . in order to relieve him, to console him, to show him that I too am in the same boat, covered with bruises, with scars . . . press close up to him, cling one to the other, keep each other warm . . . Ah! no, none of that, he will have none of it, he wants none of that degrading promiscuity, of that sort of collusion between insulted and injured. He hardened before that repugnant contact. He played dead.

He forced me to keep my distance. He intimated clearly that there was nothing in common between us, that he was not on my side.

To tell the truth, I believe—and he believed it too, probably—that if he were obliged to choose between us, it is perhaps my uncle that he would choose, in spite of everything; he would be, like her, like me, on the stronger side: my uncle is less repugnant to him than we are, we powerless rebels, whimperers, weak parasites, profiteers . . .

That satisfied look down deep in his eyes as he watched me, on the little folding seat in front of him, wriggling and struggling so comically in my uncle's fist . . . "It's made of mill-stone, the house?" . . . and when my uncle held me tighter, made me turn round and round before his amused eyes . . . "Just look at him, my dear Martereau, ha! but you don't know him . . . mill-stone, you didn't know that, it's our pet aversion . . . What we want is a thatched cottage, or an old chateau . . ."

A saint wouldn't resist, the temptation is too great. Martereau couldn't stand it . . . in this same way, terrified victims, martyred children, arouse similar reactions in others than their usual torturers . . . Martereau was unable to resist, the day we came to him, tender little pigs, bringing the money, when we stood there fluttering before him, my cousin and I, all fidgety and smirky . . . I remember how he looked at her: a caricature of her mother, coquettish, simpering . . . "Monsieur Martereau, why I just adore him, so there, I've got a real crush on him, he's so good looking . . ." but less sensitive in reality than her mother, stolid, doughy, leaden . . . he couldn't resist . . . She was ready prey, she was the hostage in his power, the mother's wax effigy which he held in the hollow of his hand . . . Here was an opportunity for exquisite vengeance, revenge for the little games, the icy laughter, the amused looks, the circus-dog training—he smiled as he looked her straight in the eyes, and she trembled under his gaze, all limp and blushing . . . He raised his finger, wagged it at her, and sang in a falsetto voice . . . *I've got a headache, you'll nev-er guess why. My grandmoth-er switched me and she made me cry . . .*

And what revenge for him, now that I think of it, what satisfaction, when he led us to the house. As we walked up the path, we made a strange little troop. I was not, as it had seemed to me, like the hero of the *Trial*, being led by "The Gentleman." I was not alone: the little far-away princess, Madame Récamier, the good fairy, was walking beside me. Martereau, who was herding us, brought up the rear. The absurd clown, the awe-inspiring knight, was amongst the prisoners, only promoted by Martereau to the rank of keeper. He was over zealous, maintaining order, forcing recalcitrant marchers to keep in step. Martereau planned for him a fate rather similar to our own. But he, heedless, carefree and certain, as he was, to be on the stronger side, intoxicated too by his own ephemeral and ridiculous power, poked fun at his companions, sought to amuse Martereau at our expense, pointed a sneering finger at us . . . "You see them? Now, do look at them . . . you don't know them . . . I know them . . . mill-stone, don't mention it, it makes us sick, we are so refined, so sensitive . . . what we want is a romantic old chateau, we dream of an old-fashioned thatched cottage." Wearing the same striped uniform, heads shaven, chained to one another, we walked along in silence. Martereau was observing her, marching beside me with lowered head. Who would recognize her now, just plain Madame Capet being led past jeering crowds, from the Tuileries Palace to the Temple . . . No more balls, midnight revels, fountains, lovers' trysts, pastoral games, come on there, princess, let's have no fuss . . . how we tremble, how we look about us in fright . . . come on now, straight ahead, this is not the moment to play the sensitive plant, to put on airs, you've got to pay, she must retrace now, on this gravel walk, under these hideous trellises hung with pom-pom roses, the path that she had delighted in making him travel, amidst smiles and whisperings, ridiculously attentive, in his hand the plate piled high with cakes . . . No use making wry faces, my girl. Here's the cement terrace. The wallpaper in the parlor is in perfect condition. Not in the least damp. You won't need to change it. The owner might agree to let you have certain furniture at a low price: the corner divan—couldn't be more practical— a couch during the day, at night a bed. The Henry II sideboard, the pitch-pine bedroom suite . . . what do you say to them? But we say nothing. My uncle gives an approving nod and looks at us, very pleased to see us mastered and brought to heel.

Martereau must have been treading on air. What a godsend, what unhoped for luck to have all three of them there, having come of their own accord to deliver themselves innocently into his hands. The clown, the swashbuckler, the great conqueror swollen with pride, has become his humble servant, happy, he too, to see her mortified, to make her pay for all that he, too, had had to put up with, the lessons in conduct—cockle-doodle-do! Excuse me, darling . . . when you leave the table during a meal—those mysterious, remote airs of being in the know that they put on before him—she and that little sissy—before him, the ignoramus, just barely good enough to make money for them, he must feel plenty of resentment, he too, is avenging himself: "Of course, we'll buy that corner divan, and how! Of course, it's very practical. They'll make the best of it, we'll cure them of their habit of wool-gathering, their poetic aspirations, my dear Martereau, you can count on me . . ." Martereau is counting on him. But his humble servant will get his turn, like the killers who, once the deed is accomplished, are done away with by the leader of the gang. We'll cure him of his desire to teach people a lesson: "Money, my dear Martereau, you'll believe me or not as you please, but for me it has never counted . . . Hammer on the same nail, have but one passion and money will come later, all by itself, more than you want . . . Is that so? and you're telling me? As a result of the war, my little chap, that you neglect to mention. Through speculation . . . By chance—your greatest virtue . . . bare-faced luck. You've never known what want means. Or tedious jobs. Your only passion, research, is that so? . . . You've always played a game that soared over and above sordid little calculations, petty interests . . . A telephone call given at the right moment can bring in more than twenty years of modest efforts and privations . . . On with the game, this is fun. This house—the latest toy, the newest hobby, a passing fancy, a simple speculation . . . But the player is not the one we think. This time it's he, Martereau, who takes the lead, and you are the pawn he's pushing about. He sees you but you don't see him. He leads you, come on now, this way, down to the basement, you're going to see the new heater, a very curious new system, look at all those spigots and levers, enjoy yourselves, you poor morons, spoiled brats, as for him, he's been called away on important business, the owner is waiting for him . . . What's got to be done now, as between men—you two are out of it— is to discuss the profit, the commission, on the price you're going to be made to pay.

He had suspected it, he had felt it the very minute he entered the house, as soon as he heard the sound of voices coming from the parlor, noticed through the open kitchen door the teatray all prepared, and the teakettle—his wife must have forgotten it for at least an hour, it was boiling over . . . That was it, all right—he was sure of it—it was undoubtedly I who was there—all that was for me, for that little lap-dog, that rotten spoilt nephew of a doting aunt and uncle . . . sent to spy on him, to try and "get a rise out of him" . . . and she, naturally, dancing sprightly attendance, all smiles and blushes, "don't look at me, I was cleaning house, don't look at my hands, at my apron" . . . think of it, what an honor, unimportant people like us, what wouldn't we do, poor tenant farmers, when the heir of the manor-house, the young Lord . . . why, there's nothing she wouldn't do, she hurries off . . . "yes, yes, you're not going to refuse, you must have a cup of tea, it won't take me a second" . . . she makes haste, he mustn't be left alone too long, quick, she fills the tea-kettle to the top, a quarter of that would have sufficed for two, but better too much than not enough, she hasn't time to figure it out, what does it matter, she's in a hurry to get back to him, she must act quickly, before that ogre of a husband of hers comes home, make her complaints, reassure him: "Ah! I understand quite well, I've suffered enough, I too, if you knew . . . but just be patient, the way I am, he'll come round, believe me, you'll get your house . . . only you must watch out, you shouldn't have hurt his feelings, he's so sensitive . . ." they needn't fear, they'll get everything they want, she'll see to it, they can rest easy . . . the water is boiling over, flooding the stove, the gas is still burning, she doesn't care, she can't be bothered . . . oh, she would give them all the water in the Seine if that gave them any pleasure, she would give them her shirt in order to get in their good graces, for them to have a good opinion of her, of

233

him, "My husband has his faults but when it's a matter of his honesty," for them to be quite satisfied, to serve them, like good faithful servants, ready, if need be, to sacrifice their own savings when their masters' fortune is threatened by unlucky speculation . . . he is suffused by a warm flush: a cat's-paw . . . they had dared to think that for an instant . . . certainly, right away, why of course, at your service, it's too great an honor, I am flattered—they believed that —by their confidence, their confidences, those bones they throw to people . . . only too delighted, hurrying about just as she does, arms laden with cakes, bottles, knocking into her, "aren't you ready yet, he's going to come, hurry up, go and change your dress" . . . she, dull-witted, docile, inert, exasperating, the way a thing, an inanimate object, can be, continues to make the same gestures, like a mechanical toy that he has wound up, you can't stop it, impossible to explain that to her, Colombin, the little fairy, and he running about with the plate full of cakes that cost a fortune—she would have a fit . . . heavens, is that possible?—distributing ridiculous tips, clowning . . . Cockle-doodle-do! . . . blind, obstinate, idiotic, she holds him up, forces him to keep going: Come on there, make your bow! Why don't you smile! Haven't you seen who's here? Who's come to see us? But it's all over. The party's over. The dance is over. We've played enough, laughed enough. Masks off. Here he is in his own home. No more affected airs, no more delicious little teas and dinners, not a glance at the little gentleman, too bad if what he sees is not to his liking, is distasteful to his delicate sense of smell, his fine aesthetic feelings, they're so keen, my dear, on "style," on good manners! They'll see. He looks at his wife—his voice is cold, hissing: "You forgot the teakettle on the stove, the water was boiling over. I turned it off. You had put in enough for a regiment." The play is over, as well as the flirting, the greasepaint—he is as he is . . . We're not rich, we aren't, my young friend, for us money doesn't grow on trees, we work hard, it's not pretty to look at, poverty isn't, you'll find that out, sordid, as you say . . . my wife is killing herself working here, she's not well . . . he's master here, he's in his own home . . . the hostage has come voluntarily to give himself up . . . he pushes me away, sends me rolling into a corner, he raises his foot: "As for you, my boy, do you know what they call that sickness of yours?" . . . All shrunken together, eyes raised in his direction, I wait . . . An immense giant's foot, an enormous hob-nailed sole . . . But he's not going to crush me. Just one not very hard tap, a saint would not resist, but he controls himself. He allows me to leave, he pushes me out . . . come on, let him get going, let him run like greased lightning to carry home the morsel . . . together they'll sniff it on all sides, turn it over and over, tear it to pieces, chew on it, continue to batten on it . . . his two powerful hands clasp our necks, rub our noses together . . . go to it, go on . . . "will he, won't he, give it back . . . you let yourself be taken in, you acted like a child, he knew what he was doing from the start . . . you're the ones who affronted him" . . . ants scurrying about in the hollow of his enormous hand . . . bold little pigs who lead the wolf on . . .

motionless and gentle, so as not to frighten us, he let us come near him, nearer still, don't be afraid . . . he permitted my uncle to sniff, and sink his teeth in . . . he let me crawl up to him, trembling: "Did it hurt, Monsieur Martereau? Do set my mind at ease, I was so frightened . . ." Please look at that, the little thin-skin, his delicate nerves can't stand the sight of blood . . . he saw us coming, he foresaw, watched all of our movements . . . those far-away looks, that wistful expression, luxury-loving women, dainty tea-parties, little cakes, little triumphs, oh! all that for two, darling, why you're mad . . . amused glances at the tip . . . He laughs best who laughs last . . . That'll do, now. Finished. Call to order: the limit he set in advance to our sport must not be overstepped. To your places. Eyes front. Look straight at me . . . I smile a little bit on the side of my mouth . . . Come on, there, smile, and better than that . . . his hot fingers tickle my neck, take avid hold of my scarf, his ogre's teeth are shining. His eyes . . . his voice grows muggy, hot, burning . . . "tell me, is it your aunt, did your aunt knit that for you?" the man jumps from behind a tree, the little girl draws back, blushes, lowers her eyes . . . "it's your aunt, she likes to knit, your aunt, she knits well, that keeps her busy, eh, she likes that? . . ."

Someone is calling me. My aunt is calling me. The door opens: "So you were there all along? Didn't you hear me? We've been looking everywhere for you. A letter from

Martereau . . ." Like a victim of asphyxiation or drowning who is being revived, I perceive their movements, their voices, as through a fog, unreal, remote . . . "Why yes, he was there, sitting in the dark . . . what were you thinking about? were you asleep?" . . . they open doors and windows, let the fresh air come streaming in, hold a paper before my eyes . . . "There, look at that . . . a letter from Martereau . . . "the house . . . at your disposal . . . October 15th . . . occupied it the time required to make repairs . . . enclosing bills." They shake me, my uncle grows impatient . . . "Well! What's the matter, you look at me with a flabbergasted expression, as though you didn't understand. Martereau's giving us back the house the 15th of October. He occupied it in order to supervise the work, he pretends that I asked him to take charge of it. He encloses the bills. He has had the figures checked. Everything is in order. There's nothing anyone can say." My aunt's little pointed laugh runs up my spine like a fine, icy jet . . . "Much ado about nothing . . . hm . . . hm . . . what a void, eh? Brr. Who'll we talk about now? Who'll keep you busy now?" The door slams. Silence. My uncle walks up and down. He stops in front of me: "Well? What have you got to say? Now you can calm down. And what a fuss you did make about it . . . When really, it was hardly worth mentioning. It's extraordinary that faculty you have of making mountains out of molehills. You had finally succeeded in getting me worked up, as well. I offended that poor fellow for nothing . . ."

Everything is like it is in a dream. Astonishingly accurate. Truer than reality itself. That was what he was supposed to say to me. That was according to the rules. It's the reward that I always expect to receive from him for all my gifts, everything which, at his tacit command, I fetch and lay at his feet, like a well-trained dog. Just as soon as it's no longer to his taste: "Come, come, that'll do. That's enough. What have you been sticking your nose into now? What's all this filth you've gone and dug up this time? What are you after, anyway?" And groveling, I withdraw.

With one of those rapid spins of his, he has gone over to the other camp. They're together again, he and Martereau, leagued against me, they're advancing towards me, arm in arm, on their faces the calm look of healthy men.

But I too know how to make spins and leaps. I can also . . . arm in arm, as before . . . as though nothing had happened. But why as though nothing had happened? There was nothing: nothing but bubbles, nonsense, mirages, smoke, reflections, shadows, my own shadow, after which I was running, round and round in a circle.

I hadn't had the wit to give Martereau the credit that was due him. I had lacked confidence. I had made so bold as to imagine that he was like us; not exactly like us—my insolence hadn't gone that far. But I had allowed myself to believe that maybe something very forceful (for us, a breath, less than nothing, suffices to make us disintegrate) something comparable to the powerful neutrons that succeed in decomposing simple elements which nothing can break open, had, as it were, disintegrated him. But apparently, he had remained intact. More stable than the nucleus of the atom. Similar to what I had thought he was at first, to what I had so ardently desired he should be.

His acts, his gestures, his words, clear pure lines that portray him, express him, perfectly. Underneath, round about, there's nothing: a sheet of white paper.

*O*nce again, as before, I follow with my eyes, fascinated, my entire self gathered in them, entirely contained in them, the delicate, precise, slow motions of his fleshy fingers, with their square-cut nails: very cautiously, they straighten or tie to their stakes, tomato plants and rose-bushes; they pick through the box of fish-hooks; they thread the silk line through the ring of the hook; they tie the tiny knot; they hold the fish-hook up in the air . . . "Look . . ." his comically saucy, teasing forefinger is beating time: "I've got-a-head-ache-Shall-I-tell-you-why . . ." His appraising fingers feel my scarf, he gives an admiring nod . . . "Tss . . . that's a nice scarf, believe me . . . nice and warm, it was your aunt, eh, who knit that for you? . . ." Nothing about, nothing anywhere, my uncle is right: there was nothing to make a fuss about.

Nothing to make a fuss about: that's what I must keep repeating to myself, whatever happens. That hardly perceptible reaction, a little while ago, when he noticed me coming through the garden gate: like a sort of very slight displacement of his expression, something that he put back in place, readjusted right away—nothing. There is nothing: surprise at seeing me, annoyance at being disturbed, nothing to make a fuss about, nothing, as he would say, to worry about. He himself, as he used to do, seems to want to help me get a new foothold on firm ground . . . Come along, come on in, come nearer, there's nothing, I assure you, I've got nothing, empty hands, empty pockets, look, I'm sitting here in the sun, it's nice weather, "the last fine days, the autumn sun is here already, towards evening it gets a little chilly, but just now it's nice, what fair wind brings you? How goes it? It's been a long time since we saw you . . . you can see, we're getting ready to move, to go back to Paris, I'm taking advantage of the last fine days . . ." He sets the box of fish-hooks on the ground to make room for me on the bench beside him; he holds his fishing-rod resting against his knees; patiently, cleverly, his big fingers unroll without haste the line wound round the long bamboo pole, untie the knots one by one; he seizes the line caught in the knot between the tip of his thumbnails and his bent forefinger, he pulls gently . . . there it comes . . .

bravo, one more untied, now for the next one . . . he takes the fishing pole in his hand, stands it up straight in front of him, shakes it, lets the line hang down, shakes it again, and as we watch, heads lifted, while a few last loops unroll from round the top, he begins to talk to me . . . a few words . . . what one does say in such cases, not worth making a fuss about, a few polite phrases of no importance . . . "Well, then . . . you've nothing to say . . . what's new? . . ." I'd give anything not to have noticed in his tone, in the sound of his voice, less in the words themselves than in their prolongation, in the silence between the words, something aggressive, a bit contemptuous . . . "What's new? . . . You've nothing to say? . . . What have you been up to? . . . How's everything at home?" . . . a rubbing sound, a light scratching . . . a sort of little whistle . . . a fine jet, acrid and hot, that comes from his words . . . but I'm exaggerating already, I'm about to lose my foothold, it's less than that, much less, hardly a shade, like a tiny, badly oiled wheel in a clockworks that is perfectly cared for and well regulated, but it's there, I noticed it, I need no more than that, less than nothing suffices now, it's become a habit between us, my very delicate balance is threatened, upset, I am swinging, swaying, and he senses it, he sensed it from the beginning, he sensed me there, beside him, all trembling, pleading, heeding . . . something ponderous, limp, clinging to him, pulling him; he felt like shaking himself in order to tear it from him . . . a fine jet of annoyance, resentment, loathing, escaped in that barely perceptible "shush" that prolonged his words . . . "Well, then . . . have you nothing

to say . . . What's new? . . . what are you up to that's nice?"
. . . almost nothing, less than nothing, trite phrases, harmless words, but there are no harmless words between us,
there are no more harmless words, words are tiny safety
valves, through which heavy gases, unwholesome emanations, escape, envelope me . . . now it has started, I absorb,
I become impregnated, as usual, I reproduce all his reactions, all the eddies, the uncoilings in him, within myself,
or is it rather my own reactions that find repercussion in
him?—I don't know, I never have known: a game of mirrors in which I lose my way—my image which I project
into him, or the one he plasters immediately, savagely, on
me, the way the other man, my uncle, does, and beneath
which I smother . . . I kick about me, trying to extricate
myself, but he holds me, I give in, he's right, I feel that I
am like that, I am that: a fastidious lap-dog, a rotten
spoilt child, extra care, special dishes, "the rich man's illness" . . . and I lower my eyes, abashed . . . "that's your
illness, my boy, believe me . . . army service, a tough life,
nothing like it to set you on your feet again" . . . weak,
docile . . . a parasite . . . who has come here to spy about,
to watch slyly, observe what's going on—the burning jet
spurts forth . . . "Well, then . . . so you've nothing to say
. . . what are you up to? . . ." a good-for-nothing, a born
failure, still making that cork-screw furniture of his, those
spun-glass tables, that must cost them a fortune, but he
has to be occupied, doesn't he, that little fellow, he has to
be diverted . . . the picture I see in him fascinates me, I
look more closely . . . the picture of all of us here: unwhole-

some, frivolous, idle, spoilt . . . I make an effort to restrain myself, something in my voice too—he notices it—rings false . . . "Oh . . . I don't know, really, nothing very interesting . . . my uncle hasn't been very well recently, he says he feels tired . . ." give him what he wants, appease him at all costs . . . behind them, safe behind them . . . I make him a gift of them, let him take them and spare me . . . on his side, against them . . . "You know how he is . . . he complains . . . he says . . ." there it is, in front of me, it's looming up in the distance, a threat, a danger, not yet clear, but I perceive it, a dark mass, a formless bulk, the obstacle against which I'm going to crash to my end, but I feel that I'm going to charge it head on, like certain in-experienced bicyclists or skiers who never fail to run into the very tree or stone on the side of the road that they were trying their best to avoid . . . but that's not what im-pels me, it's not apprehension, I'm not afraid—or perhaps I am afraid, too, at the same time—I anticipate, I'm look-ing forward to a sensation of enjoyment, the same, cer-tainly, that my uncle must experience so often in similar cases . . . let the inevitable happen, let the clash take place, let everything get under way, tremble, throb, I want to see whirlwinds and eddies . . . I release my brakes, I am racing along . . . "my uncle says that it is because he didn't go to Switzerland this winter, as he does every year . . . his doctor ordered him to take a month off every winter, without fail . . . at St. Moritz . . ." Martereau takes his eyes off the fish-hook he is examining and looks at me . . . "To Switzerland? . . . at St. Moritz? . . ." St. Moritz . . .

pleasures . . . palaces . . . somewhere at an immense distance, high up among sparkling peaks . . . The Shah of
Persia, the Rhanee of Kapurthala . . . luggage plastered
with labels, the bellhop touches his cap, all the flunkeys
dance attendance while they proceed—vessels in full sail
—through the wide foyer, and he stuck here by them, in
this hole, clinging wretchedly to this sordid hole . . . they
are flouting him . . . I dared . . . inside him something
trembles, rises up, boils, swirls, myriads of tiny particles,
gravitating worlds, unfurl from him onto me, what I was
dreading, what I was expecting . . . they're insulting him,
but it serves him right, idiot, old fool . . . he had offered
his arm, he had thought . . . he could tear himself to
pieces, beat himself, bing . . . that protective tap on the
shoulder . . . that sneer, hammer on the same nail, Monsieur Martereau . . . soft, mucid spit, but he didn't wipe
it off, don't flinch, too polite, why of course, on the contrary, don't mind me, enjoy yourselves to the full . . .
grotesque clown, cockle-doodle-do, running about red-in-
the-face, breathless, arms loaded with parcels, dashing up
the stairs two steps at a time, quick, he's about to arrive,
we must hurry, take off your apron, and she, the face she
makes, worthy helpmeet, just the one for him, he feels like
scratching her too, trampling her under foot . . . her look
of a scared mouse as she untied her apron strings . . . and
the other fellow—they knew everything, they saw—his reaction when he sank back onto the sofa . . . didn't tip
enough, must give a little more . . . and he himself, it was
marvelous, knowing everything, everything from the very

beginning, but pretending, incapable of giving it up . . . so weak, can you believe it, hoping against hope, playing the game in order to glean . . . not much, but better than nothing at that, we demand less as we grow older, we're satisfied with a few crumbs . . . flattered, in spite of everything, smiling dancing attendance, . . . "why no, it's not late" . . . pouring out a little more brandy . . . her look, that had grazed him, it had cut like a razor blade, the way she had looked at the tip . . . smooth, soft, well-groomed skin, delicate perfume, in his hand the slender fingers with their lacquered nails, fresh odor of fur, that quick side-wise glance at the banknote sticking out from under the folded check . . . from afar, they were sizing him up, piti-less, relentless, clear-sighted: cold room glaringly lighted, hermetically closed, bare walls, in which he is struggling, useless to knock, to call, silence outside, no assistance, the die is cast: a little fellow, no great intellect, a decent sort, a cat's-paw, only too flattered . . . there was a way out, however, a means of escape, he could have so easily . . . but she, it's she, it's her fault, scared mouse, so timorous, her imploring, beseeching manner, her constant insinua-tions . . . poor face washed out by infinite sufferance, in-finite resignation . . . drudging away now, you can hear the furniture being pushed about in the house, in order to leave everything in perfect condition, so there will be nothing for them to find fault with, above all, incur no criticism, no rebukes, good faithful servants . . . she forced him to walk straight, to comply, nothing audacious, no vagaries, they're not for him . . . worn, torn, shorn, they've ruined him . . . he deprives himself of everything, he doesn't smoke any more, he can't sleep, he must save even a little more than he's doing, houses cost more this year than last . . . We prevented him, deprived him . . . we fleeced him, I look at his profile, he has lost weight, there's something touching, pure, in the line of his thin neck floating about in his collar which is now too big, he feels my gaze and starts to overact . . . piteous, defenseless . . . he shrinks up a little more still . . . we've debased him, humiliated him . . . with our spoilt children's games . . . I fed him to them and they devoured him . . . but he seems to be pulling himself together a bit, he seizes the line between two fingers and threads it through the tiny hole; I admire his gameness, his dignity, he smiles, there's just a slight bitterness, a gentle irony in his smile . . . "Ah! so your uncle's going to St. Moritz . . . what does he do there, your uncle? does he go in for winter sports? does he ski?" Far off, seen through the big end of a field-glass, a brittle little puppet is rushing down the slope, unsteady on its thin legs, waving its arms, we laugh together, Martereau and I, we look at it from afar . . . from a distance . . . now it's he, Martereau, who keeps his distance. No more childish illusions, affection, impulsiveness. Now he knows, he understands: it was a last error of youth, one must learn to mature, to grow old . . . he has paid: what he had to, the highest price, without haggling. Accounts are settled, he may well try to amuse himself a bit, to enjoy himself a bit, he laughs, with no joy, however, a bleak little sneer . . . "does your uncle take part in the slalom contests?"

I laugh too—a taste at once bitter and sweetish, the familiar flavor of treason—I see my uncle rushing down the slope in front of us, his eyes bulging, I wish you'd look at him, oh! watch out, he's going as crooked as a crab, he's dropped his poles, he's rolling over and over, we're shaking with laughter, together now, nice and warm, I snuggled up against Martereau in close intimacy and confidence, we understand each other so well . . . "My uncle! oh, you know him, he plays bridge all day long . . ." something about Martereau attracts me, sucks me in . . . closer, cling closer to him, caressing, tickling, tantalizing, lightly pinching . . . "My aunt" . . . I push her right up against him . . . "It's all my aunt can do to get him to walk a little on the terrace every morning . . ." His eyes, still fixed on the fish-hook he's holding in the air, grow softer . . . frail little exotic bird, little kitten, gentle captive slave, it's not always rosy for her, life isn't, he's so peculiar, if you knew, he thinks only of himself . . . he feels in his fingers her fragile little hand . . . her soft innocent flesh, within his reach . . . he turns towards me, something in his glance wavers, a watery gleam, he points with his head to the wide strip of cement in front of the house . . . "Well! she'll certainly have a nice terrace here, your aunt will, they'll be able to take strolls, play bridge, organize, what do you call them . . . tournaments . . ." He gives a wink towards the hideous arbor covered with dusty ivy . . . "In there, you'd think it was made especially, it's just the thing, she can put a jazz-band," he laughs . . . delicate, blushing . . . the captive princess, the dethroned queen in the hands of coarse, vulgar jailers . . . she assumes an expression of loathing, looks elsewhere, lifts her head proudly, but they're finished now, all that delicacy and simpering, come along, it's useless to make a sour face, he holds her tight, he's showing her about, "there, that'll be magnificent, don't you think, it's just the thing, your cousin can dance, you can give dancing parties here, eh, what do you say?" . . . I too, with them, held tightly, damp embrace, on my face something luke-warm, soft, but above all, don't wipe it off, don't move, don't flinch, acquiesce with a smile, a bit embarrassed, I can't help it, I feel like looking elsewhere, but he can rest assured, he's playing on velvet, I won't budge, I'm too afraid . . . one single move to disengage myself, to repel him, one single a bit too brusque move, and something atrocious, something unbearable would happen, an explosion, a frightful conflagration, our clothes torn from us, noxious, deadly emanations, all his distress, his impotence, his forlornness, on me . . . our two nude bodies gripping each other . . . he lays his hand on mine, he utters a sort of satisfied, crackling "aah" . . . he shows me the fish-hook which he is holding up in the air with the taut line held tightly between his thumb and forefinger . . . "well, that's done. Now look, young man . . ." a slap to call me to order? to drag me out of the mire in which I was floundering? that made my uncle so mad, humiliated him so, when we were walking together, noses to the ground, through the meadows, and I interrupted him suddenly to show him some violets, some daisies, "Look, uncle, aren't they lovely . . ." I look at Martereau. He's sitting very erect, staring at the fish-hook. There is a certain kindliness and purity in the attentive wrinkles about his eyes . . . "Well, that's done. Is my knot well tied? A fisherman's knot, you must have learned that when you were a boy-scout. My line is ready. But I believe it's getting a bit chilly. At this time of year, as soon as the sun has set, it gets cold right away. I think we would do better to go inside. So help me, will you, to bring all that in."

SELECTED DALKEY ARCHIVE PAPERBACKS

FOR A FULL LIST OF PUBLICATIONS, VISIT:
www.dalkeyarchive.com

SELECTED DALKEY ARCHIVE PAPERBACKS

FOR A FULL LIST OF PUBLICATIONS, VISIT:
www.dalkeyarchive.com